EVERYONE AND NO ONE

E V E R Y O N E

and No One

A   N O V E L

M A R K   J A C O B S O N

Villard / New York

All rights reserved under International and Pan-American Copyright Conventions. Published in the United States by Villard Books, a division of Random House, Inc., New York, and simultaneously in Canada by Random House of Canada Limited, Toronto.

VILLARD BOOKS is a registered trademark of Random House, Inc.

Grateful acknowledgment is made to Warner Bros. Publications U.S. Inc. for permission to reprint excerpts from "Peace in the Valley" (a.k.a. "There'll Be Peace in the Valley for Me") by Thomas A. Dorsey. Copyright © 1939 (Renewed) by Warner-Tamerlane Publishing Corp. (BMI) in the USA. All rights outside the USA controlled by Unichappell Music, Inc. (BMI). All rights reserved. Used by permission of Warner Bros. Publications U.S. Inc., Miami, FL 33014.

Library of Congress Cataloging-in-Publication Data
Jacobson, Mark.
Everyone and no one / Mark Jacobson.
p.   cm.
ISBN 0-679-45656-2
I. Title.
PS3560.A27E94   1997
813'.54—dc21   96-51931

Random House website address: http://www.randomhouse.com/

Printed in the United States of America on acid-free paper

24689753

First Edition

Designed by Fritz Metsch

For my dear Daddy, gone from here.
He really loved me.

T A Y L O R

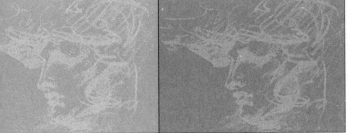

1.

The best place to start is when I died. When I was supposed to have died, that is. The first time.

It was Jimmy Dime's idea. His idea to go up in the Learjet. "Come on, Taylor," Jimmy said in his satanic toad croak when he called me that afternoon. "It'll be hot, hotter than hot. We ain't fucked at twelve thousand feet yet, not at Mach .7." Jimmy was nuts for banging in the odd nooks and crannies of the universe, even more so since he snagged the Lear off some strapped Arab prince for who knew how many millions.

"Jimbo," I groaned, splaying myself across the silk sheets. I'd been feeling logy, like Elvis must have in those last white-suited weeks when Dr. Nick was off in the Ozarks or somewhere. "Didn't we bang at Mach .7 last week?"

"Shit, Taylor. Good thing you're too big to be a jockey; you got no sense of pace. That was Mach .6 at ninety-five hundred feet. This is a whole other thing. You ain't really fucked till you fucked at twelve thousand feet. Tawn says it's to die for."

"She knows?" Tawn was a former cotillion wildcat with a body like a white Barbara Carrera, daughter of a natural-gas fat-cat out of Amarillo.

"Yessir. Tawn's very aviation oriented. She's a legend down at NASA—banged every moon walker from Armstrong on down, got their rocks off righteously. She put a round-the-world on John Glenn that made him forget all his other orbits. The girl knows her compression tables. Besides, Jennifer's going to be there."

That did it. I had unfinished business with Jennifer Cantrell, a former senator's adopted daughter turned supermodel, national spokeswoman for a major lingerie concern. So, a couple of hours later we were up in the wild blue, sonic-booming south of Vegas.

"Ever feel like you'd just like to disappear?" Jennifer asked, drowsily, in the midst of one of my legendary doggy-style downstrokes. Prerequisitely long-legged and sleek, but imbued with a plushness I deeply appreciated in the sinewy age of spandex and StairMaster, Jennifer had a torpidity that seriously undermined her sexiness, an unfortunate condition I had taken it upon myself to liberate her from.

"Disappear?" I didn't exactly catch the question. Tawn, who was riding Jimmy's stick up in the cockpit, was right on the money, pressurewise. Twelve thousand feet at Mach .7 produced an exceedingly copacetic suction effect, dick to honeypot.

"You know, just completely vanish," Jennifer elaborated. Her eyes were perfect hazel, her hair a sheen of auburn. "One minute you're here, gone the next."

It was funny that the beautiful Jennifer, a sphinxlike creature from whom I'd never heard more than a few words at a time, should choose this particular moment to ponder such a concept. Funny, indeed, because a similar matter had come up only a few days earlier, as Jimmy Dime and I were banging a pair of 250-pound hookers in the back of a Chevy Suburban at the Pomona Drive-In movie.

It was ritual, cornerstone to the friendship Jimmy and I had forged over the years, starting that night twenty years earlier when we tied for the Best Actor Oscar and got so drunk we found ourselves cruising a bunch of gamy whores out by Pedro. Jimmy stopped the car, told me to duck down. He did the same. "Hey girls," Dime said in a squeaky voice, holding up the Oscars so they could be seen above the window jamb. "Hey girls! Why not try a real hard man for a change?"

One thing led to another, we wound up giving the hookers the Oscars in payment for services rendered, initiating no small amount of freak-out from the Academy when the statuettes ap-

peared in a South Central pawnshop. POWELL, DIME BARTER OS-
CARS FOR CHEAP SEX! one headline screamed.

That's how it began: The Oscar Nite Cunt Hunt. Every year we
hit a different, anonymous, vaguely new yet already decaying
suburb, which is what led us, most recently, to Pomona. "You
ever get sick of being you?" I asked Jimmy Dime, from underneath a mountain of dark flesh who claimed her name was
Starr.

"Sick of being Jimmy Dime?" my colleague sneered, the remaining tufts of his wingy hair standing on end as he tightened
the leather reins on the elaborate Rube Goldbergish contraption
he'd festooned around the girth of his "date," Gwen. "And give up
all this? You kidding?"

Jimmy snorted a snatch of his patented neo-666 laughter, then
segued to a variation of eyebrow-raised sensitivity, another of
his reflex shorthands for long-forgotten honest emotion. "What's
a matter, Taylor? Don't tell me you're thinking of becoming a
gaffer again."

That old needle. Jimmy never tired of breaking my balls about
that time on the desert picture when I just couldn't take it anymore, when the thought of having my presence splashed across
one more movie screen seemed like more than I could bear.

It was an honest request, sincerely tendered. I called up the
studio guys and said, "You know fellas, I've about had it being
Taylor Powell. Next time I'd rather be the grip, or the gaffer, or
maybe the transportation captain, the guy who gets his nick-
name noted in the credits, like Tom 'Tuff Tommy T' Tuffalo."

Hearing of my plan, Jimmy had gone bonkers. It was as if my
suggested abdication might rearrange the stars sufficiently to
endanger his well-hewn Dimeness. "Why do you have to rock
the boat, schmuck," he'd ranted, full of bile and fear. "What are
you going to do with yourself? Program computers? Sell Xerox
machines? Everyone'll say, 'Hey, you can't sell Xerox, you're
Taylor Powell. You're the Face! The most beautiful Face in the
world. The Face that drives women wild. The biggest fucking
Face in the history of Hollywood!"

Then, soothing himself, Jimmy affected a more generous tone. "Taylor, Taylor . . . kills me to see you downcast like this. You see: We're pals, but we're not the same. I could have been anybody— a tax accountant, a Bowery bum, a civil servant stooge like my father. It's just will, luck, meanness, and talent that made me Jimmy Dime. You though, you couldn't have been anyone else. There's never been a face like yours and there never will be again. Your face is God's Gift to Women."

Jimmy turned to Starr, whom I was eating at the time. "It's true, ain't it Starr, that Taylor's face is God's Gift to Women?"

She might have called herself Starr but her real name was Thelma. She lived in some hideous housing project, and the way she looked (beat and ornery) and smelled (a definite nonbather) you'd figure most people wouldn't even want to be on the same bus with her, much less pay twenty bucks to shove their face into the sour yeast abyss between her legs.

That was the point: If I didn't eat Starr, push my perfect nose and sparkling blue eyes into the tangle of her rank pubis, who would? I took one look at her nasty ghetto body and I knew I *had* to eat her, that it was my purpose on earth to eat her, and that in doing so I was actually eating all women, each and every one of them, and what could be more beautiful than that?

I didn't worry about germs because I knew nothing sprung from a woman that could hurt me. I was invulnerable in their soft presence. The sanctity of my Face, which loved all women and was loved by them in return, protected me. I ate Starr in the back of the Chevy Suburban that Jimmy Dime had so delicately dubbed the fuckmobile. I ate her like I'd eat Princess Di, and I made her come right there.

That's when Jimmy Dime came into the picture again with his demon leer. "I ask you again, you dumb hooker," he addressed Starr, "is Taylor Powell God's Gift to Women or not?" As for her part, all Starr said was, "God . . ."

"See, Taylor," Jimmy said triumphantly, "that's the difference between me and you. I'm a rodent, a taker, a miserable human being. But I'm free. You—you're a god, a god with the face of a god. A god in chains."

That, more or less, was the reason I found myself fucking the lovely but semi-lifeless Jennifer Cantrell in Jimmy's Learjet on that fateful evening. She had never come. Untold numbers of teenage boys and frustrated married men had hauled out their dongs to wack off to the image of her perfect tush in thousands of underwear ads, and she'd never come. She was a block of ice.

"It's a job for the Face. Taylor-made and Taylor-laid," Jimmy Dime had cajoled just hours before. And now, raising up Jennifer's bottom to afford myself the optimum-insert angle, I was so moved by the hermeticism of her glacial beauty that I almost broke out crying. I redoubled my resolve to help Jennifer, return her to the realm of the living, present her with an orgasm that matched her astonishing loveliness.

"I can't disappear," I told her, in answer to her earlier question. "I'm Taylor Powell. The Face. I have a purpose on this earth."

That was when I noticed the plane moving in an irregular fashion. My prick, previously perfectly positioned within Jennifer's divine vagina, began wobbling erratically in its human sheath.

"There's something wrong with Jimmy!" Tawn screamed, throwing open the cockpit door. Snow white in her nakedness, her russet hair flowing over well-formed shoulders and casually upturned breasts, Tawn's ultra-hotness outshone whatever panic might have been evidenced on her vaguely cheerleaderish face. "I think he's having a heart attack! The controls are stuck—the plane's out of control—we're going to crash!"

This news piqued even Jennifer's interest. She lifted her head and said, "Heart attack?" I felt it immediately: The specter of impending doom had kindled a hitherto-dormant spark of desire within her. Until that moment I'd been carrying the full load of the fuck, but now, hearing of the terrible danger we found ourselves in, Jennifer writhed her body backward, pressing against me. "Ohh," she moaned.

The situation was impossible: Clearly I had no other option but to run to the cockpit to see what could be done about the increasingly wild pitch and yaw of the plane. On the other hand, Jennifer wanted me, needed me. "Touch me," she said, grabbing my hand and placing it on her clitoris. I would have thought of the idea myself, but now Jennifer was several steps ahead of me. After so long, her moment of sexual fulfillment was rapidly approaching.

Tawn was becoming hysterical. "Didn't you hear me? We're gonna die! How can you fuck when we're gonna die!" She started pounding on my sweat-riven back.

"Go away!" Jennifer shouted. "Go *away*, Tawn!" She flailed her bony arms backward in an attempt to strike the frantic Tawn. In this effort she hit me in the mouth with an elbow. An electric charge serrated upward through my brain and out the top of my head. I felt around in my mouth with my tongue. I had no front teeth! Jennifer had knocked them out in her frenzy! They were lying bloody on the left cheek of the supermodel's bucking posterior.

I peered down at the still-gleaming incisors. Once big and bucky centerpieces of my irresistible boyish smile, never once victimized by mundane cavities or subject to ignoble cosmetic replating: My two front teeth, the most coveted of Christmas presents, they were now nothing more than a pair of insignificant, tiny slivers of anonymous bone.

"Fuck!" I dug into Jennifer's open purse, pulled out her tiny compact mirror. I couldn't believe it. I'd never even cut myself shaving. Now there was a bloody hole in the middle of my face, big enough for a pollen-drenched bumble bee to fly through. I looked like a moron hockey player, or a sugar-addicted Eskimo.

"Don't stop," Jennifer moaned, her sobbing barely audible above the increasingly erratic jet engine thrum. The plane was falling now, moving in great jolts and darts. "Please don't stop," Jennifer gasped, low, insistent.

I didn't stop. How could I? I was the Face, God's Gift to Women. I could not, would not, abandon Jennifer now, leave her high and dry. She'd have her orgasm. If I died in the midst of this quest, I had no quarrel. It was the essence of who I was, the final personal truth of a man named Taylor Powell.

Jimmy Dime understood. He staggered to the cockpit door, his jowly mug twisted and bluish. His breath came in spasms, with great effort. Whatever had exploded inside his chest hadn't touched his soul, at least the running mate part of it. A huge grin sheared through the agony when he saw Jennifer.

"Shit, Taylor, she's about there. I knew you could do it," Jimmy said, stumbling forth, hacking blood. He steadied himself on my shoulder and kissed me on the cheek, staring admiringly into my bluer-than-a-Japanese-sea eyes. "Taylor . . . the most beautiful face that was ever in the world . . . the Face . . . hope I see it in Heaven . . . we'll bang some babes up there all right."

Then he let out one of those sinister-clown Jimmy Dime chortles. "Well, no one can say we didn't go out flying and fucking."

"Men are so goddamn sick, don't you ever stop bonding?" Tawn yelled, and she was right of course, but what really was to be done about it then? The jet was in free fall; Death was charging up from the desert floor below. When Jimmy offered Tawn his quivering hand, she took it and the two of them went back into the cockpit and slammed the door.

Lovely Jennifer. How beautiful she looked when she came. She craned her long swan's neck to peer back at me. Relief and gaiety informed those wonderful, no longer moribund features. She smiled, sweetly, contentedly. No words came, nor were they necessary, in that instant before impact.

2.

How do you figure out you're not dead yet? Even now, it remains difficult to accept: the living through, the persistence of self.

To this day I have fantasies that it never happened. That Jimmy Dime shook off his heart attack, managed to skid that Lear on its titanium belly until it came to rest against a Joshua tree. Then we crawled from the wreckage, the four of us, me and Jimmy, Tawn and Jennifer. "Shit, Taylor," Jimmy Dime says in my fantasy, "I knew we should have taken the collision."

The truth is: I have no recollection of those few crucial seconds during which I was somehow thrown clear of the doomed plane. Nor can I begin to explain by what agency I found myself basically unhurt, lying buck naked halfway up a stark hillside overlooking the desert floor as the jet's gas tanks ignited, tossing a fireball a thousand feet into the starstrewn sky.

I scrambled toward the burning plane. I tried to save them. I want to be very clear about that. My arm was bloody and my famously bushy eyebrows were singed off by the heat, but no one—*no one!*—can ever say I didn't at least *try* to save them. Not that it would have done any good. No human could have survived that crash.

Those are the words I heard inside my head as I struggled toward the burning wreck: *"No human could have survived that crash . . . Whoever was in that plane has to be dead!"*

A huge plume of flame shot from the ruined tail section. I saw faces in the fire: Jimmy, Tawn, Jennifer, but others, too, hundreds of people whose lives I'd passed through, dozens of women I'd fucked, fucked, and fucked again. God, they looked good, even in the midst of that inferno.

Transfixed, I imagined these burning phantasms symbolized all women, females back to Eve and cave people. These were the women who had died before I, Taylor Powell, the Face, had been born on a wintry Tuesday morning in a North Dakota army hospital forty-six years before. It was as if, in this moment of my strange nondeath, a crease had opened in the mysterium of Existence, an opening that would enable me to find and fuck each and every one of these women. That was a good thing, I knew, because these women needed me; I could help them, make them happy.

Onward I charged, to enfold myself in the embrace of eternal sexuality. But as I got close enough to feel the fire's heat on my exposed balls, I couldn't take another step. It was as if the unknowable energy that zealously polices the demarcation between Life and Death had stopped me cold. Again my mind was filled with a singular, incessant thought: *No human could have survived that crash.*

I smelled the bodies now, the reek of frying flesh melding with the stench of burning Jacuzzi casings, wiring, and seat covers. Jimmy Dime was in there; Jennifer, too, her body charred to nothingness.

"No!" I screamed and heard my echo in the night. "No . . . no . . . no . . ." And I ran. I ran away from the smoking wreckage. I ran naked over the canyon wall, out to the highway beyond. It was empty, a two-lane nowhere road. The cold shrunk my prick to the size of a stunted rhododendron bud. No one saw me. No local single mom just off from the late shift at directory assistance came over the rise in her beater Ford, slammed on the brakes, and stuck her harried head out the window to bat her eyes and say, "Hey, you're Taylor Powell, what you doing running down Highway 317 in the pitch dark? You know you're kind of naked, don't you?"

I could always depend on the kindness of strangers, except to Taylor Powell no woman could be a stranger. But no one came up the road that evening. I may have been among the living, but I might have been the only one. I was the last man on earth. Or so it seemed on that moonless night.

I came to a gas station with sagebrush growing through the cracked cement slab. Two big holes like gouged-out eyes remained where the pumps once stood. The Fina sign, leaning up against the pole from which it once hung, had been shot through with bullets of various calibers. I stuck my hand through the broken glass door of the sagging wooden building marked OF-FICE and went in, out of the wind. There were some old clothes lying on the floor, a grayish mechanic's jumpsuit caked thick with motor oil and grease. Shivering, I pulled on the uniform. Surprisingly, it was a perfect fit, snug in the crotch, the way I like it. Embroidered in red thread, the name above the breast pocket said DEAN.

"Dean," I said absently, fingering the stitching.

Fatigue washed over me. I sat in the cracked-leather swivel chair, the broken springs digging into my ass, wondering what I'd say if anyone pulled into the station. *"Dean at your service. Check your oil, ma'am?"* Wouldn't that be properly James M. Cain–ish? Just the sort of stuff they were always trying to cast me in. But no one came by, not a single car. I looked at the sky, thinking I might see some light generated by the burning plane. There was none of that either.

On the desk was an old telephone, black and heavy, a 1960s desk model. It was plastered over with yellowed stickers hawking local gasoline-related businesses. Taped to the ponderous receiver, the sort that mystery writers often considered as potential murder weapons, was the number of someone identified as GRACE'S LAWYER—555-4965.

Grace—it was a name I'd always liked, old-fashioned, comfortable and proper at the same time. I'd always felt a special coziness moaning names like Grace. *"Grace, Grace, Grace, you're some girl Grace."* How smoothly words like these entered the deliciously sweat-slicked realm of passion. The name summoned up an image of smoky gray but lively eyes, a straight, small nose. Grace. I could hear her pleasingly basso voice. Grace: There was an appealingly Western roughness to her skin, perhaps she was an equestrian, a stern but compassionate breaker of quarter horses.

It was in the midst of this reverie that I saw the real Grace, in a snapshot held by a rusted paper clip to a five-year-old bank-issue calendar. She was a redhead, a little brassy and slightly plump, freckles across her big-cheeked face. I recognized her right away. It was probably five, maybe six years earlier, when Jimmy Dime was on that peyote kick. He'd heard about some Paiute shaman working a day job at the Taco John off Highway 89 who was supposed to have bodacious peyote buttons. I was between pictures, so I went along in the Suburban fuckmobile. We'd passed through here, screwing redheaded waitresses, part of Jimmy's Lucille Ball jones. Most of these redheads were the usual just-glad-to-be-here types, happy to grope in the backseat with a famous movie star. Grace was different.

She worked the swing shift at the Blue Star Diner, but it wasn't what she'd hoped for. She wanted to go to college, learn accounting, or maybe travel abroad as an airline stewardess. There was a real sweetness about her that touched me. She said she'd never done anything like this before and she was telling the truth—I always knew when women were lying about cheating on their husbands. Her man, Dean, was a "good man," she said, a hard worker who never got a break. She'd never want to hurt him.

When we were done, she shook my hand, which was a first. "Thanks," she said. "You were kind. I knew you would be. I could see it in your face."

Incidents like these were the worst part of being Taylor Powell. The last thing I ever wanted was to cause trouble for my fellow American males, even if most of them were nothing but jealous lowlife assholes who did not deserve the celestial women they abused daily in so many ways. I hoped I hadn't caused Dean too much pain. In his way, he was probably a much more admirable individual than myself. He just couldn't fuck very well. He didn't understand how important that was to Grace.

Sitting on the desk at which Dean had no doubt spent hundreds of hours scouring the empty roadway for errant customers, I turned back to the phone. I knew it would still work. It was typical of Dean's bad luck that the telephone company—some avaricious, deregulated monopoly no doubt—would continue his service, and the fees for that service, long after the demise of his business. This was evident from the stack of bills scattered on the floor, some dated as recently as only two weeks before.

I opened my clenched palm, regarded the business card I'd carried since the crash. It'd been so strange, having been thrown from the plane, to come upon my wallet, lying on reddish sand. The leather was shriveled, the credit cards melted together into a plastic layer cake, the embossed TAYLOR POWELL on my special-issue Amex plate smeared to illegibility. Only that one thin paper card had survived, unsinged.

The card was *his* card: DR. VINCENT PARRY. HOURS BY APPOINT- MENT.

The tone humming clearly in my ear, now I dialed the number on the card. It was a "private line," I'd been told, reserved for "special" clients. I should call anytime, day or night, it made no difference. I regretted using Dean's phone for what would likely be a costly international call, but there was no other way.

It took three or four tries to get through, rapid-fire Spanish intruding on the line. Finally someone picked up. "Yes?"

"Is this the office of Vincent Parry, Dr. Vincent Parry?"

"Dr. Parry speaking." The voice was dark and somber, as if sprung from the depths of a bottomless well.

"This is Taylor Powell. I want to see you."

"Mr. Powell. I knew you'd call. Come quickly. There's no time to lose."

3.

I had met Dr. Vincent Parry eight months before in Big Sur, sitting in a hot tub overlooking the Pacific Ocean. The place had been a beatnik hangout since the '50s, until the owners turned to crack, which more or less blew the vibe. Dolph Swinetti, the Sardinian munitions and art profiteer, bought the property at foreclosure and handed it over to his wife, Sally, a health food/ leather freak, whom I'd been banging on and off when I could hack it.

Me, Jimmy Dime, and some former Dallas Cowboys had flown in for the weekend, Jimmy being heavy into health food pussy since his prostate operation. Everything was mellow until one of the football players, a down lineman, got paranoid during zazen meditation and started waving around a .45 he'd been carrying under his Nike warm-up suit. He blew the heads off a couple of reclining Buddhas, causing Sally to run around screaming, "I told you once, I told you a hundred times, you can't give LSD to black people. It just doesn't *work!*"

Fried, I lowered myself into the resort's shallow mineral pools, allowing the combination of the night air and hot sulfured waters to soak away the evening's inanities. Within moments I was dozing off. I have no idea how long I slept, but I awoke with a terrible claustrophobia, as if the boundless ocean sky was pressing down upon me.

At first glance he looked pelted—like a bear, or a very hairy dog. A full, tightly tufted beard met the similarly curled helmet of his scalp at the midpoint of his nearly circular head. The rest of his body was similarly lush, great jet-black corkscrews springing from every follicle of his barrel chest.

Being Taylor Powell, I'd gotten used to people gawking at me. This hairy man's stare, however, seemed to slice through the salt-spray air. I found myself rubbing my cheek, to see if it was bleeding. An odd, almost Cheshire cat–like smile creased his beard before he spoke. His accent was decidedly foreign, but difficult to place, a strange amalgam of the guttural tones of the Near East and the melodic, floating timbres of a South American aristocrat.

"It's such a gamble when you get a face," he said.

"Excuse me?"

"Think of it. Two eyes, a nose, a mouth, two ears: Almost every species on earth works with these basic components. Yet every face is different. The smallest shift creates a totally distinct look, another feel altogether. A cruel game of chance, the ugly might say. Your face, on the other hand, is something of a miracle, don't you agree, Mr. Powell?"

Shit. You just want to soak your ass and here's some bushy-faced weirdo coming on all cryptic and bizarre. "It's a face like any other."

The hairy man chuckled. "Don't you ever wonder how, out of all the possible combinations of features, you came to possess such a phenomenal face?"

I should have blown him off right there, told him two's a crowd in my hot tub, bub. I've been known to be curt with the unwanted. Still, this very question had vexed me for quite some time, especially since my father died.

The old fuck. "You little pissant. I'll see your pecker cold in the ground. I'll bury you." These were his last words to me. As far as he was concerned the rest of the human race existed as nothing more than an expendable tangent to his stay on the planet. But there was nothing he could do about that dot. The little black spot under his eye that he was too vain to do anything about— until it was a big black spot, a runaway melanoma.

Well, I didn't look a thing like Dad. No chip off that block. He had brown hair, I had black hair; he had dark eyes, mine were blue; the whole shape of our heads was different. This isn't to say he wasn't a handsome man, in that square-jawed, chest-thumping way. He just wasn't as handsome as me. Not by a long shot.

Poor ole Dad, he couldn't take me being better looking than him. Couldn't take me getting laid more either. He thought I'd fucked his second and third wives, which was a lie. I'd only fucked the second one, and that had nothing to do with him, since they were already divorced. Rotten as he was, she really needed someone to be nice to her.

I didn't look much like Mom either, not that I have any memory of her. She died before I turned two. I have pictures. One, anyway. She's standing on a dock, wearing a long white dress. People float in little rowboats. It's an old-fashioned spring, the men in straw hats, the dresses billowy and over the knees of the women. Mom's soft half-Irish face is partially in shadow, but she's smiling. Happy. I'm in her arms, a little baby, decked out in a sailor suit. She loved me. I can tell that. I know the way women look when they love you. But I didn't look anything like her either. Except for the eyes. At least that's what the old fuck used to say: "You got your mother's eyes."

It drove him crazy. "Stop looking at me with those eyes," he'd yell. He was out of the army by then. He'd been a major, in the first waves into Normandy. A big hero, took out a couple of Nazi pillboxes. I never understood why he quit the service, except that he knew he'd never make general. He went into insurance and spent the rest of his life hating himself, which, as far as I was concerned, made it unanimous.

We'd go around the country in the car together. I was only seven. He'd leave me sitting in the backseat of the big black Dodge while he paid calls to his clients, mostly housewives. That's when he said it, coming out the houses of those women. "Stop looking at me with those eyes!" he'd yell, still zipping up his pants. I wouldn't stop looking. I'd bear witness to his treachery, testimony to his desecration of my mother's trust. I'd keep on looking at him with my mother's eyes. Then he'd hit me.

"You are upset, Mr. Powell," the hairy man across the hot tub said. "I'd like to help you. My name is Vincent Parry. Dr. Vincent Parry." I could see his red-knobbed dong floating like a buoy on the surface of the gently oscillating medicinal waters. It was the only visible part of him without hair.

"Who says I need any help?"

"You do. Your face tells me so. It's crying out. Screaming in pain. So beautiful. So anguished."

That did it. "Can't tell you how fabulous this has been, Doc." I started to get up, but before I could step out of the pool, Parry lurched toward me, blocking my exit. He couldn't have been more than five foot six, but there was a solidity to him, a primal stumpiness. Hairy as he was, it was like facing a werewolf.

"Tell me, Mr. Powell, if you were no longer yourself, if you could become anyone, anyone at all, whom would you be?"

It was an idiot question, but I felt compelled to answer. The words came out uncontemplated, unexamined. "Someone else. Anyone else. Joe Anonymous. I'd be no one. Everyone. Everyone and no one."

"Everyone and no one." Parry repeated the words, his eyes shining brighter in their sockets. "Everyone and no one. Yes, that would be it. Perhaps that would save us."

"What do you mean, *save us*?" I tried to sound petulant, faintly threatening. "You some fucking Christer or something? I didn't know Sally invited wacko—"

In the darkness, I never saw it coming. Parry reached up and covered my face with his outsized hand.

"What the—" I spasmed backward, but Parry's grip stuck like a steel-fingered lamprey. He was palming my face as one does a basketball. The man's strength was incredible. I could feel myself being raised from the tub floor. I felt the heat immediately. It was as if my face was melting underneath Parry's palm, becoming fluid. I tried to speak but no sound came. I couldn't catch my breath. Then, I felt my face begin to move. My features were breaking free of their moorings, my eyes and nose were suddenly caught up in an irresistible force, swirling like vast cloud formations around the eye of a hurricane. Everything was being drawn down, down, and down, as if Parry had inserted a massive drain right in the middle of my head. Then it was over, as quickly as it started.

"What happened?" My face still felt hot, molten. I felt I could press my thumb through my forehead, plunge it into my brain.

"When you are ready, call me, Mr. Powell," Parry said, pushing his business card into my wavering hand. "It's a matter of life and death. More than that. You have no idea of the stakes." Then he walked off, his dripping, hairy form disappearing into the night.

"Hey!" I tried to run after him but slipped, falling back into the tub. A curtain of steam rose as my face hit the sulfured water. When I scrambled back to my feet, Parry was gone.

Up at the house, the party, which had begun with communally administered high colonics and evocations of the Goddess, had degenerated to the usual sulky group grope. Everyone looked up when I came in, no surprise since every woman in the place would rather have been with me than whoever they were currently going through the motions with. That was when I became aware of the incredible bone I had on.

"Oh, Taylor," cooed a half dozen women in unison, "you're so rough, you're so ready."

When I asked if anyone knew anything about a hairy doctor out by the hot tub, however, pained and puzzled looks came over the well-chiseled countenances of the languid orgyists. No one admitted to seeing such a person; the name Dr. Vincent Parry was greeted with a twitching stonewall of silence.

"Maybe you saw a bear, Taylor," fretted Marge Dilfork, the dim-bulbed studio exec I once fucked on a rickety card table in the middle of an empty 747 hangar. "Or an exceedingly large raccoon," suggested the agent Tepper Shantz.

The hirsute man was obviously some star-struck party crasher, said hostess Sally Swinetti, dispatching several steroid-stuffed bodyguards to investigate. Suddenly everyone was on edge. The mere mention of Vincent Parry's name had dried up every pussy in the house, wilted every dick. Except mine, of course. My cock was so rigid I feared it might detach from my body and soar through the room like a blood-engorged cruise missile.

"Would you knock it off, Taylor," Sally Swinetti whined. "Why do you have to be so hard all the time?"

It wasn't until a couple of days later, as we lay side by side on massage tables at the club, with Helga and Dusty belaboring our backs with oak branches, that Jimmy Dime set me straight.

"Vincent Parry's the tummy tuck king of Beverly Hills. He's been into more noses than Peru, contoured more cleavage than Maidenform ever dreamed. He probably snipped and stuffed everyone at the party. That's why they flipped. Parry knows where all the liposuction is buried."

"They bury liposuction?"

"Sure. Fatty globule landfills, squishes under your feet, but very ecologically sound."

"If Parry's so big, how come I never heard of him?"

This pissed Jimmy off. "Why haven't you heard of him? Fuck, Taylor, sometimes that whole naïveté act of yours is too damn much. You haven't heard of Parry because you're perfect. You're the Face, the only guy in the whole damn town who doesn't need Vincent Parry." Jimmy grabbed at the skin below his eye, pulled at it. "See this shit? You think this is me? Any of it?"

I felt chastened. Jimmy might have been a prick but he was my friend. My best friend. Maybe my only friend. Huge as he was, he was still essentially a character actor with attitude, never a total heartthrob. On the dark side of fifty, panic was setting in. I knew he occasionally rode my coattails to get babes but that was fine. There were more than enough to go around.

"Sorry man," I said quietly. "Maybe there's a portrait of me up in the attic covered with warts and loose skin."

"Still wouldn't even things up," Jimmy muttered, wounded. "Creepy fucking guy that Parry. He makes you swear."

Helga was really digging into my trapezius. "Swear what?"

"That you won't tell the parts he touched. He intimates freaky ninja shit is going to come down if you let on. He's got some rap about the sanctity of the face."

I mulled this over a moment. "He's good, though? He's a good plastic surgeon?"

Jimmy smirked. "He's the best, best in the world. Check into his joint in the morning, your face hits the ground running. You're eating pussy for dinner."

I replayed this incident through my head as I headed south through the Central American night in that clatterbox bus. It wasn't long after our encounter in the hot tub that Vincent Parry, tummy tuck king of Beverly Hills, had mysteriously disappeared, leaving a roster of despairing Rodeo Drive models and matrons. He'd left no forwarding address, only a note saying he was going "to the jungle" to do "what had to be done."

Yeah, it was something to think about all right, I thought, the stray headlights of the Third World night blaring in my eyes as I thumbed through a Spanish newspaper detailing the lurid "facts" of my untimely demise. I got top billing over Jimmy, but I'd always been huge in Latin countries. ¡EL AMANTE SUPREMO TAYLOR POWELL MUERTO! said the headline. Forensically speaking it was an open-and-shut case: Even though the corpses had been totally incinerated by the fire, rescue workers found the two front teeth that Jennifer Cantrell, in the throes of passion, had knocked from my mouth. A quick dental-record check sealed my fate. The paper had a picture of me, taken from some old biker film, one of my first. The reproduction was shitty, my famous face barely decipherable. Still, I pulled down the brim of the hat I'd bought at the bus station, pressed my face closer to the rattling window.

Not that the people on this bus were likely to recognize me, missing two front teeth or not. They were dirt-poor jungle dwellers, half of them transporting goats, pigs, and other underfed animals. They carried large baskets and lugged torn cardboard boxes that they lashed to the top of the bus with plastic rope. Everything they owned was in those parcels that could, at any moment, slip from the rusted roof rack, the contents to be scattered along the pocked roadway by the buffeting winds. What would they do then? Look in the ditch, shake their heads, and simply go on.

These were the real people of the world, the salt of the earth, God's legitimate children. Why should they care if a shitbag actor like myself was dead or alive? They had problems of their own. Real, human problems. They were better than me. Now, however, shuddering through the jungle night, I felt closer to these people. My baggage had slipped off the bus, and I was going on.

4.

I was looking at the faces. Faces on heads, women's heads, severed at the neck and stuck on poles, garish red lipstick slathered across mocking mouths, shocks of animal fur bonded by blood to form riotous brows above bulging eyes. Skin hung like the rotting rind of month-old cantaloupes. I knew these faces, and the bodies to which they were formerly attached. I'd fucked them, each and every one, loved them. They belonged to Parry now. The plastic surgeon, unshackled from Beverly-Wilshire niceties, was no longer content with mere face-lifts. Here he took the whole head.

The doctor was close now, very close. Lightning stabbed through the jungle canopy, illuminating the face directly before me: Jennifer. Lovely, frigid Jennifer: the lonely supermodel. I'd seen to it that she died happy. Now she was here with the rest, her shampoo-ad mane mockingly replaced by a Norman Bates wig.

Except there were no faces, no heads, just the night, the insects, and the shriek of nocturnal birds. "Please, sir," Josias said, shaking me awake. "We must continue on."

"Sorry," I replied, opening stinging eyes. "Guess I fell asleep."

It was Josias who had met me at that wretched dung-strewn "bus stop" in the small market town. Apparently in his late twenties, at least six and a half feet tall, he towered over the other Indians milling about. Even through the mucky bus windows I could see the dull shine of his eyes, the cataracts metallic like the side of a tarnished pot. Not that his blindness appeared to hamper him. He seemed to operate according to an interior radar, making a path between the beggars and the fetid corpses of flattened dogs, stopping directly in front of me.

"Come please, sir," he said in serviceable English as he picked up my bag. "We have a long walk."

I followed him into the jungle, our every step taking us deeper into a dense, primeval world of ever-thickening photosynthetic fecundity. In we walked, past huge slithering vines, creepers and crawlers both. Above, in the trees, mica disklike eyes of hungry, unseen beasts glinted, replacing the stars of the obscured sky.

After two days of leeches and wet feet, we came upon a compound of weathered wooden buildings. In the middle of the tumbledown structures was a large corral or holding pen, inside of which lay a large pile of rocks and a cache of rusted, heavy hammers; someone, or several someones, had once been employed breaking those rocks. I didn't imagine it was of their own volition. Directly behind the corral was an old wooden church, its cracked steeple soaring above the vegetational riot.

"The doctor is there," Josias said, motioning me forward.

I got within twenty feet of the church before the shouting started. "There's nothing! *Nothing at all!* Nothing below the surface! It's madness! Evil madness!"

That did it. Whatever Doctor Moreau scene was going down inside that building, I didn't want any part of it. I was getting out of there. I'd go back to L.A., turn up one morning at my old Bel Air Hotel table, put on that irresistible shit-eating grin, and say reports of my death were greatly exaggerated. It'd play. Bigtime.

One glimpse of Josias, however, told me there would be no turning back. The blind Indian had situated himself between the corral and the church, blocking any escape path. His machete was no longer safely tucked into his belt; now he held the fearsome knife in his hand, seemingly at the ready. "Go," he said with steely insistence. "He waits for you."

Another terrible cry came from Parry's lab. "There's *nothing*!" he screamed. "*Nothing at all!* Only an emptiness . . . He's stolen the soul! Sucked it dry!" This was followed by an anguished weeping, a despair the likes of which I'd never heard.

With much trepidation, I approached the warped wooden doorway of the tin-roofed church. "Dr. Parry . . . It's Taylor Powell." There was no answer, only the white noise of jungle hum. I opened the door, went inside. Immediately the stale odors of alcohol and formaldehyde assaulted my nose.

Parry was sitting on the floor of the anteroom, bearing little resemblance to the powerful, frightening man I had encountered in the hot tub only months before. Propped up on a pile of satin pillows like a rummy pasha, his head wobbling about on his shoulders, the plastic surgeon appeared to have shrunk, his previously trunklike arms reduced to mere sticks. The jet-black hair, once plush as a proud winter pelt, seemed to be molting; it was as if he'd contracted a mange-like disease.

"Parry, are you all right?"

"Oh, Mr. Powell," Parry finally replied. "I didn't expect you for several days." He looked around the room sourly. "I would have tidied up a bit."

A few ceramic plates containing half-eaten food lay around. What caught my eye, however, were several syringes, sitting on a stainless steel tray. It was like entering a junkie's lair. Bruises covered Parry's arms.

"Sodium Pentothal," the doctor said, picking up one of the needles, pushing the plunger so a fine stream of liquid spouted from the needle's tip. "The truth drug."

Mainlining sodium Pentothal! How kinky could you get? "I thought they only gave that to spies."

Parry sighed. "We are all double agents in the house of our own nature, Mr. Powell, are we not? What better drug with which to travel within? Unfortunately, I have only succeeded in reaffirming my long-held fears." Parry coughed several times, finally catching his breath. "The soul, Mr. Powell, the Spirit unseen, which was once assumed to be the Breath of God within us, has withered and died. It is nothing but an item of nostalgia now, a mocking reflection from the past to be cruelly exploited by priests."

"You saying there's no soul, no inner life . . . no hope?"

Parry blinked his rheumy eyes. "I didn't say that. Not at all. There is hope. Now that you are here."

The doctor shouted for Josias to show me to my quarters. "Your journey has been an arduous one, Mr. Powell. You should freshen yourself."

Dinner was served inside the "chapel," a windowless hallway-like structure at least one hundred feet long and barely fifteen feet across with a vaulted tin ceiling rising perhaps forty feet above the hardpacked mud floor. A long table ran lengthwise, a line of burning tapers shoved at various angles into an undulating mound of wax that rose from the tabletop like a dragon's spine.

"Javelina, Mr. Powell?" Parry said, passing a ceramic bowl filled with stewed, stringy meat. "Caught and freshly butchered by Josias."

"Josias caught this?" The Indian had set the food on the table without a word and now stood out on the chapel porch, holding a gas lantern and facing into the vacuumlike darkness of the jungle.

"He's quite the hunter," Parry said, peering through the screen door. "It's remarkable watching him stalk the beasts. He became blind as a young man, but knows where things are." Showered and shaved, attired in an elegant forest green smoking jacket and dark twill trousers, the doctor appeared vibrant once more.

"Javelina, huh?" I said, smelling the plate of steaming meat before me. It was seasoned with oddly aromatic spices. It was only after I began eating that I realized how hungry I was; I hadn't had a proper meal since the plane crash.

"Smoke?" Parry handed me a large, hand-rolled cigar.

"Sure," I said. I'd long since quit smoking, for the usual reasons. Now that I was ostensibly deceased I saw no reason to refrain. What was the use of being dead, if you can't abuse your body a bit?

Parry lit my cigar and rose from his seat, opening the ornately carved doors of a large mahogany cabinet and bringing out a cut-glass decanter. "This cognac is very old. I think you will notice the difference." He poured a bit into my glass, did the same for himself.

I've never been much of a drinker, but this was obviously not an ordinary cognac. The amber elixir seemed to burnish the sides of my throat as I sipped it. "Excellent," I allowed.

"Yes, it is," Parry replied, fingering the rococo decanter. "It was brought here by the murderers. They killed dozens in this place. Tortured them to death, many right here in this church."

This bit of news turned the cognac to blood in my mouth. With one hacking spew, I spit out the liquor, spraying myself and the earthen floor.

Parry thought this was funny. "Don't worry, Mr. Powell! The decanter conforms the cognac to its particular shape, but former ownership imparts no lasting properties."

The stinking booze was all over my already reeking gas station attendant's jumpsuit. "That what you do for fun down here, make up stories like that?"

"If only it were made up." A scrimlike shadow fell across the doctor's face. "Many were tortured outside, in the pen. The worst of it occurred here, where we sit right now. Sometimes their cries echo, and the suffering faces invade my dreams. Tell me, Mr. Powell, do you have such dreams?"

"I dream about women, nothing else."

"I envy you, to have such a fecund paradise for an unconscious. Of course you would . . . being who you are . . . the Face. That is why I was drawn to you. The two of us have had a symbiotic relationship for some time. You've made me quite a bit of money over the years."

Parry took another sip of cognac, savoring it. "So many of my former clients spoke your name even as the anesthesia took hold, the image of your face penetrating that deep fog of the mind. That was why they came to me in the first place: because of you. You were the focus of their lives. They could think of nothing else but to look sleeker, younger, more lustrous—for you. I took professional pride when they called me with thanks. 'He told me my eyes were beautiful,' they'd say. Or: 'He spent ten minutes talking about the wonderful curve of my chin.' 'He was crazy about my nose,' 'He didn't notice a thing.' I took such pride in these reports. To have you, the ultimate lover, be pleased by my humble alterations. For an artist, this can be very gratifying."

Parry drained his glass. "There's one thing I don't understand, Mr. Powell. Imagine, a face like yours. A face with so much power over women. Why would you want to give it up?"

"Who said I wanted to give up my face?" I shot back.

"You did. That night. You wanted to be anybody but yourself. That is what I asked, how could anyone be unhappy to have a face like yours?"

"I'm not unhappy."

"But you are." Parry stared at me, dared me to deny it.

It was as if I'd been slipped one of his sodium Pentothal Mickeys and I was bound to tell whatever version of the truth I could muster. "I don't know. I used to be happy. I was the happiest guy in the world. Then, I don't know. Something happened. It's the pressure. I can't take the *pressure* . . . all those women . . . wanting me . . . needing me. I'm only one guy."

Parry reached out, gently touched my arm. "You underestimate yourself, Mr. Powell. The pain you feel comes not from the overload of responsibility. But rather from *too little*. As much as you've done for the women of the world, your capacity to help is even greater."

"What more is there?"

"The fate of humanity, Mr. Powell," Parry intoned. "The continued existence of this world as we know it."

"Stop saying that creepy shit."

"Sorry, I didn't mean to upset you," Parry said, sincerely. He finished his drink with one gulp and looked at me solicitously. "Would you care to hear the story of how I came to this place? It is a long tale, but we have time. Who knows how long it will be before dawn."

Sure, I thought, why not. Tell me the story of your life. This life and every other one. Time was an inexhaustible commodity in the jungle, or so I'd been told. "Let's hear it. My appointment book's a six-lane blacktop and not a car in sight."

An unexpected gratitude infused the doctor's haunted face. "Thank you. I have been here some time. I need someone to listen. To understand." Parry filled my glass once more and motioned toward Josias, who continued to stand outside the door, his lantern a thin beacon in the close jungle night. "It's his story, really. But ours, too. All of ours." Then, leaning back in his chair, taking deep, hungry sucks on his black-leafed cigar, Parry told the history of the place where we were.

5.

"It began as a nightmare hatched, as so many nightmares are, in the sober halls of government and commerce. An imported nightmare, a modern plague, a virus in the hearts of men, traveling from far across the seas, to this oblivious, uninocculated place." This was the manner in which Parry began his story of how several European powers came to this remote jungle to create the short-lived rubber boom of the 1920s.

"The idea was to compete with the British markets in India and Malaya. To accomplish this, a workforce of unprecedented size and diligence was required. The Indians of this area were river dwellers. They practiced no agriculture, possessed no written language, built no great hidden cities, worshiped no mysterious and bloodthirsty gods. They walked naked. To the eye of supposed civilization, they were men of no consequence, barely men at all."

Parry opened a drawer, took out a small, oval silver frame containing the photo of a dark-haired, dark-eyed man of perhaps forty-five. It was an unremarkable face, a mix of Spanish and Indian features, not atypical to the area. The nose was slightly flattened and too large, as if it had been broken at one time, the eyes set relatively far apart. There was an uncomfortable look to the man, a formal stiffness, but I attributed this more to the primitiveness of early photography than to the subject himself.

"His name was Arana," Parry said. "Julio Cesar Arana, a clan leader from the city with a shadowy reputation. He was given license by a European consortium to 'secure the full-scale production of top-grade rubber by whatever means seen fit.' To Arana and his men, *Los Muchachos,* a group of local toughs outfitted with emblematic stovepipe hats, this meant invading the villages of the forest and coercing every able-bodied man into the rubber fields. *Los Muchachos* would arrive without warning, ruthlessly rousting the people, bringing them here. Those who resisted, or were too sick to work, were killed.

"From this building, from the very chair where you now sit, Mr. Powell, Arana administered his Empire of Death. He ordered the mass floggings, maimings, blindings, personally presiding over the more intimate tortures, some performed with the well-sharpened points of a crucifix. To Arana, the Indians were his own personal property. The forehead of each man, woman, and child was branded with the date 'Marzo 22.' That was the birthday of Arana's mother, whom he held in great regard.

"The business of rubber production was largely forgotten, the tapped plants left seeping like wounds, the pots unattended. Only enough to satisfy the European sponsors was produced. It was a delirium of terror which continued for nearly a decade, halted only by a dispassionate letter sent by an Amsterdam banker informing 'Foreman Señor Arana' that while his work had been 'highly commendable' the rubber produced in this region was found to be inferior to the subcontinental variety, therefore unsalable on the international market. His funds cut off, Arana and his men left one evening, never to be seen again."

Parry's story left me stunned. "All that, in this room, this horrible, horrible place!" Suddenly possessed by rage, I picked up the frame containing Arana's picture and tried to crush it inside my fist.

Parry's hand covered my own, loosened my grip. "You are angry at these terrible crimes, Mr. Powell. That's good. I do not, however, tell you these things as yet another saga of human darkness. What happened here was dreadful, but this is not a zone of terror. Indeed, this is a holy place. Evil reigned here, but it was also banished, chased from this very building by the bond of men."

Josias was now standing beside me. I hadn't seen or heard him come in. For such a large man he moved like a ghost. He picked up the story from Parry now.

"They beat and killed us until we forgot. They would shout, 'Who is your father; who is your mother? Who is your grandmother; who is your grandfather?' Those who answered were killed. If you said you didn't know, they beat you more. There was no way to fool *Los Muchachos,* they were river people like ourselves, they knew our ways. 'He's lying,' they'd say, 'he remembers.' It was only when they were convinced that you knew no one, not where you came from or where you were going, that they let you live. This was their way."

The candlelight was casting an unsettling glow upon Josias's silvery eyes as his trancelike baritone droned on. "Then, one day, the killing stopped. Those still alive stumbled along the banks of the river, which was now unfamiliar to them. For a thousand generations we have lived here, on the boats and in the forest. Now, a monkey screeched, and people looked into trees. 'What a strange sound.' They said, 'What beast might make such a noise?'

"My grandfather was a very strong man. He convinced *Los Muchachos* he'd forgotten all that he was. This was not so. He placed himself and the world he knew in a part of his mind where they could not reach. He was a living echo, the only one of us who could remember. He tried to remind the others. He told them stories of their lives, drew them pictures of their parents, but still they could not recall.

"One day my grandfather went into the jungle and began to pick roots. Roots and leaves. He gathered parts of the forest, pieces of the earth. The earth cannot forget itself, he thought. It has seen what has happened here, it will make us remember. He put the things he gathered into a large black pot and boiled them for days.

"My grandfather called the people. He made them come here, to this very house. This place of torture and forgetting. 'Sit in a circle,' my grandfather said. 'Sit in a circle as we have always done!' The people did not move, they'd even forgotten what a circle was."

Josias thrust out his arms now, spreading them to either side of his body. His reach was long, the wingspan of an eagle. An excitement came into the Indian's face as he approached me. "My grandfather sat right there, in Arana's chair. Where you, Mr. Powell, sit right now. He said: 'Everyone! Come here. Link arms, *drink this!*' He poured each person a cup of the drink he had made from the earth. The liquid was bitter; people gagged and were sick. In their agony they reached out for each other, joining hands around the circle. Within one hour the remedy took hold, and the people saw what the earth had remembered for them. They saw themselves as they were before Arana. They were not happy about all they saw. But they saw these things together and again they knew who they were."

Then Josias stopped speaking, becoming as stolid as before.

Parry was behind me now, his hands on my shoulders, massaging my muscles. "So there it is, Mr. Powell," Parry said, "the story of this place, up to now, that is. You may wonder what this has to do with you. Why should a man so blessed as yourself care about the fate of a remote tribe of Indians? The two of us, we are cosmopolitan individuals. Men at the top of our respective professions. It begs the question: Why are we here, in this dank, mosquito-ridden hell, not still sitting in the luxury of a hot tub overlooking the rolling Pacific?"

Parry's backrub was so relaxing, I was spacing out. "I dunno. Why?"

"Because the war against evil will never end. It goes on and on. That is why we are here, you and I, Mr. Powell. To learn how to fight. It is a battle each generation must take on anew, on its own terms. For us, there is no remedy in Josias's grandfather's elixir, it is just another desultory drug experience, one more instance of self-aggrandizing spiritual adventurism. We cannot expect the earth to remember what we have forgotten. We've paved the earth over, drained its blood, put out its eyes. It can't even see us. How can we expect it to bear our witness?"

With that Parry shoved a mirror into my hands. It was an elegant piece of work, sporting a tooled handle of solid silver. Embossed on the frame were the words MARZO 22. Arana's mirror!

"This is what we have instead of the earth," Parry said, pushing the mirror closer so my reflection filled the glass. "The Face, the face of man. It is the only universality we understand at this late date. We have allowed ourselves to be cut off from the interior, the soul, and all that is left is the surface. That is our commonality, the surface of ourselves."

I stared at myself in Arana's mirror. It was funny, you know, me being the Face, but I rarely looked in the mirror. "Most beautiful guy who ever lived and you ain't even vain about it. Ain't fucking fair," Jimmy Dime used to bitch. "With Narcissus, us ugly guys always knew he was going to get so hung up on himself he'd turn to stone. You don't even care."

Parry was closer now, his voice insistent. "The face is our only hope, Mr. Powell. That is why we are here. The two of us." The plastic surgeon tapped his index finger to his temple. "You see, up here, I have every face. Every face ever made. All God's copyrights, memorized, cataloged. It has always been my gift . . . to never forget a face, so to speak. Even the ones I've never seen." Parry grew quiet now. He appeared to be in deep meditation, as if an impossibly large Rolodex of face cards was flipping at tremendous speed past his mind's eye.

"Shall we begin now?" Parry asked, with sudden sharpness.

"Begin what?"

"What you've traveled so far for, Mr. Powell. To become everyone and no one."

I took a deep breath and felt myself transported to Fat Vito's barbershop in Paterson, New Jersey, where my father used to take me to get my hair cut. There were any number of barbers closer to where we lived, but Dad insisted I see Vito. "He was one of my men, we fought together," Dad said, by way of explanation.

It was the same every time. Vito would usher me to the chair in his dowdy shop as if I were the young prince ascending his throne. Flapping his cotton sheet with regal flourish, he would inquire, "So what'll it be today, sport?"

"He'll have a crew cut," my father always said, before I got a chance to open my mouth. One time, however, when Vito asked his ritual question, I blurted, "I thought I'd have a pompadour."

"A pompadour!" Vito exclaimed with approval. "The pompadour is very popular these days. If I was a handsome young man like you, I, too, would want a pompadour." Vito was clicking his scissors, gleefully twirling them about his finger as a gunfighter might a six-shooter, when my father said, "He'll have a crew cut."

"Crew cut it is," Vito replied dutifully, laying down the scissors and picking up his buzz-clippers.

"Don't you *ever* contradict me in front of one of my men," my father said when we got back to the car. Then he smacked me across the face, hard. Now, in Arana's mirror, I could see the spot where Dad's battalion ring tore my skin, below the right eye. It was a weird thing, that scar, because other than that, my face had seemed more or less invulnerable. Like that time Jimmy Dime and I got jumped by those irate husbands outside Tulsa. They were putting quite a hurting on us until they realized who we were. Then they got goony, asking for our autographs, buying us beers; the fact that we'd banged their wives in the Suburban just moments before was suddenly of no consequence. Anyway, Jimmy got his nose busted, took twenty-five stitches under the eye. I was, as always, unmarked. That's when Jimmy asked me how many souls I'd sold to the Devil to get the Face.

Dad's ring was the only thing that ever marred my peaches-and-cream complexion. I'd always treasured that little divot; in case I forgot, it reminded me how much I hated the old man. Now the mark would be gone, along with the rest.

"Are you ready, Mr. Powell?" Vincent Parry asked, his mouth covered with a surgical mask, bidding me to lie down on the dining table.

"Ready as I'll ever be," I said, stretching out on the chapel table on which Parry apparently planned to operate. "Just leave some in the front to comb, you know, like a pompadour."

Parry did not answer. He put his hand over my face, as he had that night in the hot tub. I felt my face begin to move, after which the lights went out.

6.

"The butterfly . . . the butterfly . . ."

The journey between life and death and life again is that of a single atom propelled by the faintest breath across the incalculable arc of the heavens and earth: It is a voyage beyond the recognition of the traveler. You can't find yourself. Especially when you have no idea what you look like. Or if you even exist.

Then, out of blackness, widewinged and soaring, came the butterfly. A single monarch butterfly, orange and black, like so many I'd chased that lone summer of bliss, when Dad rented an apartment across the street from a vacant lot in North Jersey. All day long I'd run through the muck with my friends, Billy, Joe, and Carroll, in search of our fluttery prey. We didn't have nets, only our hands, and we didn't bother with dumb little cabbages or even viceroys. Monarchs were what we cared about.

Once I caught one, cupped it against the cinder-block wall with my hand. I peeked through my fingers and saw that the butterfly wasn't panicked. It knew I would let it go and I did. That was between the bug and me: It would always be free to fly above the landfill and all I had to do to see it was raise my eyes. It wasn't until the next year, in junior high school science, that I learned how long butterflies really live, not to mention the effects of DDT.

An actor lives a roster of fakery, and now, cast into Parry's anesthetic blackness, the face of every moron character I'd been paid so much to play passed before me. The feckless drifter, the feckless comedian, the feckless bankrobber, the feckless assassin—each feckless manifestation of my famous face flickered and faded before me. All that remained was the boy with the butterfly.

"The butterfly . . . the butterfly . . ."

It was Parry speaking. He was right beside me, inches from my gauze-wrapped head. "The butterfly," the plastic surgeon said again. "The beautiful butterfly . . . returned to the cocoon . . . from where he might emerge again . . . as something beyond beautiful."

That's when I heard the gun cock. Even through the muffle of the bandages the sound was unmistakable: the cocking and un-cocking of a pistol, the spin of the cylinder of a revolver.

"Ah, Mr. Powell, there you are. At last." There was a numb weariness in his voice, as if he'd been without sleep for days. The gun cocked again. Uncocked. Parry must have been playing with it, bringing the weapon to the brink of discharge and then back-ing off.

"Don't try to speak, Mr. Powell. Nor should you move. The healing process is not a very long one, but it must not be inter-rupted. Remaining still is the key." Then, after a long pause, Parry said: "Of course, you have many questions. Let me tell you this: The operation went well. Very well. In one week's time, when these bandages are removed, you will see for yourself.

"As for the other questions . . . as to who you are . . . and what the significance of your existence may be, these are for you to answer. You and you alone. I have done everything I can. There is nothing left for me." Again the gun cocked. This time I didn't hear it uncock. I turned in the direction of the sound.

"I SAID DON'T MOVE!" Parry thundered. "If you move you'll ruin everything! It'll all be for nothing! So help me I'll kill you if you move!"

A moment passed before he spoke again. "Please, Mr. Powell. Your destiny, perhaps the destiny of us all, lies before you. You must allow yourself to heal properly. It's the only chance." I felt Parry's hand on my wrist. How soft it felt, so warm in compari-son to the clammy coldness of the straps lashing me down.

"Mr. Powell, I ask one thing of you. A promise." He gripped my wrist more tightly. "I ask because I feel entitled to ask. We have come so far together, you and I. You must promise me you will never, under any circumstance, the imminence of your own death included, reveal who you once were. You must come back into the world as a totally New Man. There can be nothing of the old you to inform this new face of yours—at least on the surface. Will you promise me this?"

I felt the warmth of his breath through the layered bandages. "Please! If you agree to promise just wiggle your finger and I will know of your decision." He was pleading, desperate for my assent. "Do you promise never to tell? *Do you?*"

I wiggled my finger.

"Thank you, Mr. Powell. And may we be successful in our common battle, against the evil which infects us all." I felt his lips kiss the gauze that swathed my head. A moment later came the roaring explosion, followed by the sound of Parry's body hitting the floor.

7.

I have no notion how long I lay there, afraid and unable to move. The impulse was to shout for help but Parry had warned me against that. Besides, what good would it do? The surgeon was dead, probably before he even hit the floor. I never heard another sound from him. Inside my mummy's casing, it was impossible to avoid the image of two faces. His: decaying, dead, a gaping hole blown through it. Mine: new, waiting to be born.

I wondered when Parry would start to smell. The stink would attract animals who wouldn't priss about like picky-eating city pets. These were jungle animals, they'd be on Parry's body in a flash, ripping the brains out of the surgeon's shattered head with their spiky claws. Then the beasts would see me and it wouldn't matter whether I was dead or not. They only care if you're moving.

I must have passed out again then. The next thing I knew was Josias's quiet, steady voice. "Please, sir," the Indian said with measured insistence. "You must get up." I could feel him cutting the ropes with his machete.

"I . . . I . . ." Speech was next to impossible. I wondered if Parry had sewn my lips together as is done with shrunken heads.

"We must go. The killers approach."

"Killers?" My skin felt tight, every utterance, each movement, was torture. If I rose prematurely, my as yet unfinished face might shift like a newly iced cake turned on its side, the cheeks and chin oozing like wet clay, eyes drooping from their sockets on elongated stalks.

Josias was working faster now. "The doctor's death will only anger these men. They are beasts. They come from Arana."

"Arana? Arana is alive?"

"Arana cannot die. That is why we must leave. We cannot allow him to see your face. Your face is dangerous to him. He will try to destroy you. *Los Muchachos* are coming here, right now!"

"*Los Muchachos?*"

"Yes. They come with their machetes and rifles. We cannot allow them to catch us." Josias finished freeing me, gently helping me sit upright.

"What's burning?" A nauseating odor permeated the gauze, clinging to the mesh.

"The doctor," the Indian replied, as he pulled me off the table. "It is better this way. Now they will not mutilate him and use his parts as talismans of their evil cause. The doctor was a good man. Talented. But very strange."

Josias did not elaborate. He laid me down in the back of his donkey cart, snapped a whip at the animal. The heels of my dangling feet bumped along the rocky pathway as we traveled away from the encampment. We hadn't gone more than a mile or two before I heard a scatter of gunfire.

"They have arrived at the camp," Josias said. "They see that the doctor is dead and we have escaped. So they shoot at each other in frustration. They must kill someone, even if it is themselves. It is how they are. But they are relentless and good trackers. They will come after us. I was a fool to think we could escape them on this roadway." The Indian stopped the donkey and came to lean over me. "Drink this, sir."

I felt a thin straw probe through the bandages and find its way between my raw lips. I sucked reflexively, as a newborn might. "It will make you sleep," Josias said. "It will make it easier for me to carry you through the forest." The Indian's wiry, powerful arms cradled my body and he began walking, my 180 pounds seemingly no impediment to his increasingly brisk pace.

"Arana can't die?" I asked groggily, the drug's effects beginning to take hold.

"No. His dark blood flows through us all. He can appear at any place or at any time. Even from the heavens above. That is why you must be protected, lest they find out who you are."

"Who am I?"

If the Indian answered this question, I didn't hear it. The hint of daylight seeping through my bandage cocoon disappeared and once more I saw nothing but blackness. The next thing I knew I was on another of those rattling buses, *conjunto* music blaring scratchily through half-blown speakers. I could tell from the clamor of horns and the smell of acrid air that we'd reached the city.

Josias's cousin Emilio ran a long-distance telephone service. People came to the small storefront on a gritty side street near the main square to call their relatives in the United States and other points north. From what I could glean, the two cousins had very little contact with each other, Emilio's family having moved from the jungle more than twenty years before. Nevertheless, Josias was certain his cousin would help.

"You will need papers, a passport. Emilio can make these things for you," Josias told me as we clambered off the bus and made our way through the bustling marketplace. It must have been quite a spectacle, a blind man leading a bandaged man, but if anyone bothered to notice, they said nothing.

The long-distance office was crowded. Emilio was attempting to get a line to Texas. "Hello, Texas! Hello! Hello!" he shouted into the phone. When he finally got a connection, he barked, "San Antonio!" and handed the receiver to an anxious customer. He seemed less than happy to see his long-lost cousin and strange companion.

"Take him in the back," Emilio snarled, and soon I was lying on a sagging bed that smelled strongly of semen, sweat, and beer. Still under the influence of whatever potion Josias had given me, I fell asleep once more, only to be awakened by the sound of scissors close to my face. My bandages were being snipped off.

"No!" I'd gotten used to the darkness, to my dense gray world.

After a life of being gawked at, it was restful not to see, not to be seen. The thought of leaving this quiet place was terrifying.

"Do not be afraid," Josias soothed me, spooling the gauze away from my face. With the first glimpse of the dim light, I felt a great surge of emotion.

"There," the Indian said, giving one last stubborn piece of tape a sharp pull.

"Hey! That hurt!" Stale air hit my face like the slap of a sadistic maternity doctor, and there I was, back in the world. All sight was exaggerated. Light from the single, naked hanging bulb attacked my irises. The drip of a nearby faucet was a veritable Niagara. I tried to orient myself. I was lying on a rusted, iron-frame bed in the middle of a storage room filled with piles of cardboard boxes and automotive parts. On the floor beside my bed, like the peel of a gigantic fruit, was the pile of discolored bandages.

I put my hands to my face. The skin felt smooth. If Parry's handiwork had left great networks of railroad track–like stitches crosshatching my cheeks and forehead, I did not detect them. "I need a mirror," I croaked, trying to rise on unsteady legs. There was no mirror, however, only Josias, the blind Indian.

"My face," I sputtered. "What does it look like?"

Without reply, Josias extended his huge hand and clamped it around my head, much as Vincent Parry had done in the hot tub so long ago. His palm cradled the bottom of my chin, his fingers probed the contours of my forehead. He pulled on my nose, folded his knuckles into the sockets of my eyes. He was taking an impression, creating for himself a tactile print of my newly forged features. What seemed at first to be a clinical survey soon turned sensual. The Indian was caressing my new, unknown features. A shiver went through me. He was making love to my face. Then, removing his hand, Josias started to cry. It was a striking thing, watching a blind man cry.

"Why are you crying? Is it that horrible?"

"No . . . it is not horrible. It is wonderful . . . It is . . . everyone and no one . . . It is hope."

It was right then that Emilio entered the room holding a Polaroid camera. Small and seedy in a Ban-Lon shirt and sporting a pencil-line mustache, Emilio was an ugly little man who bore scant resemblance to his taller, younger, angelic cousin. Unpleasant in his manner, he seemed a natural-born hater. "Okay you, get up, I got no time for this. I'm busy. Very busy!" he blustered, aiming the camera at me.

I sat there, expecting Emilio to recoil at my new face, but he took no notice of it whatsoever. "Listen, you want your picture taken or not?" the knobby man shouted impatiently, circles of perspiration spreading under his arms.

I looked around the room. "Don't you have any mirrors?"

"What do you need a mirror for? It's only a passport picture. You look fine." Emilio reached into the pocket of his checked gabardine slacks and drew out a small black comb. "Here, comb your hair if you have to."

I regarded the greasy, dandruff-specked comb. "No . . . it's not that . . . I just want to see what I look like . . . You see, I don't know."

Emilio frowned impatiently. "What do you mean, you don't know what you look like? You look like you." He readied the camera.

How many thousands of times had I had my picture taken? How many millions of feet of film bore my celebrated likeness? I knew the camera, understood its ins and outs, its wants and its needs, how to coax sadness and gladness from its phallic lens. As was said, ad infinitum, the camera loved Taylor Powell. Me and my famous Face. What would it think of this one? I smiled my unseen smile. *Cheese.*

Emilio's Polaroid was one of the old models. Talk about a watched pot! The sixty seconds seemed an eternity. I used the slowly passing time to ponder the difficult process by which a child comes to recognize himself, to differentiate his own face from others. Names are so much easier. Children know what to call themselves long before they fully grasp the picture of the face that goes with that name. We go through a significant part of childhood being anonymous to ourselves. For many, no doubt, this condition persists to adulthood, onward to the grave. It's only photos and mirrors, secondhand indicators at best, that give us what passes for a sense of ourselves. Thinking of this as I waited for the first view of my new self to be peeled from the gummy emulsion of the camera filled me with a loathing for the modern world.

"There. Perfect," Emilio said in a clipped voice, giving the photo the most cursory of glances. But then an odd thing happened: Emilio seemed to freeze. An inch from brusquely handing me the photo, the unpleasant little man now withdrew the picture from my anxious grasp. Moving robotically, he looked at the print again, hooded eyes widening, a tiny gasp emitting from his thin, wormish lips. He stared at me, then looked back at the picture, his face a twist of incomprehension.

"What?"

Emilio shook his head violently as if he had a crick in his neck. "Nothing. Here." He shoved the photo into my hand.

And there I was, the new me, inside that two-inch square: a genial-looking guy with light brown, slightly kinked hair. My complexion was on the swarthy side, but not excessively so. My eyes were dark brown, moderately deep set beneath a vaguely protruding forehead of the slightly oval head. My teeth were all back in their proper place, but my smile was no longer the dazzling eye-catcher of old. This face had everything a face ought to have. Nothing was left out, there just wasn't anything particularly distinctive about it.

Whoever the unassuming man in the photo was, he sure wasn't Taylor Powell. The Face was gone, its perfect features scraped off life's own negative. There was nothing in the thin-faced, hollow-cheeked man before me that shouted *Star*. He could have been a supermarket manager, a second-string catcher, a day laborer, an airline pilot. He could be anyone. Or everyone. Everyone and no one.

"What's your name?" Emilio demanded.

"Name?" I drew a blank.

"You want a passport, it's got to have a name on it."

"Oh." I understood now. If that thing currently residing on the front half of my head was my face, a name was required to complete the conventional existential portfolio.

Still attired in the filthy jumpsuit I had donned inside that abandoned desert Fina station, I ran my hand over the soft cotton denim, tracing the stitched letters over the pocket on my chest. "Dean," I said.

"My name is Dean . . . Dean Taylor."

There was no time for second thoughts, as Emilio was already scribbling the name on a piece of paper, along with some other lies. Instead of being born in Baltimore on May 23, 1951, I now came into being on April 15, 1957, in New York. I made myself younger. Wouldn't you?

When he got it all down, Emilio turned to me with a scowl and said, "Josias believes in ways I do not. Old ways that have gone from me. He is my family and if he asks me to give you a new passport even though you have no money, I will not refuse him. But you must pay. When you return to the States you will send me a thousand dollars. Do you hear me? *One thousand dollars.* This is a debt I shall not forget."

"Don't worry," I spat back. "You'll get your dough."

Then Emilio sent me to wait outside in the phone office. He would print up the passport and send me on my way.

I walked down a narrow hallway and went through thick, draped curtains into the storefront where seven or eight locals were waiting to make or receive calls. I scanned these faces. Primarily round, black-haired, of Indian ancestry, a few looked happy, some sad. There was an old man with a teenaged boy I imagined to be his grandson. A woman wearing a red dress was pregnant and bounced a child on her lap. If any of them took note of my presence, they didn't show it. One by one these people took their turn using one of several phones. They might have been poor, of limited prospects, but at least they had someone to take their call. Someone they knew, and who knew them, would be there when the connection, however static filled, finally went through. I was a man who didn't even know his own face. I didn't have anyone to take my call.

I squinted through the smeared plate-glass window to the street. It was crowded out there, the standard pandemonium Third World vehicular traffic: ratchet-engined motorcycles, monoxide-spewing lorries, a thousand impatient hands hard on plastic horns—a migraine-inducing, lung-savaging, yet ultimately invigorating tumult. Inside the phone salon, however, I heard nothing, the rude tableau passing by as nothing more than an ecologically incorrect mime show.

Then I saw Josias, standing in the middle of the street, seemingly oblivious to the traffic. I'd often marveled at the blind man's sensory awareness of his surroundings, but now he was heedlessly putting himself in harm's way. "Watch out," I called, running out the door. But it was too late. A huge truck, done up with colorful paints and hanging trinkets, swung around the corner, slamming right into Josias.

I pushed through the crowd and knelt down beside him. The truck had run over his middle, his intestines were pouring onto the oily asphalt. "Josias," I cried. "It's me. Please don't die . . ."

If he was in pain, he showed no evidence of it. Instead, he smiled and extended his hand, once again stroking my face. "You must find yourself in this New Man. It may take a long time, but you will. Then you will be able to do what you must . . . You will know what it is . . . when the time comes."

A trickle of blood came from his mouth. "There is one more thing . . . Keep the promise you have made to the doctor . . . Never reveal yourself or how you came to be who you are now. This is most important."

"Yes. I swear."

Josias reached out now, once again placing his huge hand over my face, probing it again, as if making a final test. Satisfied with his findings, he motioned me forward and kissed me. *"Vaya con Dios, Dean Taylor."* And he was dead.

I sat a moment looking at his lifeless face, before I felt Emilio pulling at me. "Here." He handed me the passport he had made, featuring the photo of the new me. "You have what you came for. Now go."

I wasn't going to let this creep keep me from Josias's side. "Let go of me."

"Go," Emilio rasped. "We will bury our own dead." He was no longer alone. Several men surrounded me now. Short, squat men with impassive faces who appeared to be on intimate terms with death. Could they be *Los Muchachos*—-awaiting a signal to unleash their terror? I didn't want to hang around and find out. A pedicab came up and Emilio pushed me into it, telling the driver to take me to the station.

"Don't forget your obligation," the mean little man said as the cab pulled away. "One thousand dollars."

My itinerary was straightforward. That night I would board a river steamer leaving for the coast, then onward to Tampico. From there I would take a train, eventually making it overland to the American border. So many others—desperate, hopeful people—would make a similar trip that same night. Twenty or more souls would cram into an eight-by-twelve, false-bottomed pickup truck. A thin line of women, children lashed to their backs, plastic-soled shoes sinking in the muck, would attempt to ford the moatish river. Some would make it, some would be turned back, a few would die trying.

Emilio foresaw no such problems for me. "You look so normal," he spat as if uttering an oath. "They will just wave you through."

Which is exactly what happened a few days later at the border as a red-faced Immigrations man in the middle of hassling a hippie waved me by without a question. And then I was back on U.S. soil, an alien man who looked like everyone and no one.

DEAN

1.

Flat on my back in the squalid alleyway, I summoned my repertoire of erstwhile surefire tricks. The sidelong wink, the rising eyebrow that keeps rising, the pursed lip petulance: Each of them had been big-money moves when I was known as Taylor Powell, a.k.a. the Face.

Now, however, these building blocks of my formerly matchless career were pointless gestures, fleeting swipes at a fading shade, corrosive nostalgia. In the newly forged context above my neck, my every trademark facial trope had become a meaningless mug, a nonsequitorial twitch. Nothing was as before. Taylor Powell's mouth featured blinding dentition and lips like plush pillows. Dean Taylor offered what might be a limey sailor's smile, a gate-mouthed affair perimetered by lips thick and wide. Taylor Powell's complexion was a pleasing pink, a soothing off-white. Dean Taylor's skin was ruddy, mottled by pocks and moles. And so it went, right down to the brown doggy eyes that stood in the sockets once occupied by Taylor Powell's legendarily dazzling blue duet.

But the difference between the me I knew and the me I'd become was far greater than the simple inventory of features. A face is more than a biologic work-up of eyes, ears, nose, mouth. A face is the front half of the Mind, the filter of experience. Life is lived through a face. The face currently residing on my head might as well have been that of a newborn. It still had training wheels on.

"Did you hear me? I said who the fuck are you looking at?"

Oh, the cop. The one hitting me with the nightstick. I'd almost forgotten about him.

It'd been like that since I crossed the border. Given an opportunity to see myself, I'd space out, become oblivious to all else. It happened in front of store windows, or at car washes, where I'd hang out waiting to gawk into the gleam of newly Simonized hoods of Oldsmobiles. It happened in the crummy coffee shops and shelter lunchrooms where I'd stare into the polished scoop of spoons (if the place used plastic utensils, I'd just walk out, leaving my food untouched). Now I couldn't stop looking into the twin gold-framed reflectors of the cop's metallic sunglasses: a double-chromed cameo of the new me, albeit a tad fish-eyed.

"I said, *who the fuck you looking at?*" The nightstick jabbed at me again, finding my liver, the back of my neck. My assailant was a twentyish, beer-bellied cracker, one of those slow-moving-peckerwood, former-high-school footballers the LAPD sends out to dispense the department's particular brand of service and protection. He was one powerfully peeved copper too, my incessant staring cramming him ever deeper into the cruel little corner of fear and hatred where he was born and no doubt still dwelled.

"Answer me! Who the fuck *are* you looking at? You must be looking at me, there ain't nobody else here!"

That dreary old "you looking at me?" De Niro riff. I never cared for those so-called signature moments, to tell you the truth. Three weeks after the picture comes out fry cooks at Denny's are doing it better than you.

"Shit," I said, my throat raw. "I ain't looking at shit."

The cop's mouth twisted to a malignant gash. "You damn bum. I'll bust you up." I didn't get the porker's problem. My new face was a tinge on the dusky side, suggesting a touch of the ole tarbrush so to speak, but it wasn't as if I looked black or anything. And still, the guy was going nuts on me, trying to break my ribs. Not that it hurt that much. In fact, I barely felt a thing. Initially I attributed this lack of somatic sensitivity to Parry's having left out a nerve ending or two when he sewed me back up. But it was more than that; there's an invulnerability to parts that don't belong to you. I was a man who needed a cheat sheet to tell the color of my hair; it was easy enough to pretend the pain was happening to someone else.

Moreover, I just didn't care. You see, my famous face wasn't the only thing changed. My famous dick, sometimes referred to by admirers as "Little Taylor," was not quite itself either. "Face bone connected to the dick bone," Jimmy Dime always said. "The face-dick continuum, a grand symbiosis. Face-dick, dick-face."

"The Dickface Continuum, maybe Ludlum can use it as the title for an international semen-smuggling thriller," I joshed Jimmy then. Now I wondered. Since the termination of the Face, the dick had not risen.

Before, everything had been so automatic. It pissed, it fucked, stayed hard as long as it had to. To me, impotence was a myth to be invoked by unscrupulous doctors on bus billboards along with hair replacement and the lasering of hemorrhoids. There was no outward sign of sabotage, no evidence of tampering with the hallowed hydraulics. Little Taylor seemed the same rosy-crested, cream-shafted sweetheart it had always been. Problem was, it just lay there.

I kept a diary of those woeful times, the earliest days of Dean Taylor. The entries are odd fragments, cryptic in spots. I reproduce them here to attest to my state of mind during that time.

Saturday: again, I can't breathe . . . it's the face . . . it's pressing down on me . . . too tight, like a suffocating scuba mask . . . too tight . . . the claustrophobia of the face . . .

Sunday: still no hard-on . . .

Monday: walked by a Ferrari showroom . . . I don't know, it was just instinctive, a new year, time to check out the new models . . . the salesman came over, same asshole I always used to buy from. Sharaz, used to be third penholder to the

Shah or some shit. He was as fawning as ever, treating me like my checkbook was out and ready. Then he asked, "Like this car?" I said I did. He said, "You'll never have it," and had some ex-Savak guys toss me out.

Tuesday: still no hard-on.

Wednesday: I see hate and I see fear . . . sometimes I'm significant, with a gravity as encompassing as Jupiter's. Sometimes I'm as small as a pebble on a beach . . . I have a terrible thirst. I will quench it by walking to the sea and sucking all the water into my mouth. Then all the boats will run aground. When the boatmen holler, I will quiet them by pissing until they drown . . . At least the dick still does that.

Tuesday: threw a brick through the Ferrari showroom window. The alarms went crazy, Sharaz shaking his torturer's fist . . . thought the exhilaration would get the juices going but, still no hard-on . . .

Friday: . . . was screaming in my sleep again . . . they said I yelled "I don't fuck for money . . . I do it for fun . . ." Still no hard-on . . .

Saturday: . . . like Lugosi I crave dark, fear light . . . a man who has forgotten his face is only free in the dark . . . still no hard-on . . .

Monday: went for temp work at the cannery again, they asked me for a social security number. I made one up. No one said a thing. I was outraged. Identity shouldn't be so easy to forge. It's a damn scandal. I'm going to write my congressman about it . . .

Wednesday: some guys in the shelter lobby were watching one of my old pictures, that weird old Western in the snow. I was banging Julie on a brass bed, through half a dozen layers of bearskins. Shot the whole thing in a giant refrigerator, the idiot director going on and on about wanting to see our

breath. Julie, damn. If I'd been a normal man, not Taylor
Powell, not the Face, she would have been the one . . . kept
watching the movie, hoping her memory would stir me.
Adjust the angle of the dangle. But no . . .

Friday: I walk the streets and I am alone. An exile. I am
different. The only one with a real face. Everyone else is a
blank with hair. Indian head nickels, rubbed flat and smooth.
Everyone else lives with the face they were born with. Only I
am new, only I am modern . . .

Monday: still no hard-on . . .

Tuesday: still no hard-on . . .

Friday: it just lies there . . .

Monday: . . . limp . . .

The only way to remain sane, I decided, was to call someone.
Someone I'd fucked, which was about everyone. It couldn't be
just anyone, she had to be hot and able to keep a secret. Maybe
Tanya Smerl, who'd utilized those muscly gams of hers in the
Service of Our Nation, whoring for the CIA. No, her phone was
always tapped. I thought of Sandy Dayton, the casting director.
What a magical mystery tour it was, spelunking her stalactite
clit. She was hip, had a cool van too. She could pick me up, we'd
drive out past Twentynine Palms, bed down amongst the yuccas.

I stood there, on the soup-kitchen line, rehearsing the conversation. "Baby . . . it's me, Taylor . . . No, this isn't some sick joke.
It's *really* me, you want me to do a psychological work-up of the
Rorschach beauty mark on your right inner thigh? . . . Guess you
can't believe everything you read in the papers . . . If I'm a ghost
that proves there's fucking after death, okay . . . now . . . I'll tell
you all about it when you get here . . . *but don't tell anyone. No*
one!"

I never made the call. What was the point? The Sandy Daytons of the world lived to fuck Taylor Powell. They didn't want to fuck a guy who *used* to be Taylor Powell. Especially a faceless, dickless former Taylor Powell. I wouldn't have done it anyhow. I *promised* I wouldn't. Promised never to reveal that Taylor Powell and Dean Taylor were one and the same. I'd promised Parry and I promised Josias. I could never go back on that.

I was in a tough spot all right. Limp-dicked and anonymous in a back alley, getting the crap beat out of me by an enraged yahoo of a cop. At least it figured to be over soon. It was becoming apparent that this particular cop would not be satisfied simply to leave me bloody in the alley. The way his steel-tipped boot kept banging into my pancreas, I had the distinct impression he was trying to kill me.

Life, death: This was something of a pick-'em affair for me at this point. I searched my mind for a rationale, even a fudged-up one, that might justify the trouble it took to keep breathing. Then I saw it: the policeman's shield. He hadn't even bothered to cover it up with black electrician's tape, the way other killer cops do. He was just that arrogant, just that ruthless. The nametag said: ARANA.

"I'll teach you to look at me!" the cop yelled, thrashing away.

I doublechecked the nameplate. ARANA, that's what it said all right. It didn't compute; this kid looked like Bull Conner's nastier grandson, not the descendent of a Latino mass murderer. The cop stopped now, pursed his lips. *"Te rompo la maldita cara,"* he seethed, in the same sick-ass Southern drawl he'd said everything else.

"¿Mi cara?" Good thing I had a working knowledge of whorehouse Spanish.

"Su cara mehere. ¡Yo lo aplastare! As if a face like that could hurt me."

"No!" I threw my arm up to block the force of the incoming blow. The nightstick came down hard on my elbow. Even through the suddenly exploding pain, I recalled Josias's warning. Arana could not die, his evil blood ran through the veins of all people, not just in the jungle, but everywhere. Always. Arana would be after me, Josias said, somehow my face was dangerous to him.

"Ahora tu muerte," the cop said, pinning me to the ground. The guy was incredibly strong. His fist, gnarled and pronged with rings, was traveling at a rapid rate toward the middle of my new face. A moment before, I might have simply closed the eyes that weren't my eyes, clenched the teeth that weren't my teeth, girded myself for the end of the life that wasn't my life. Suddenly, it seemed unthinkably important that I stay alive. If Arana wanted my face, Dean Taylor's face, obliterated, then it was up to me to preserve that face just as Vincent Parry constructed it.

"Fuck you, asshole!" I screamed, managing to move my head just as the huge man's fist flew past my cheek and cracked against the pavement below. This was no ordinary foul policeman, I knew now. The man trying to smash my face was *un Muchacho,* an emissary from Arana, if not Arana himself.

To tell the truth, I've never been much of a fighter. Ole Jimmy Dime loved to walk into dim cowboy bars, smack his lips loudly, scream how he liked the tush on a particular eighteen-wheel driver so much that he couldn't wait to "eat the dingleberries right out" of their shorts. It wasn't anything personal. Jimmy always said the occasional head beating made him feel like a man. He never pressured me to join in. "It'd be bullshit for you," Jimmy would say, happily spitting bridgework, "you're a lover, not a fighter."

Very definitely, a lover, not a fighter. Now however, with the alleyway neon glinting off the huge blade in the cop's hand, I felt a warrior's surge in my breast. Suddenly I was very conscious that the stakes in this backstreet struggle amounted to a good deal more than whether my own particular next destination would be a metal drawer, a tag on my toe. I was seized by the belief that the very Fate of Humanity hung in the balance. This conviction gave me strength. I punched the assassin harder than I've ever hit anyone. I wanted to drive his porcine nose up into his programmed brain. I heard his bones crack, saw his blood pour. He reeled backward, fell over. I grabbed hold of the nightstick he'd beaten me with and hit him in the stomach, then broke it in half over his skull. I picked up a trash can cover and began bashing the cop's face. I drove the metal saucer down onto the *Muchacho,* hit him a hundred times, until he stopped groaning, stopped moving. I'd killed him.

I hovered over the man's body uncomprehendingly. Lying beside his smashed face were his mirrored shades, in a dozen jagged little shards. I wouldn't be able to stare into them anymore. That was fine. I knew quite well what I looked like, now.

2.

You never know when Fate will stumble from behind the counter of a Stuckey's and lay its liver-spotted hand upon your shoulder. Certainly I had no inkling of what awaited me as I rode in the back of a truck to Pardosville, a small gulf shore town that only days before had been more or less flattened by Hurricane Tom, the biggest storm to hit the region in decades.

What a horror show. The feds said 739 people were dead, but that was an outright lie since everyone knew someone and their brother who had drowned when the swamp waters jumped the levee. But these were primarily migrants, gnarled Mexican pickers and the like, hardly worth counting. Among the living, street life had gone seriously freelance. Gangs shot it out with uniformed protectors of property, fighting pitched battles over waterlogged furniture in the parking lots of wrecked shopping malls. Squatters took over abandoned subdivisions and set car fires visible miles away. Piles of debris grew, vied for the title of being the highest points on the seaboard. Damage at the Mega-Gro factory dumped tons of the plant stimulator into the water system, choking the sewers with wild foliage. The land was returning to itself, to a time before air-conditioning and mosquito control, prior to so-called civilization, a time when bodies were burned at pyres and the hideous waft of Death was nothing but routine.

All things considered, the area seemed a fitting destination for a man like myself, indigent, without friends or relations, a cop killer. I'd hitched down to the Gulf Coast, along with half the drifters in the lower forty-eight, with a notion of picking up day labor. A TV commentator, talking over footage of a grand piano floating down Main Street, said it would be the biggest cleanup "ever." If you could hammer a nail, you could get flush: Nearly all the buildings—most of them fairly new but shoddy—needed serious repair, if not total rebuilding. This couldn't have come as a surprise to the cheap-crook Rotarian Club contractors who'd built the drywall-and-plastic-rivet deathtraps to begin with. Weimaraner farts could blow over houses in Pardosville, to say nothing of a 150-m.p.h. gale. It was a whole town not up to code.

You had to be careful which crew you hooked on with. The scene buzzed with stories of ad hoc foremen hiring dozens of guys, putting them to work hauling debris or drying in roofs. When payday came, however, instead of a check the unlucky workers received a bullet in the back of the neck.

I fell in with a mixed bag of losers in one of the sprawling tent cities popping up along the nearly impassable main highway routes. Most were Haitians, voodooists and boat people, who'd washed ashore, naked and starving, only weeks before, much to the chagrin of package-tour vacationers. After the storm hit, the Haitians stole several huge rolls of tar paper from a ruined construction site and declared themselves roofers. Likely they figured having an English-speaking white man along might be good for business, so I became a roofer, too.

Which explains how I came to be knee-deep in pink piles of mildewed fiberglass insulation, trying to patch the roof of a ravaged apartment complex, when I heard the shouting.

"Please! Leave me alone!" It was a woman's voice, a sear of pain across the ruptured land.

At first I could not figure out where the voice was coming from. The Haitians kept their women back at the tent camp where, underfed and underloved, they spent their days cleaning clothes by beating them on rocks and cursing after small children. Life on the rafts had not ennobled these people. When the men returned from work, dour and drunk, the women were fucked for a few haphazard moments and then tossed aside, their gaunt bodies dumped onto the hard tent floor. Perhaps, when I was Taylor Powell, I would have felt responsibility for these discarded women. I'd have slipped out of my tent and found one of them, the thinnest and most disease-ridden. I'd dry the tears from her bloodshot eyes, show her tenderness she'd never known. But I wasn't Taylor Powell anymore. I was Dean Taylor, and as Dean Taylor, I felt only irritation with the manner with which the women allowed themselves to be treated. I had problems of my own.

"Stop it! Go away, this isn't right!" I'd located the source of the anguished shouts now. It was coming from inside the ruined town house below. No one was supposed to be in there. The entire area had been evacuated; eleven people had drowned just around the corner when the canal overflowed, burying the pump station in mud and hopping toads.

I could see her through the gaping hole in the roof, standing in the middle of what was once her kitchen. From my vantage point she looked to be in her mid-thirties, slim, and sandy-haired. As was the case with many storm victims who wore whatever they could salvage, she was dressed idiosyncratically, in a starched, pleated tennis dress, blue cashmere sweater, with old-fashioned high-button shoes on her feet.

A man in a familiar gold blazer and maroon slacks was moving closer to her. "Come on, honey, how about a itty-bitty little kiss."

She threw a water-damaged Mr. Coffee at him. Then a chair. Both missed and he kept coming, his voice taking on a more sinister tone. "You ain't going hold out on me, are you? Shitty little policy like you got, me helping you make out that claim form like I done. Don't be a little tease, I don't like that."

The patch on his blazer identified him as being in the employ of the Quick Pay Insurance Company. Their ads were all over, vowing "fast, honest assistance at difficult times." The guy was an adjustor called in to deal with the extraordinary number of claims in the wake of the storm. In disasters, adjustors ruled. They arrived in their rented late-model Fords with their tape measures and clipboards, sauntered squint-eyed and cocky through the shattered hulk of a family's home and proceeded to mete out a form of frontier economic justice. The phrases that dropped from their lips—"remove and replace" or "not covered"—were imbued with the power to resuscitate life or scuttle it.

I knew a good deal of this firsthand, of course, having accompanied my father on several such assignments after his discharge from the army. Not that I ever got a chance to see the old man adjust anything. I was always left to sit in the back of the car, a volume of Milton or Dante thrust into my small hands. "Memorize that," he'd order, saying he was going to test me on it when he came back. Probably I'd be a lot better educated today if I'd followed his dictates, rather than routinely pulling out the comics I stashed under the seat. Of course, if the "client" was a woman, Dad wouldn't be back for hours. By then he'd be too soused to remember my name, much less make me recite any verse. Thirty-five years later, it still turned my stomach, how much I continued to hate him.

Below, the woman kept yelling. "I didn't promise you anything!" She was brandishing a carving fork now, jabbing it toward the adjustor. "You can't do whatever you want. You're not God." The adjustor laughed menacingly. "Little lady," he said, kicking the fork out of her hand. "I'm as close to God as you're ever gonna get."

"That's what you think, asshole!" I shrieked as I jumped down through the hole in the roof. The adjustor didn't know what hit him, I was on his back like a cat, my dirty fingernails digging deep into his eye sockets. I'd become an avenger, I wanted to destroy that adjustor. Kill him like I killed the cop in L.A.

I might have done it, too, if it hadn't been for her. "Please stop!" That was the first time I ever saw her pink-white skin, her green-yellow eyes, her smallish mouth, a gold cross around her neck. "Don't! He's a human being." It was a sad face, a little puffed up. But comfortable, the face of someone you could talk to. Right off, I knew she was an alcoholic.

"All human life, all life, is sacred," she said, slowly. Her voice was quiet, steady. She touched the hand I was pressing against the adjustor's throat. With a gentle but unyielding insistence, she unclenched my fingers one by one. My hand was shaking, a violent electricity coursing through it. Her touch soothed me. I could feel the frenzied wrath fall away from me.

"Sacred . . ." I mumbled. She was right. The adjustor was a human being. Human life is sacred. I had no right to take his. I removed my knee from his stomach, helped him up. "You all right?" I asked the man, grudgingly.

The insurance man was in his fifties, swoop-haired and sun-burnished, like a low-level golf pro. He didn't speak at first, just kept looking at me, his bloodshot eyes widening. A little awestruck terror on his part was understandable, after all I'd been responsible for bringing this licentious creep to the verge of his final breath. Still, I didn't like the way he kept staring at me.

"Don't I know you?" he finally managed to say.

I swallowed. It was weird, but a lot of people had been asking me that same question ever since I'd officially become Dean Taylor. Just the other night, in the package store, some pasty-faced cracker stopped dead in his tracks, swore I looked real familiar. Down by the border, it was a young Latino who was certain he knew me from El Centro "or somewheres." Sorry, I told him, never been to that barrio. It kept happening though. Men or women, old or young, all of them seemed to know me from somewhere. At first I thought Vincent Parry, as his last act on earth (did I screw his wife? his daughter? his mother?) had made me the butt of a vicious, intricate practical joke. I wanted anonymity and he'd made me look exactly like some gangster, or rock star, a celebrity somehow even bigger than Taylor Powell—someone everyone knew on sight. That's where it ended, however, for almost immediately after saying they knew me, the person making that claim invariably withdrew it, shaking their head. "Sorry," they'd say, "you looked so familiar there for a moment."

Which is exactly what that scummy adjustor said—"Sorry, I

thought I knew you from somewhere"—before he scuttled away, like the rat he was. I was going to go after him, make him apologize, but she stopped me. "I don't think he'll try a thing like that again," she said. "You taught him quite a lesson. My name is Mary Grant. How can I ever thank you . . . Mr. . . ."

"Taylor . . . Dean Taylor." So often, in my pathetic career, I'd saved a damsel in distress; but I'd always been cool about it, tossed it off with a wink, or a suitably ironic line. Here, I found myself suddenly very shy. "There's nothing to thank me for. Anyone would have done the same thing." All I left out was the "aww shucks."

The Haitians, who'd been clustered about the hole in the roof rooting for blood, had grown bored by this time and were moving to the next job. "Well, good luck," I told her, and started for the door.

"Please," she said, reaching out to grab my arm. "Don't go . . . not yet. Please."

Her face was flushed, her eyes were red. "It's not every day someone drops in and . . ." She peered up through the hole in the ceiling to the blue sky beyond. "Please let me buy you dinner, at least."

I was kind of hungry. "Guess I could do with some of that."

3.

We went to La Continentale, one of those awkward places where the red-and-black Formica is meant to impart a hoary Queen-for-a-Day elegance. This effect, however, was compromised by the sandbags that had been piled high against the shuttered windows to guard against mudflows during the storm.

Mary was endearingly overdressed, in a mustard yellow silk shawl and teal velour dress. She'd likely lost a good deal of weight of late, because the slightly threadbare dress draped over her shoulders like a sack. Her hairdo was equally unfortunate, an off-center bun that teetered uneasily atop her head. Not that I cut a finer sartorial figure, clothed in the gas station jumpsuit I'd worn almost exclusively since the plane crash. At least I'd given one of the Haitian women fifty cents to wash the coveralls so they didn't smell too bad.

This was the least of my self-representational troubles. I'd broken out in acne, from forehead to chin. It was quite a shock, running my fingers across my cheek's blotched and bumpy terrain. Taylor Powell never had acne, not a single blackhead. At first I judged the pimples to be the product of sheer pore-clogging dirt, but diligent scouring only aggravated the afflicted area. Eventually I came to believe that my face, having lived through its infancy immediately following the operation, was now in a stage of adolescence. Understanding this concept, however, did little for my personal esteem as I skulked amongst the nerdish teenagers near the zit-care rack in the discount drug store.

Perhaps we did appear to be a pair of geeks, Mary and I, but this was not Spago or some such fast-lane fishbowl, this was starch-and-grease America, and within the hokey confines of La Continentale, we fit right in. That was obvious enough when our waiter, a lumpen high schooler dressed in a Gallic black vest and long white apron, handed us a pair of hefty Naugahyde-bound menus. After a recitation of "today's specials" rendered with C-minus seventh-grade French skills, the waiter allowed that none of those items were available.

"Weather's cut off what's come in fresh," he said, reverting to his native tongue, "so we'll be serving from cans."

"Steak tartare from cans?" I inquired, more haughtily than I wanted to. The waiter said he wasn't sure about that and went off to check.

"I'm sorry," Mary said, abashed. "Ordinarily I'd never come to a place like this. I just wanted to do something nice. Do you want to leave?"

"And miss a chance at a plate of Green Giant LeSueur peas?" A lame joke to be sure, a tinny echo of my former unbeatable wit and charm, but she smiled with a warm appreciation.

"Maybe we could feed them to that guy over there," she returned, nodding toward the ridiculous suit of armor standing in the corner of the restaurant.

"Looks like he's already had his fill, see the rust under his armpits?"

She laughed. It was a warm and purring laugh and it lifted me up. The Haitian women laughed sometimes. Off by themselves, speaking in Creole, they would break out into dry cackles that shook their desiccated bodies. When I drew close though, they'd stop, solemnly go about their business.

"Thanks," I said. "I haven't heard a woman laugh for quite a while."

"I should laugh more," she said. "I heard it makes you live longer, as if that's supposed to be such a great selling point." With that she reached into her tiny sequined purse. "Mind if I smoke?"

I shrugged. I never liked it when women smoked, didn't care

for the acridness of their tongues against mine. Now it seemed a very small point. "Just don't blow it on my peas."

She shoved the cigarette in her mouth with an addict's alacrity, as if she'd had nothing else on her mind since we entered the restaurant. If my acne-affected face was prematurely young, hers was going in the other direction. She'd tried to pancake away the dark circles under her eyes but it hadn't worked. In the restaurant's "romantic" underlighting she looked tired, desperate. She was in trouble, there was no doubt of that.

Growing more talkative with the nicotine influx, she carried the majority of the conversation as we picked at the barely thawed Pepperidge Farm croissants in the plastic breadbasket. Mostly she belittled herself, criticizing her endless ignorance, her crushing provinciality. One of several children from a Kentucky mining family, she'd been a whiz at school, her success the lone bright spot of a bleak upbringing.

"No one had ever seen a girl as good at math as I was. I scored the highest on the comprehensive test in the whole state," she said. When she went off to Vanderbilt on full scholarship, half the high school came out to see her board the Greyhound.

"They even had the band out there, because I used to play the flute at the football games. I looked out the bus window and saw Herman Sawyer with his tuba. He was a boy I'd liked. Once I let him kiss me, but he just ran off to his friends and told how he'd put his hand down my dress. There he was puffing away on that tuba with 'Porkies' written across the top of it in chipping red paint because we were the Pinkerstown Porcupines. He kept puffing, Herman Sawyer did. 'Puff your guts out, Herman Sawyer,' I said to myself. 'Puff until you get into the philharmonic, because that'll be the day I come back to this town.'"

She smiled sourly. "Thinking back on it now, maybe that was the high point of my life, sitting on that bus. I was going to go everywhere and do everything."

She lit up another coffin nail. "I lasted about two weeks at Vandy. Once I saw those sorority girls I went into shock. They looked at me like I was dirt, and I became dirt. From that moment on, I couldn't do math anymore. The talent went right out of me. Even now I can't add up a row of numbers. I'm dyscalculitic."

With palpable self-disgust, she reported failing in her attempt to major in oceanography, a choice made after seeing a *National Geographic* undersea documentary. "What I really wanted to be was a fish, alone in the quiet dark, not being spoken to, not having to speak. Oceanography was just more classroom, so I cut out the middleman and became a beach bum." She laughed ruefully, picked at a roll. "It went downhill from there."

Listening to women's regretful commentary on their compromised lives was, of course, nothing new to me. As Taylor Powell, patient reception of the postcoital confessions of laconic fashion models and harried housewives were my stock and trade. I'd been party to the unlocking of many hitherto mnemonically sealed Pandora's boxes.

Still, I was taken aback as Mary revealed the great, unending horror of her life: Six years before, her husband, with whom she had lived in the now storm-wrecked town house, left her, taking their son, the then nine-month-old Shawn, with him.

"Your husband stole your child? Just left in the middle of the night?"

"Shawn was Martin's child, too," she said, guardedly.

"You're the mother! Where are they? Can't you get to them?" I asked, my voice rising. Knowledge of the situation had made its existence instantly unbearable to me.

"Don't you think I've tried?" She was sobbing now. "Don't you think I've done everything I can do?"

"But the guy's got your kid!" I was ready to devote the rest of my life to tracking down the kidnapping father and missing child. I'd find Martin Grant, kill him, and return Shawn to Mary so they could live happily ever after.

Mary drew back. "No! You can't look that way! . . . *It's wrong!* . . . I can't bear that *hatred* on your face . . . it's not about vengeance . . . it *can't* be about vengeance!"

Her voice calmed me. "Sorry . . . It's just so awful. I got . . . upset."

She wiped at her decomposing makeup with the synthetic cloth napkin. "It is terrible, I shouldn't have told you. I never talk about it. But there's . . . something different about you. Something in your face."

"What about my face? Is there something wrong with my face?" My teeth dug into my bottom lip.

She was rumpling the tablecloth between her thumb and forefinger. "No, not at all. It's a very nice face. A normal face. I feel at home with it. It's just so hard . . . lying to you . . ."

"You're lying?"

"I lied about that man . . . in the house. The adjustor." She took a deep breath. "He said my claim was to be disallowed. I was behind in the payments. They weren't going to give me a dime. I couldn't let the house go, simply abandon it. That's where Shawn was born . . . I knew what kind of man he was. A woman knows. When he started talking about a courtesy grace period for tardy payments, I smiled at him. That was all I had to do. I never said I'd sleep with him, but I didn't say I wouldn't. I played on his weakness, that's all. And he almost died for that . . . I almost made you a murderer, for that."

There was an imponderable loneliness in her red-rimmed eyes. "No one has ever done for me what you did. Maybe no one ever will again. I'm certainly not worth it."

I reached over to take her hand, to offer a degree of solace. She pulled away, refused to let me touch her. There was a fierce, quiet fury to her now. I could feel the pierce of her unyielding gaze on my alien skin. "Who *are* you?" she asked.

"Just a guy." I shrugged.

"No. Who are you, really."

What was I supposed to say? That I used to be Taylor Powell, maybe you caught a couple of my pictures, maybe I passed through your town once, fucked some of your girlfriends. Maybe I even fucked you before, it's so hard to keep track. Except then

I decided I didn't want to be Taylor Powell anymore so I went to see some insane doctor in the jungle, got plastic surgery, and became this person you see before you now, whoever that is.

The truth was, it was getting harder and harder to even remember being Taylor Powell, especially now that the "coverage" of my demise—mostly composed of inane talk-show roundtables during which my former lovers compared notes—faded away. "As a celebrity death, Taylor Powell's has short legs," said an industry analyst. Petty vanities aside, I recognized that I was no Bruce Lee or John Lennon, dead stars whose fans were actually upset at their passings. Nor did I arouse the campy necrophilic delight associated with Jim Morrison or James Dean. For certain, I was no Elvis, who transcended all category of celeb death. I'd lived, fucked, made money, fucked, died. Over and out.

No, I couldn't tell Mary—or anyone else—about being Taylor Powell. I'd sworn I wouldn't. But as she claimed she had trouble lying to me, I found it difficult to be untruthful to her.

"I was in a plane crash . . . a terrible fiery crash. Everyone else died . . . except me."

"My God."

"I thought I was going to die. I was even ready to die . . . but then, I don't know how, or why . . . but I was thrown clear, flung out of the plane . . . Somehow, I wasn't hurt." Even in these vague terms, the mere summoning of these inexplicable and harrowing events made me dizzy; for a moment I thought I might pass out, my reconfigured face splashing into the steaming tureen of reconstituted onion soup before me. But I couldn't stop there. The next few lines were the most important, and I must say, I delivered them as perfectly as any in my career.

"After that, everything's been kind of a blur. It's like I'm another person, I can't remember a thing. Amnesia or something. My entire life just knocked out of me."

She looked with quiet wonder. "Your name's not Dean Taylor?"

I glanced down at the name on the front of my coveralls. "I found these clothes, took this name."

"You don't know who you are?" Her eyes, which I now realized were a shade of green I'd never quite seen before, gazed toward the ceiling, scanning from left to right. It was as if she were tracing the arc of an unseen object through space.

"You were thrown from a doomed plane . . . you alone, among others, flung free . . . a man without a past, who doesn't know himself, soaring through the sky . . . And you fell to earth through the hole in my roof . . . to me . . .

"My angel . . ." That's when she reached over and brushed my cheek with her hand.

Josias and that killer cop in L.A. aside, it was the first time my new face had been touched by another human being. The warmth of her fingertips spread almost instantly from the acne-ridden veneer of my synthetic countenance, through my head, cascading down through my entire body. "Huh," I said, with a small spasm.

"Sorry," she said, blushing, "you had this." She held a piece of pinkish fluff that she'd picked out of my unwashed hair.

"Fiberglass insulation," I said, "it's all over me, little splinters of it, digging into me. You can't wash it off. It's in most of the roofs around here."

"It looks like cotton candy."

"Cancer cotton candy. It'll turn your insides black."

She frowned in disgust. "Same as always. Same as when they sent my father down into the mine. Twenty-five years, from one hole in the ground to another. That was the way of death in Kentucky, nobody questioned it."

She threw the fiberglass puff onto the restaurant floor. "Now they make it look nice, like something children ask for at the circus. My father was a dumb country boy, he cheated on my mother and never paid attention to me and my sisters. But he tried in his way, and he didn't deserve to die like that."

There was zeal to her, a righteousness I found absolutely

thrilling. Sitting there with that silly bun sliding off the top of her head, velour dress hanging off her thin shoulders like a smock, she seemed the most remarkable woman I'd ever met.

"All over the world there are people turning other people's lungs black. Torturing other people to death, stealing their birthrights. This sort of evil is everywhere. It has to be stopped. Stopped in the right way. Power is nothing without compassion. Vengeance is murder without self-knowledge."

"Self-knowledge. Yes. Absolutely . . ." Suddenly I found myself straining to concentrate on her words. "Ah," I groaned.

"Are you all right?" she asked.

"Yeah," I said, truthfully. "I think I am. I think I really am." It was her touch that had done it, the contact of her fingers on my cheek. That's when it began rising. Now it was as hard as it had ever been, pressing against the jumpsuit crotch, a fleshy bottle rocket straining toward launch. "Face bone connected to the dick bone," I muttered, under my breath.

"Excuse me, Dean?" Mary leaned forward.

"Oh, nothing."

The waiter had returned. "Steak tartare does not come in cans. Sorry about that. We could fix you up some deviled ham," he said, in his narcoleptic drawl.

"That's okay," I replied. "Just the check, please."

4.

We went out into the drizzly night. Even though there had been little or no electricity in the weeks since the storm, it was still difficult to get used to the astonishing blackness that descended as evening pushed toward night. Neither one of us said a word as we got into her rumpled Corolla. She didn't start the car, we just sat there in the oppressive dark.

"They say lights at night are a mark of civilization," she remarked, lighting another cigarette, the match's flare casting a fleeting reflection of our faces on the streaked windshield.

"I wonder," I replied. "Sometimes I think the world's already over. Except there wasn't any atom bomb or plague. It just stopped without saying so, and down deep we know, except we can't admit it, so we keep on walking around because we can't figure any other thing to do."

"I don't believe that," she said, firmly.

I turned toward her. In the chiaroscuro of the Corolla her eyes were diamond buoys, far off across uncharted, possibly fatal seas. I steered for them.

"Maybe you're right that the world stopped," she said, through a curl of smoke. "That just means this is the beginning again. The beginning of another of a million beginnings. And we're here to . . . witness it."

She put out her cigarette, extended both of her palms, put them on either side of my face. Then she pulled me forward and kissed me on the lips. "I've been waiting for you, Dean Taylor. I've been waiting for you all my life."

We fucked in the backseat of the small car. I ripped off her clothes and she ripped off mine. She said she'd never done anything like it before, but then again, neither had I, not this current me. The act was so much more immense now. As Taylor Powell, I was like the Willie Mosconi of fucking. Ole Willie, we shot a couple of racks together when he was the tech adviser on that pool movie.

"Always leave yourself something, boy," Mosconi told me, chalking his cue. "Give yourself somewheres to go, cuz the shot you're making this time ain't shit less it leads to the next, and the next." Under the obligation to run the table of all the women in the world, I took this advice to heart. I was always looking to leave myself something. Now the next fuck didn't exist, and there were none that had come before.

It figured to be sloppy and it was. At one point I got poked in the eye with the door handle. There was no book on how to fuck Mary Grant; the intuitive sexual compass that had guided my every move as Taylor Powell no longer functioned. What was occurring now was a teenage thing, like the pimples on my face. A pure passion beyond proficiency, empiricism, or genius. Even as I entered her that first time, I'd already totally accepted the magnitude of the act, that I was now in a realm where I would stay, forever and ever. This was the beginning of things, a new Genesis; Mary and I, through the grace of our immediate yet already eternal love became Adam and Eve, that dented Toyota our tiny Eden.

I was awakened at dawn by the rumble of trucks. A long caravan of army vehicles was rolling down the trashblown boulevard. Such processions had become fairly common since the storm, but still, this being America, there was a strange and frightening novelty to the military presence. The trucks were loaded with supplies bound for the swamp. Malaria had broken out down there, not that anybody in authority was publicly admitting it. Everything was like that now, rumor and denial, denial and rumor. Either way, people kept dying.

She'd been there when I awoke, peering down at me. "What are you looking at?" I asked, groggily.

The scratchy morning light filtered through the smudged car windows. Her hair, gummed with spray, stood away from her head like the rays of the sun in a child's painting. "It moves, you know."

I smiled. "Galileo said that about the earth and the Pope threw his ass in jail."

"No, silly. I'm talking about your face. It moves when you sleep."

"Everybody's face moves when they sleep," I replied, warily. "It's called breathing."

"It's like the hands of a clock. You can't really see it go," she said. "But it moves. It never stops."

I knew what she meant. I'd seen my face moving, during the hours I spent studying it, trying to commit its features to memory. There was a fluidity there, like the movement of pressure zones on a TV weather map. I'd discounted the impression, putting it down to the stress of my neo-reincarnation.

Still, try as I might, I couldn't dismiss the idea that my features were not in any way fixed. Often times, I awoke in terrible pain, as if my facial tissues had been used as the rope in some particularly ferocious tug of war. This was usually after one of the horrifying dreams that had beset me ever since the operation. Florid stereotypes of mushroom clouds, bloated capitalists, disgusting subterranean dragons stalked my sleepscape, sinister comic-book demons scarring the lives of innocent multitudes. Other times the dreams would center on small, offhand acts of cruelty, the deliberate forgetting of a child's birthday, a seemingly innocuous yet devastating remark made at a critical time. Gnashing apocalypses and barely noted but deeply rending slights: They were evidences of palpable evil in my dream world. Always, at the core of the nightmare, was: Arana.

Arana. He could appear at any time, in any guise. Sometimes he'd be an animal, a possessed, rabid dog, or more surreptitiously, a harmless-seeming beetle, idly munching away at a leaf in a forest. Except then the bug's jaws would grow, the mandibles swelling to the size of an unthinkably huge strip miner. Deafening sounds of mastication would fill my sleeping head, an endlessly voracious chomp to devour the planet. Arana's bug ate the world and didn't even say "excuse me" when it belched.

"My face moving, migrating like continental drift . . . That's crazy," I told Mary, with an attempted scoff. "If that's the case, how come my nose doesn't just fall off my head?"

Mary shrugged and started rearranging her sticky tresses. "It's late. I've got to go to work."

"It's eight o'clock Sunday morning, who goes to work now?"

"It's not a regular job. It's just something I do for extra money." After wiping away her makeup, which made her much prettier, she pulled a long black robe out of a small satchel she kept under the front seat. "You can come if you want. It won't take too long."

We drove down through the tangle of wrecked cars and up-rooted trees toward the swamp. The stoplights hadn't worked since the storm destroyed the central switching center, but this being Sunday morning, traffic was little problem. Soldiers manning the checkpoint set up by the National Guard waved us through.

We were going to a small church in Reymonds, on the edge of the mangroves. The church had been seriously damaged during the storm, its roof blown off, walls caved in. All that was left were the pews and the pulpit, open to the wet, pungent air.

"They need an organist," Mary said, as we pulled up alongside the ruined church. Perhaps fifty men and women, and a like number of children, primarily black and Hispanic, were milling around in what were most likely the best clothes they had left.

"I pinch-hit around here almost every Sunday. I know the tunes. I learned them back home." She opened the trunk of the car, took out a portable Casio keyboard she had wrapped in a powder blue crocheted blanket.

The preacher, a large, stout black man in his mid-forties came forward to greet her. "So glad you could be with us this day, Sister Grant," he said. "Your playing raises the tired Spirit. And so thoughtful of you to bring this machine. As you know, our piano was demolished in the maelstrom."

"Reverend Watkins, this is Mr. Dean Taylor," Mary said to the preacher. I flushed with unexpected embarrassment. Our clothes, mine certainly, were rumpled, stained with bodily secretions. We smelled of sex, sex in the backseat of a car. At least that's what I thought Reverend Watkins was responding to as he stopped in his tracks and stared at me. "Have you ever prayed with us, Brother Taylor?" the preacher asked.

"No, I haven't."

"Strangest thing. For a moment I was certain I'd seen you here before." Then, shaking his head as if to rid himself of the impression, Reverend Watkins placed his hand on my shoulder. "Tell me, son, are you a churchgoing man?"

"Not really. I haven't been inside a church in years."

The reverend spread his powerful arms outward to where the building's walls once stood, craned his huge pious face upward toward the vanished roof. "Well, you're not *inside* a church now, are you, Brother Taylor? This is the meaning of this storm: To teach the impermanence of man's work. We build ourselves a church and then, our chest puffed out, we stand back to admire our glorious accomplishment. We gaze upon a structure of lumber and drywall and declare it to be a House of the Lord, *His House.* But God will not tolerate such conceit, such self-congratulation. He raises His Hand and unleashes the great coiling force of the universe to sweep asunder the façade of our vanity. In this, He shows us Truth: that these walls were illusory even when they stood.

"That is the lesson of this so-called disaster, Brother Taylor, that whether we drive in our car, walk down a city street, or place a loving kiss on the cheek of a child at bedtime, we are *always* in His House, *always* within His Sight."

With that, the preacher called the congregation to order. Once composed primarily of older black ladies in pink hats, Reverend Watkins's flock had grown threefold in the wake of the storm, now embracing people of all description. Bluish-haired white ladies who'd formerly attended the flooded-out Methodist church around the corner came, as did a seemingly endless flow of Mexican migrants, their tent cathedral blown down. Families of pious and demure Lutherans appeared as well, telling of how their chapel steeple snapped off in the winds, soaring wild until it pronged into the concrete enclosure of the maximum-security prison, thereby setting off the largest single jailbreak in the state's history.

Mary played for these disparate souls. She sat on a rusted metal folding chair, her thin white fingers gliding over the Casio keyboard hooked to a battery-powered amp set up on the sodden carpet in front of the pulpit. She sang into a small microphone in a thin, unearthly alto. It was a very old-fashioned voice, I thought, something you might hear on an unremastered 78.

Her first number was Thomas A. Dorsey's "Peace in the Valley." My father, probably out of guilt, often tuned into gospel programs. "Peace in the Valley" was the theme song of one of these shows, so it became one of my favorites. Mary sang the intro, followed by the congregation, Reverend Watkins's spacious baritone providing a mighty foundation of sound.

"There'll be peace in the valley, for me, someday," they all sang, their voices spilling from the wrecked church, through the ravaged town, to the ocean beyond. "The bear will be gentle / The wolf will be tame / And the lion will lie down by the lamb . . .

"The host from the wild will be led by a child / And I'll be changed, changed from this creature that I am."

At this point Reverend Watkins stopped and turned to me. "Join us, Brother Taylor. Raise your voice with Sister Grant and sing!"

And I did. Loud and clear.

5.

The Feds opened several derelict motels, which they had seized for tax arrears during the tourist slump, and set them up as temporary housing for those left homeless by the storm. With Mary's condo condemned, we found ourselves in Room 423 at El Cielo Azul, until quite recently a Cuban-run hotbed establishment. Our twelve-foot-square, cinder-block-walled room contained only a sagging double bed, a disconnected telephone with a cigarette-scarred receiver, and a black-and-white TV bolted to the ceiling. Mildew pervaded everything. This mattered little to us.

We'd fuck and then Mary would play church songs on the Casio. Then she'd play again and we'd fuck some more. She was insatiable. No sooner would we finish, she'd want to go again. Her ardor was endlessly thrilling to me, but I just couldn't keep up. "Baby . . . baby . . . ," I'd gasp. "My turnaround period just isn't what it used to be."

That would get her embarrassed. "I'm sorry. I've never been like this before. I don't want you to think I'm a wanton strumpet."

"You're always wanton more, that's for sure," I joked, but this change in my sexual capacity vexed me at first. In my days as Taylor Powell I was a sixty-minute man, twenty-four/seven. Starlets blew into town like gunslingers, their magnificent bodies bearing invisible notches marking the conquests of onetime high school cocks o' the walk. "So, you're the great Taylor Powell," they'd say, "try to fuck *me* under the table." Which I did, of course. Every last sweet-snatched one of them.

I never did it out of malice, not for domination. Other stars, Jimmy Dime and the rest, would forever be lamenting the lot of the Hollywood Lothario. "Just because I call you Peaches, that doesn't mean *cling* Peaches," Jimmy would grouse, mocking his unfortunate conquests: " *'But you SAID you loved me'* . . . Shit. Everyone's so damn *needy.*"

Taylor Powell wasn't like that. Never once did love, or rather the *illusion* of love, come into it. I never lied, never had to. As I knew what to expect from women, they likewise understood that I would never fall in love, that I would always be out of reach. It was a given, intuitively known; in that way I never broke a single heart, never spread bitterness or mistrust. Everyone said Taylor Powell's face was magic, and it was; the Face was pure Spirit, it passed through, was gone again. That was the glory of being Taylor Powell. And the emptiness.

But I wasn't Taylor Powell anymore. Strange, I thought: You fuck a hundred women, you stay hard day and night. You fuck one, she wears you out.

"I love you, Mary Grant," I said.

"I love you, Dean Taylor," Mary said.

Then she'd touch my face and my beleaguered pecker would stir to life again. *Face bone connected to the dick bone.* "Where'd you get a face like that?" Mary would ask, sometimes goony and giggly, sometimes almost weeping.

"Around," I'd say, raising one of my ersatz eyebrows. "What's it to you?"

"I don't know, but when you look at me, it makes me feel like everyone on earth is here with us, holding hands, and our love is their love. Your face is a church, Dean Taylor."

Yes, we had some kind of fun in those days. Mary had a real flair for sexual hijinks. One evening, after going to sleep as she played a wondrous version of "Just a Closer Walk with Thee," I awoke to find her dressed in only a black leather bandolier and glossy red panties. She had purchased the items at the adult bookstore, which, as chance would have it, was one of the few buildings in the area left unscathed by the storm.

"They're edible," she said, coquettishly referring to the crinkly-looking panties. "In the mood for a snack?"

"Maybe a little nosh," I remarked, lowering my head. It was only a moment before my mouth began to burn and I rushed into the grimy motel bathroom and began to spit up.

"They're taco flavor, extra hot sauce," I heard Mary say as I plunged my head toward the algae encrusted toilet bowl. "They also had sloppy joe, but I thought a Mexican motif might be more exotic. You're all right, aren't you, honey?"

"Never better," I said with a loving retch.

The day Mary was a quarter short for a pack of cigarettes we decided we better get jobs. Mary had experience as a court stenographer, but always hated the job. "It is the profane facility of my fingers," she said, noodling a gentle version of "The River of Jordan" on the Casio. "Playing God's message, and touching you naked, is the proper, sacred labor of these bitten-down digits."

Work is work, however, and post-storm Pardosville was awash with an unprecedented number of sleazy damage suits. Each specious claim and lying counterclaim required accurate transcription, for such is the law. So Mary put on her gray skirt, her cantaloupe-colored top with the big gauzy bow at the neck, and went off to the Quonset hut that was serving as the Pardosville courthouse.

With Mary absent, our motel Heaven turned back to the cubicle of Hell it truly was, so after the third day of supposedly "catching up on my reading" (I'd gotten to page fifty-one of one of those dreary P. D. James mysteries Mary favored) I decided to return to the roustabouts. I saw no alternative. What other opportunities were knocking in this devastated landscape for a fortyish drifter with no work history, no history of anything?

I went down to the highway, looking to catch on with a crew. The Haitians were gone, their hovel camp burned down, now just another charred pile by the roadside. I thought a cooking fire had grown out of control but closer investigation revealed a more sinister scenario. In the drainage ditch behind the camp, carcasses of animals were clumped together like a dam built by demonic beavers. Then I came upon the human fingers and toes, dozens of them, arranged in a neat pile beside the dripping pipe where the women once washed clothes.

I was about to run, when I saw the hammock I'd put up so many months before. Somehow it had survived whatever havoc had befallen the camp. Strung between two shady trees at the rear of the camp, the hammock had been the only place I could find peace when I was with the crew; I'd whiled away many hours resting there and had come to consider the place to be my own. Now I saw a dead body enmeshed in the low slung weave.

It was Alphonse, one of the few Haitians with whom I actually had any personal dealings; he had a small cache of marijuana and would share an occasional bowl with me. Alphonse's life in Haiti had been better than most. He'd been trained as an electrician and was often employed wiring the estates of the local elite. One evening, however, he got drunk and made some politically inopportune remark; the next day the Tonton Macoute were after him. Seeing no alternative, Alphonse left the country in a rickety raft that soon foundered on the high seas.

"We were in the water, each of us clutching to a piece of wood," Alphonse said, as he passed the marijuana. "One by one my boatmates lost their will, letting go, their heads slumping beneath the dark waters. The surface of the sea appeared to be the border between Life and Death, ever shifting, changing. I felt a great temptation to stick my head in the water, for just an instant, to peek at Death. So many of my friends, my whole family, had died. I longed to see them again. One peek, I thought. One glance cannot hurt. I stopped myself, for I knew: This is how Death works, once seen, it cannot be escaped. So I did not peek below, and soon I found myself washed up on a beach near here.

"This made me happy," Alphonse said then, exhaling a mouthful of the pungent smoke. "It made me feel that I might find a great destiny here, in this new land."

His great destiny unrealized, Alphonse now lay in my former

bed, dead, his torso stiff and bloated. Beyond this was what had happened to Alphonse's face. It wasn't there anymore, it had been burned off. This set me reeling. Alphonse had been dumped in my hammock for a reason, I knew. Someone was sending me a message. I covered the dead man, said a hasty prayer over his faceless body, and ran from that place.

The newspapers had taken note of the murders, the stench over the city being too omnipresent to ignore. Everything was blamed on what the papers called "roaming bands of so-called roofers, pool pumpers, and wreckage haulers." There were dire warnings not to utilize any freelance laborers in the cleanup process. Instead, people were instructed to sign up with "locally reputable" construction firms sanctioned by the chamber of commerce and the official Rebuild Pardosville Committee.

Foremost amongst these was the Elliot and Abrams Company, a division of Stipe/Schneiderman, which had recently been awarded an extensive contract calling for the wholesale demolition and replacement of a large number of Pardosville edifices. "It seems foolish not to avail ourselves of this opportunity to cast aside the old in favor of the new," the mayor, a major stockholder in E&A, declared. The fact that a good deal of the buildings in question were less than ten years old and could have been repaired went unmentioned.

What did I care? Avaricious skullduggery is a given in times of chaos. Plus I needed the work. I signed on as an all-purpose helper.

I'd been on the job about a week when I devised the game, mostly out of boredom but also as a silent commentary on the crappy construction practices. I'd about had it with the shoddy materials the bosses handed out. The nails were inferior, bending more often than not when hit solidly. The plywood was no better, splintering and cracking under the slightest pressure. The game, as I developed it, was to try to drive one of the cheap nails through the cruddy board in a straight line with a single shot. To make it interesting, I assigned imaginary stakes to each swat. You know: If I manage to get this nail through the wood without it bending, then ... I can drink two beers tonight ... idiot stuff like that.

One particularly bright morning, atop a brand-new condo complex that Elliot and Abrams planned to finish within a matter of weeks, I decided to raise the ante. I pulled a nail from the brown paper bag and held it up before my face so the gunmetal gray stalk appeared to split the sky. This one nail would decide the fate of the universe, I decided. If I drove the nail straight through the board with a single shot, the world would survive. If not, pestilence and corrosion of the Spirit would be irreversible.

I placed the point of the nail against the blotchy grain of the plywood: one shot, for the future of the universe. Preparing my singular blow, I peered around. From my perch on the roof of the three-story condo, I was afforded an uninterrupted 360-degree panorama of Pardosville and its surroundings. What a load of shit this place was, I thought. No wonder the storm changed course at the last moment, suddenly veering forty miles north to hit here. How could it resist the mobile home underbelly of this cheesy county? The logic of cosmic retribution could not be refuted: We made a world, it blew, therefore it was blown away.

I didn't have a problem with that; what's past is past. What was intolerable was the specter of an even shittier world rising from the tainted ashes of the old, another epochal sediment of corrupt humanoid biogeology larded onto the beleaguered land without a moment's pause to consider former sins. The weather service called Hurricane Tom "a hundred year storm." Did that mean we'd have to wait an entire century for a wind big enough to sweep away the forthcoming layer of crap? Was this truly the best our species was capable of?

I turned back to the one nail that would mean everything. Surrounded by such shit, striking a perfect blow would be a supremely subversive act. It was as my hammer reached the top of its arc, the maximum of its potentiality, that I saw it. My face. Dean Taylor's face, moving, shifting, just as Mary described. My face was reflected in the head of that nail, which, driven true, would save the universe.

"Hey! You! What are you doing?" Someone was yelling from the ground below.

It was Overton, the foreman, yowling through a red plastic megaphone. Universally despised, Overton was three hundred pounds of stark white jelly, a dyspeptic gasbag, and a mean motherfucker to boot. One might take some solace from the obvious fact that in a sane world there was no way a pig like Overton could ever get laid without paying for it. But the world wasn't sane and Overton didn't pay, he took; everyone had heard stories of him forcing himself on the workers' wives and sisters. "We're moving to Phase C," Overton growled. "We're done up there."

"Done?" I looked around at the roof. There were plenty more nails to hammer; the job was half finished at best. "There's a lot to do up here."

"The shingle guys are coming in."

"You can't shingle this, it isn't hammered down yet."

"It's good enough. I said we're done!"

I looked back at that nail with my moving face upon it. *"I'm not done!"*

"Get off that roof before I throw you off."

I didn't answer. I didn't care what that fat asshole said. I was going to play out my game, drive that one all-important nail through the plywood. I lined up the shot, lifted the hammer above the nailhead.

"Who do you think you're looking at?" It was Overton. How had a guy that fat gotten up on the roof so quickly? "I said: Who the fuck do you think you're looking at?"

I knew then, without raising my head. I could feel the malignancy, the sheer corruption, hovering upon me like a barbarous, suffocating cloud. Overton was Arana, just as that cop in the alleyway had been Arana.

He knew I knew. "It is as before," he said, "you stare at yourself, and what do you expect to see? What do you think of a man who doesn't even know his own face, eh, *mis Muchachos*?"

There were at least a dozen of them, closing in, a seething knot of violence. Just an hour ago I'd leaned against a wall sharing a beer with these same guys, most of them rootless drifters like myself. We'd laughed, cracked lewd jokes, imitated Overton's gross waddle. How could I have known these were the same *Muchachos* who'd raped and killed millions in a hundred towns, for thousands of years. It was true, what Josias had said: Arana was everywhere, a protean evil able to assume any form at any time; he dwelled in the land, flowed in our blood, he *was* us.

"Come on, Dean, tell us what you're looking at," Overton/ Arana mocked in a hideous whine. Then he kicked me, hard, in the side, his tasseled white loafer thudding like a wrecking ball against my kidney. I heard the obscene catcalls from *Los Muchachos,* slurs on my manhood, threats to use me like a prison whore. But I did not respond. I was focused only on the reflection of my face on the head of that singular nail. I raised the hammer, steadied my hand. Down swept my arm. The blow was swift and sure. The nail pierced the wood, straight and true: a perfect shot. A shot to save the world.

"Die, asshole!" I shouted as I jumped up, catapulting myself toward Overton. My head and shoulders slammed into the fat man's gut. Air flew from his mouth and ass. "Ooof!" He had a surprised, uncomprehending look as he skittered backward, the momentum of his great bulk driving him perilously close to the roof's edge. At the last moment, however, the large man managed to balance himself.

"Many more will follow me," he said, teetering on the brink. "I am not the last." Through Overton's foul jowls, Arana's loud, mocking laugh resounded across the dispirited landscape.

"I killed you before, I'll do it again!" I raged.

"No time like the present." With that the fat man smiled and took a step backward, pitching himself off the roof.

It was a moment often seen on Saturday-morning cartoons: The snarling dog, or the crazed coyote, moves his feet madly, only to realize he's running on nothing but empty air. There's a dreadful moment of recognition, then gravity takes over. This time it took less than a second, but that was long enough for Overton, suddenly himself again, to scream in horror before plummeting to his death.

I ran to the roof's edge in disbelief. In a month or so, some sucker who'd spent his life savings on this crummy condo would pull his heavily mortgaged four-by-four into the gently curving driveway below and tell himself he was glad to be "home." But now Overton was splat against the concrete, the wind riffling the folds of his blue nylon jacket, those stupid white shoes flung from his tiny feet.

The next hour or two was kind of a blur. I expected *Los Muchachos* to set upon me, to beat me to death. I'd killed their leader, hadn't I? But they didn't. They only milled around, blandly looking down at Overton's lifeless body, trying to figure out what to do next. Someone must have called the cops, though, because about twenty cruisers soon roared up, and after a few obligatory nightstick sappings, they took me over to the trailer being used as the temporary police headquarters and threw me into a small room with corrugated metal walls.

6.

"So you're the guy who likes to throw people off roofs," Sergeant Rex Tarpley said when he came into the room. Somewhere in his late forties, the cop was a balding, stringy-looking man dressed in a cheap olive green poplin suit.

Tarpley slammed the door behind him. It was a flimsy, hollow-core trailer door, but it crashed shut with the frightening finality of six-inch-thick iron in Torquemada's dungeon. The cop sat opposite me in a child-sized chair, the furniture borrowed from the grammar school across the street. There was a steely rectitude to his gaze as he leaned across the diminutive desk between us and stuck his index finger in my face.

"Listen mister, maybe this world's really gone crazy, and nothing matters anymore. Maybe everything we always thought we knew about right and wrong was bullshit from the start. That doesn't matter to me, see? I'm a cop and I enforce the law. That's what I'm going to do, even if I'm the last person on earth who feels that way. Understand?"

I'd seen something about Tarpley in the newspaper. He'd singlehandedly stopped a drive-by shooting by throwing himself onto the hood of the assailant's car. Tarpley cuffed the shooter, the intended victim, too. It was some drug thing, both of the guys were killers. Tarpley brought the two of them in. People said he should have let them shoot it out, who cared about scum? Tarpley said that wasn't how he worked.

The policeman looked drained. He'd been working double-time since the storm hit. Still, a moral fire burned through the exhaustion. In my twenty-seven-picture career as Taylor Powell, I'd never once played a cop, pretty incredible considering that half the jerk scripts they sent me called for such a role. "What are you, antiauthoritarian?" Jimmy Dime used to snigger. "You too good to be a copper?" As usual Jimmy had it right and wrong. Maybe I did think I was too good to be one of those cocky, self-righteous, law-and-order, race-baiting bullies, but to be a real cop, a public servant, a true guardian of genuine moral society, well, I wasn't good enough to be that.

"You understand?" Tarpley repeated, his finger still pointing at me.

"Yeah. I understand." I felt honored to be in Tarpley's custody. I'd killed two people. The fact that I was under the demented impression that both of these men were not men at all but incarnations of Julio Cesar Arana, the embodiment of Evil in the universe, was no defense. No sane defense, anyway. So what if I was crazy, these people were still dead. Even a scumbag like Overton had a mom; her wails of grief filled the police yard even now. I was a killer, I had to be stopped. Rex Tarpley, a good cop, a beacon of justice in deviant times, would stop me.

"You're entitled to a lawyer," Tarpley said.

"I don't need a lawyer. I know what I did. I waive my so-called rights."

Tarpley looked at me quizzically. "You want to confess?"

"Yeah, I'm guilty. Give me a piece of paper, I'll make out a statement right now."

The policeman stared at me another moment. I knew what he was thinking. He was trying to place me, figure where he'd seen me before. It took him a moment or two to discard the impression. Then he handed me a blank legal pad and a pen with a Pizza Hut logo on its barrel.

I'd just written THE FULL CONFESSION OF DEAN TAYLOR on top of the yellow sheet when there was a knock at the door. It was some strutting junior cop with a .45 prominently displayed in his shoulder holster. "Here's the poop on this prick," he said, handing Tarpley a blue folder. The younger detective placed his townie face so close to mine that I could smell the wintergreen on his breath.

"You're going down, shithead," he roiled. "You think you're tough, huh? A real hardcase. Well, listen, buddy, ten minutes upstate and you'll be crying for your mommy. Your mommy and your teddy bear. Well, all you'll get is some big buck making you a punk, greasing down his giant johnson, zeroing in on your backside, and you'll squeal then, like the little pigheart you are, but there'll be no way out, in a minute you'll feel it, that big throbber beginning to split your sphincter, ripping through the fudge pipe—"

"Thanks for the chart, Bob," Tarpley said wearily, cutting off his fellow officer. He waited for the younger cop to leave, sighed again, and read through the preliminary information the front-desk cops had taken from me.

"Mystery man, huh?" he said. "As far as the computer's concerned, you don't exist. Nothing you said checks out, no date and place of birth, no record of your prints." Moving quickly, Tarpley grabbed my wrist, pulling my hand closer to him. "Done a little renovation on these fingertips, Dean?"

I didn't answer.

"Come on, Taylor! There's something funny about you." Tarpley stared at me again, then picked up the eight-by-ten mug shot the cop photographer had taken of me in the booking room. He scanned the photo a moment, put it down. He was about to say something when he grabbed the picture again. The policeman's heavy-lidded eyes narrowed. So steady a moment before, Tarpley was now uncertain, jumpy.

"This picture . . ." Tarpley squinted at the mug shot, moving it back and forth in front of him. It was as if he was looking into a funhouse mirror and trying to find the exact right angle. He ran his right hand tentatively across his cheek, as if correlating the contour of his face with what he saw before him. It was eerie to watch.

"Where'd this picture come from?" Tarpley asked, not looking up, his voice barely audible. Sweatbeads dotted the cop's nose, he went pale. I didn't get it. It was just a cruddy mug shot, at least a stop and a half overexposed. I never even saw the photographer, only an amorphous shape behind an old-fashioned camera and a blast of light. "You took it."

"Me?" The cop was shaken by this assertion.

"Not you yourself, the cops. The ones who booked me." A moment earlier I'd been so happy to be in Tarpley's surehanded custody. Now the cop seemed drugged, profoundly disoriented.

"Booked you? They booked you? For what?" Tarpley exhaled deeply, put the photo back in my folder. He was calmer now. "Let's see your statement."

I started to say that I hadn't written my statement yet when Tarpley snatched the legal pad from the desk and scanned his eyes across the yellow page. He appeared to be reading text where there was no text. It seemed as if the cop had lost his mind.

"Well, this is fine," he said after a moment, his normal color returning. "Jibes with what we got from the witnesses: Overton had it in for you, been riding you, when you talked up for yourself he flipped out and tried to throw you off the roof. You sidestepped him, he fell. A clear-cut case of self-defense."

"It doesn't say that there. It doesn't say anything."

Tarpley shrugged. "Hey, Dean, don't blame me, I'd love to throw your ass in jail. Good for the old quota, you know. But you can't argue with eyewitnesses. We got twenty of them in the next trailer right now, each one corroborating your story."

"Who's in the next trailer?" What manner of police trick was this?

"The guys on the crew, your fellow workers."

"*Los Muchachos?*"

"Call 'em what you want. They all say the same thing. You're totally blameless."

Tarpley reached over, touched my wrist. "Dean," he said quietly, "I've got a little confession of my own to make."

My head was spinning. What confession could Tarpley make? Was he going to say *he* threw Overton off the roof?

The cop leaned closer. "You see, Dean, I've been trying to quit smoking for years. Drives the missus crazy. She's right, too. But I can't do it. Vietcong had me in a tiger cage for a year, bamboo sticks shoved under my fingernails, and they couldn't break me. But I don't have the physical and mental discipline to put down these cancer sticks. I'm a damn addict."

Tarpley took out a Winston, put it between his lips. "They got a new rule here: We're not allowed to light up in the interrogation rooms. Some secondhand-smoke deal, like it might soil the lungs of some killer of old ladies. So bear with me, okay, Dean?"

The cop got out of the kid-sized chair. "I'm going to go down the hall, out to the parking lot, okay? I'm feeling kind of nervous, so I'll probably have to have at least two, so maybe you could read a magazine or something until I get back. Okay?"

Then he walked out, leaving the door wide open.

7.

I ran through the shattered Pardosville streets, picking my way through crumpled aluminum siding flung across the ground like Reynolds Wrap tumbleweeds. I didn't know if I was a fugitive or not. I'd killed two men, I knew I should pay. Not that I was about to go back into that police station and tell them there must be some mistake. Plus, Tarpley's crazed assertions aside, I knew *Los Muchachos* were out there, laying for me with their moss-toothed leers and rusty machetes.

Who was Dean Taylor? Why was he being tracked by the forces of unspeakable evil, set free by stern jailers? Tarpley, after all, had not been the first to be affected by a picture of me. A lady in the storm-relief office went white at the sight of my passport photo. She pressed the picture up to her face as if she hoped to merge with it. I just about had to rip the document out of her hands to get it back. Two days before, in a scummy package store, the guy who carded me just to be a fuck broke into tears when I pulled out my Red Cross ID. Even Josias's repugnant cousin Emilio had been startled when the original photo curled from his ancient Polaroid camera.

I didn't have time to think about that now. I had to get to Mary, tell her everything. Who I was, who I used to be. I had to tell someone, or else I'd go nuts. It didn't matter what I'd promised Parry and Josias, I told myself. Screw them. If they were going to pit me against Arana and his minions, shouldn't they have given me a little hint as to the significance of the face they stuck onto my head? A little working knowledge, a manual to Faceship Dean? Besides, I convinced myself, I made that promise in the mindset of Taylor Powell, a wholly other person. Taylor Powell loved all women; Dean Taylor loved only one. Somehow, that raised the stakes. If I had a secret, Mary should know it.

She wasn't supposed to get home from work for hours, but when I arrived at the motel, I could hear her crying. "Mary!" I rushed in, fearing *Los Muchachos* had already been to the room, done unspeakable things to her.

"Aren't you supposed to be at work?" she wailed when she saw me.

The ratty suitcase she'd salvaged from the condo closet was open on the floor, some clothes thrown into it. "What's this?" I asked. "You going somewhere?"

Mary turned away, covered her face. "This was never going to work out between us, Dean. You can see that, can't you? We had our fling . . . I'm leaving."

It felt as if I'd been kicked in the stomach. "But Mary . . . I love you."

Suddenly, she was hysterical. "How could you? How could you love someone like me?" With that she began attacking herself, smacking the side of her head with her fists, tearing at her skin. "I'm not . . . I'm not who you think I am," she cried. "I'm someone else altogether."

Having arrived with the intention of telling her the same thing about myself, I was taken aback. "What do you mean?"

She handed me a newspaper clipping. It was recent, just a month old, ripped from a small-town paper. There was a picture of a plump, bearded man who looked to be in his mid-thirties. Wearing jeans and a plaid Pendleton jacket, he could have been an ex-hippie, a Grateful Dead fan. Beside him stood a small slip of a woman, somewhat younger than the man, either Thai or Filipino. Arrayed about them were seven or eight children of various ethnic groups. Everyone was smiling.

Below the picture was a long caption:

BIG WELCOME HOME TO THE GRANTS, ADOPTIVE FAM-
ILY OF THE YEAR: Martin Grant and wife Toshi, Lenior residents, have returned from the Far East, where they formally
adopted Suret (in wheelchair, left), a five-year-old girl. Many
of Suret's family were victims of Pol Pot terror. She is the
eighth orphan saved from a war zone in the past few years by
the Grants. "Her legs were blown off by a land mine, but she's
the sweetest little kid you'd ever want to see," Mr. Grant said.
"We're blessed to have her come live with us here in Lenior."
Asked how many disadvantaged children he and Toshi plan to
adopt, the Adoptive Father of the Year said, "the world's a
huge, hard place, but then again we've got a big house."

"Martin Grant? Your husband . . . the man who took your
child?"

She did not reply, only looked away. Since that first night in the
restaurant, Mary had never again mentioned Martin and her
missing boy, Shawn. But it was with her always, a weight, a veil
of sadness. The sight of a five- or six-year-old boy in the street or
at the mall was enough to bring her to tears.

"Lenior," I said, a terrible fury rising inside me. "I could be up
there in eight hours."

"It wouldn't do any good, Dean." There was a coldness to her
voice I'd never heard before.

"Why not?" My fists were clenched. At that moment I hated
Martin Grant more than any man on earth. All I could think of
was savaging him and bringing Shawn home to his rightful
place.

"You'd like to hurt Martin for stealing Shawn, wouldn't you,
Dean?"

"Someone who steals a child deserves it."

"Absolutely," she said flatly. "Harsh punishment should await
someone who steals a child. Swift vengeance. But what retribution awaits a person who *kills* a child?"

"What are you—" I stopped when I saw the revolver in Mary's hand. It was a rusty little police special I'd purchased from a Russian plumber a couple of months before. In a place like Pardosville it didn't seem smart not to have a gun. "Mary, I don't understand . . ."

She looked me straight in the eye. "I told you I couldn't lie to you . . . I mean, I have . . . but I can't anymore. Martin Grant is the most gentle man who ever lived. He didn't steal Shawn. Shawn's dead. I killed him. I killed my own son."

She was twenty-five, long flunked out of Vandy, fired from a half dozen jobs, and drinking heavily when she met Martin, one of the local fishermen working out of Kateswell docks. Only twenty-one, Martin wasn't like the rest. Martin was quieter, smarter, but less confident, at least outwardly. His mom had died when he was a boy, which is why he kept to himself, people said. He said he'd never met a girl like Mary before, someone who didn't mind talking, someone from somewhere else. It didn't hurt that she was older.

He wanted a big family. A lot of kids, "crawling all over me, that's my bit of heaven," Martin told her. He was a virgin that first time, a fact he kept secret until they were naked. Eight weeks later he asked her to marry him. She was already pregnant.

Shawn was a colicky boy. Mary feared she was a terrible mother because she couldn't soothe him. Sometimes the boy would cry for hours, bawl his head off until dark when Martin came home. Martin had the touch. Within moments, Shawn would be smiling, happily looking around.

Then, Martin's boat ran aground one evening, stranding him. Mary found herself alone with Shawn for more than a week. On the second day, the boy became more agitated than usual. He cried nonstop. It went on day and night. In the middle of the fourth day, Mary, after hours of trying to rock the boy asleep in his cradle, picked him up and began to shake.

The doctors said it wasn't that uncommon, something about their spinal cords not being knitted together yet. "Sharp jolt'll do

it all right," the doctor said. "A woman can be driven to it," con-
soled one of the West Indian nurses. "Even the Virgin shook the
Baby Jesus. You just had bad luck."

Martin was crushed. He bravely made the funeral, dug
Shawn's grave with his own hands. It was God's Will, he said.
They would have more children. A dozen more children. Then
he found the bottle. All the bottles. The vodka mostly, but the
pills, too.

"Everyone in town came over to offer sympathy. Martin never
told any of them what happened. He graciously accepted their
condolences and let them think what they wanted," Mary said
blankly. "Then, after a while, he left. All he said was he'd never
be party to bringing another child into a world where there were
people like me. He said maybe the cops wouldn't call it murder,
but he knew better. Someday I'd pay, he said."

She put the pistol in my hand. "You're my angel, Dean. But I've
seen that you can destroy . . . an avenging angel."

For years I'd catered to the ardent desires of women, imagin-
ing that my sole function in life was to give them what they
wanted. Now the one woman I truly loved was asking me to kill
her. I was capable, too. I'd killed before, I could again. I wouldn't
need a stupid little gun either. I could strangle her with my bare
hands.

"Oh, Mary! Don't ask me to do this! Please don't! Life is sacred!
All life. You told me so yourself! . . . I can't feel what you
must feel, but you have to believe things can be different. I
know!"

"It's no use. I'm bad, I'll always be bad."

"That's not true!" I grabbed her arm now, swung her around,
made her look at me. "You can change. Everyone can."

She tried to turn away, but I wouldn't let her. I made her stare
at me. Vincent Parry had stitched a mysterious power into my
face. That much was for sure. Now I drew upon that nameless
force.

"Look at me, Mary. Look at my face." She did. She stared at my
ruddy checks, my slightly too large lips and nose, my undistin-

guished but comforting brown eyes. After a moment she stopped struggling, a small sweet smile came to her lips.

"It's moving, Dean," she said, quietly. "Moving more than ever. It never stops. It's like the ocean. Eternal, ever changing . . . It's all there, Dean, in your face . . . every bit of rage in the world . . . but the kindness, too. The forgiveness . . . the door to freedom."

She held me tightly. "I'm pregnant, Dean. I'm pregnant with our child."

"Our child?"

"Is that all right, Dean, knowing what . . . you know?"

"Oh yes," I said. "That's more than all right."

8.

Of the next fifteen and a half years, I will be as brief as possible.

First of all, we moved out of Pardosville, to Feltside, a handsome and up-and-coming community some forty miles up the coast. Money, at least for a time, was no problem, owing to the surprisingly large insurance settlement on Mary's storm-wrecked town house. "One hundred and twenty-eight thousand dollars," Mary said, over and over, running her fingers along the numerals on the check. Her policy, one of those department store jobs, called for a replacement max-out value of $75,000, but we'd long ago given up the notion of getting anything close to that. Yet there it was: $128,237.87. Years ago, Jimmy Dime and I would roll into Vegas and blow an easy 128 grand in a couple of hours, on craps and hookers. Now, however, it seemed an unthinkable sum.

"Look," Mary said, showing me a handwritten note that accompanied the check. It was from Hal Koeninger, the insurance adjustor I'd almost killed back in Pardosville. It read:

> . . . with this check I am officially out of the insurance adjusting business. It was only at the very point of dying, on the floor of your town house, Ms. Grant, that I realized what kind of man I'd allowed myself to become. Sometimes it seems like the whole world is set up to bring out the worst in people and maybe insurance is more like that than most things. But I'm not blaming anything or anyone. Here's hoping you'll find use for this check, which you should cash quickly. God bless.
>
> Hal Koeninger.

There was a PS.:

Ms. Grant: Should you ever see that gentleman who stopped me from committing an act I'd have regretted all my life, please thank him for me. Tell him I'll never forget his face.

"Just goes to show you never know what's in a man's heart," Mary said, then.

We used the money to buy a hundred-year-old ramshackle Victorian house built by Mortimer Cartland, a pioneer robber baron. As the richest man in the area, he got to be governor, had a county named after him. The Cartland Residence (he never actually lived there; it was a house for one of his mistresses), by now the oldest structure in Feltside, was almost completely overgrown and widely assumed to be haunted. On dares, grade-school kids opened the creaking gate of the house, threw a stone through one of the paneless windows, and ran away, fueled with exhilaration. Perhaps it was this supernatural aura that accounted for the house's uncanny ability to escape the omnipresent bulldozer. Nothing else in Feltside had.

Mary fell in love with the place on the spot. She'd grown up in miners' housing and Airstreams. Later, it'd been doublewides and subdivisions. With the baby coming, she felt a need to be surrounded by walls that had been in existence longer than she had. "The real-estate agent said it'll take some TLC," Mary said, smiling bravely, as we walked through the creaky interior, "but it'll be ours."

"TLC, huh," I said, coughing as I leaned against the bannister, toppling it into a pile of dust. But what the hey? Rich as Taylor Powell had been, I'd never owned a house or even held a long-term lease. Like my dad before me, I was always between things. Shiftless. So big deal if TLC included decidedly unromantic items like a new plumbing stack and a septic system? We put thirty percent down and moved in one early spring day.

As our child grew inside Mary's body, I worked on the house. By summer it was almost a home. We passed warm evenings on our charmingly rickety wraparound porch, drinking iced tea in tall glasses garnished with fresh mint from Mary's fledgling garden. The Space Center was barely twenty-five miles north, and the vibrations of the blasts sometimes rattled the warped floorboards, massaging the soles of our shoeless feet. We leaned back in fraying wicker chairs, watching the contrails of the great ships, prototypes of rockets that would one day carry men to Mars. Perhaps our own child would ride in one of those ships, Mary and I thought, as we sat on the porch, hands linked in the indestructible love of the here and now, feeling attached to both the future and the past.

Then, one day as I was presstyping letters spelling out THE TAYLORS to the side of a newly purchased mailbox, Mary stumbled out the doorway and said she wasn't feeling so good, it was time to go to the hospital.

We got stopped by the drawbridge over the canal just as Mary entered the transition stage of her labor; waiting for the stupid cabin cruiser to pass through I tipped over the Styrofoam cooler full of the ice chips I was supposed to put into Mary's mouth at regular intervals.

"Ohh, Dean, cold," she shrieked as the ice landed in her lap. Amazingly, we managed to get to the hospital birthing room in time. Forty minutes later we had a son.

Mary wanted to call him Dean Junior because all the firstborn males in her family had been named in that fashion. If it had been a girl, she thought Deanna would be nice. I said one Dean was more than enough, suggesting Nicholas, on the puerile grounds that the name "Nick Taylor" might look good painted on an old-time detective's office door. Insisting that the boy at least have my initials, Mary said she had always liked the name Dyson, which sounded to her both heroic and distinguished. Then, her voice breaking, she wondered if I had any terrible objection to the middle name being Shawn, in memory of her dead son. I said I had no problem with that. So it was: Dyson Shawn Taylor, 7 pounds, 11 ounces, auspicious numbers with which to enter this world.

"Isn't he beautiful," Mary said, our son suckling at her breast.

"He's hairy, all right," I said, calling attention to the dark fuzz covering the baby's head. The infant stared at me with big blue eyes, tracking my every move.

"See how he's looking at you?" Mary said. "He knows you. He knows you're his father." Mary smiled with weary contentment. "Oh Dean, I hope he grows up to look just like you. Then he'll be a handsome man indeed." With that, she yawned and fell asleep.

As we sat there, father and son, I couldn't help but think of all those women I'd screwed when I was Taylor Powell, those uncounted vaginal cavities into which I'd ventured. Trillions of sperms must have wriggled from the tip of that divining-rod dong of mine over the years. Yet not a single baby had resulted. Jimmy Dime used to ride me about it. "Half my fucking fortune goes to buying off babes and their paternity claims," Jimmy railed. "I gotta have two morons from the permanent legal team on it twenty-four hours a day. They got orphanages the size of Albania named after me. How come you got no such problem, with all the wide open spaces where your wanger's ranged? You shooting blanks, Taylor?"

Shooting blanks. Yeah, that's what I thought. What else could it have been? Hundreds and hundreds of women, thousands and thousands of fucks, and not one baby. No known abortions either, not a miscarriage, or even a late period. So much seed spread, none taken root. It troubled me at first: the thought that my sperm packed no reproductive punch, that they lacked proper motility, moved with the alacrity of Quaaluded paramecium. After the tests came back normal, I came to attribute the condition to the particular mystique of Taylor Powell. Mine was a metaphoric jism, divorced from everyday biological function. I dispensed my salty remedy into gaping chasms of emotional need, moved on. If I was shooting blanks, they were sanctified blanks. Silver bullet blanks. Taylor Powell was a passionate ephemera; he left no tracks, no sign of his presence beyond treasured pleasure. Children, on the other hand, they were tangible; like bugs against windshields, they stuck.

The hospital room was quiet except for Mary's rhythmic breathing and the occasional sharp squeak of nurses' shoes over the hallway linoleum. I sat there looking at my son. He wasn't finished being born, I understood, cognizant of the fact that babies are far from fully formed when they arrive in this world. Bones are still milky, heads soft, faces not totally set.

"Fluid, almost like me," I said to myself, rubbing my chin. One thing about Dyson, however, did seem quite fixed. That stare, the ever-present watchfulness in his eyes that Mary had declared to be "so beautiful." I knew those eyes. I knew them better than I knew my own. I used to have those eyes. They were Taylor Powell's eyes. No wonder they were so beautiful.

The term "breadwinner," and its dreary counterpart "man of the house," is a Dickensian gnash that erodes the heart just as the steady rain wears the topsoil from a hillside. After Mary quit her court stenographer job to stay home with Dyson—a decision I supported emphatically—the noose of financial obligation tightened about me, a garrote of the spirit.

As a movie star I'd refuse to come out of my trailer unless another trio of zeros was added to my already obscene fee; now, skill-less, I found myself scrambling to put food on the table. One humbling episode followed another, shame mounting with each misstep. Convinced that managed aquaculture was the wave of the future, I purchased a small catfish farm with most of Mary's remaining insurance settlement. At first it seemed a stroke of genius, the hatchling crop doubling within weeks. By harvest time, however, a hitherto undetected flow of toxic effluent leeched into the pond, poisoning the majority of the usually hardy fish, adding unpleasant irony to the phrase "belly-up."

I stood on the anaerobic banks of my doomed investment, appalled by a stupidity I never imagined within me—it was incredible, actually believing something you read in *21st-Century Entrepreneur Magazine*. Almost immediately dunned by mendaciously creative collection agents, I sold the pond and packaging facilities at a loss, and took a job at a gypsum mine twenty miles inland.

Every day I would come home covered with white dust. Dogs barked and children hid when I got out of the car, thinking I was a ghost, which wasn't far off. After I developed a wheezing cough Mary insisted I quit. "My father died of black lung, can't have you die of white lung," she said one night as we lay in bed, a lovely four-poster she'd found for twelve dollars at a church sale and painstakingly restored.

"Maybe I'm not cut out for this husband and father deal," I told Mary. "You guys would probably be better off without me."

"Don't be silly, Dean," Mary purred. "You're just a little worn out. You need to recharge your battery."

"Benjamin Franklin and his whole key ring couldn't recharge my battery. A hundred guys from the Sears auto-parts department couldn't recharge my battery."

"How about this?" Mary said, reaching for her Casio and playing a few bars of "Peace in the Valley."

"Stop it. You know how hot that song always gets me."

She kept playing, singing softly.

"Quit it. The kid'll hear."

"We'll just have to be quiet, then," Mary said, veritably whispering the last passage of the hymn. When she was done, she turned to me, her mouth bee-lining for my already impossibly rigid cock. "Oh," I moaned. A moment later my tune changed as I felt a nipplelike plastic object enter my anus, followed by rushing, ice-cold spray.

It was another of Mary's little tricks. She'd inserted the nozzle of a can of Reddi Whip into my backside and was filling my rear with the nitrous oxide–propelled cream. What a woman! One minute she was Miss Prim in a pew, the next she's giving you an ozone-layer-destroying enema.

"You got quite a zero-to-sixty on your nice-to-nasty," I laughed, momentarily free of my obsession with our financial woes. How I loved my wife! Childbirth only made her sexier, her stretch marks nothing less than permanently etched warpaint acquired in the most sacred of human battlefronts. We fucked that night, silent and slow.

When we were done, Mary told me about a conversation she'd had with Pudge Slater, a woman in the AA group she'd recently joined. Pudge's husband, Dick, ran a lumberyard over in Stylo, south of the canal. Dick had built up a decent business selling cheap quarter-inch plywood and drywall to the local construction trade. After a recent tumor operation, however, his eyesight was failing and he wanted to get out of the business.

"Sell shit materials to make shit houses? No thanks." I snorted.

"We could restock," Mary said. "I've heard a lot of women saying they wished they could buy ornamental things. Moldings and trims. Gingerbreads and the like. Most of the houses around here are so bare, they could stand a few details."

"You're right about that. But it'd still be retail . . . standing behind a counter, trying to cut costs. I don't know."

Mary stroked my arm. "You're a man who needs a creative outlet. There's a workshop behind the showroom. All the tools are already there. It would be a great spot for a carpenter."

"I'm not a carpenter. You've got to have talent to be a carpenter. I don't."

Mary smiled. "Oh yes you do, dear. I've seen you working with your hands. It's beautiful to see, the way they move. It's an inborn thing, you can see that in things you've done around the house. You've got talent."

"I'd never make enough money."

"Don't be so defeatist, Dean. Have a little faith in yourself."

With Mary handling the bookkeeping and the front office, we made it work. We sold the subcode materials and reordered from catalogs hawking Victorian details. The business took off, condo owners came from miles around, anxious to transform their vapid environs with an influx of pseudo-drawing-room styles. My shop was out back, in a separate, low-slung building. In the beginning I was wary of the place, only spending an hour or two a day there. Within weeks, however, it was up to ten and twelve.

Mary was right. I did have talent. As my fingertips had previously skimmed over the skin of women, guided by a mystic assurance that in touching one I was somehow touching all, I now regarded the texture of a piece of pine as a gateway to a realm beyond the physical and temporal. All I had to do was lay my hand on the grain of a piece of oak to follow its ethos beyond the gnaw of bandsaw teeth and lumberjack's hack, to the virgin forest, on back to a moment when the first tree pushed through primeval loam. Suddenly it was as if nature itself was flowing through me, as if I were the appointed human custodian of the planet's remains.

My hands taught my head. With startling rapidity, working without plans or even the barest of sketches, I produced several odd bits of furniture—a dresser with a looming mirror frame in the shape of a cobra's hood, a large oak table with fluted, mermaidlike legs, bookshelves that rose in the manner of inverted pyramids. Within weeks all manner of marvels filled my little shop.

My professionalism as a carpenter stood in sharp contrast to the sloth of my acting career. Back then, I sought only the easiest possible roles, things I could walk through on looks alone. Even Jimmy Dime, his head turned by those blowhard, red-meat-eating Montanans, took harder parts, once tackling Othello-in-the-Park. It was a disaster, of course, but at least he tried. Now, however, I measured myself according to the quaint concept of the job well done.

Indeed, I was feeling pretty good about myself the afternoon when a strange visitor came by. I'd been out back at the time, experimenting with different hues of homemade varnish when I heard someone inside the shop, going through my things. My first reaction was that I was being robbed. A young woman tending the convenience store on the interstate connector had been gunned down three weeks before and everyone was still talking about it.

I picked up a hammer and slowly made my way through the back door. "Hello?" I shouted. "Can I help you?"

No one answered, but I had no doubt the intruder was still inside, waiting for me. Immediately I had the sense this wasn't a simple robber, or even a homicidal escapee from the nearby state hospital in Starkston. Something more irrational, more malevolent, was inside my shop. It was Arana; it couldn't be anyone else. No one else could inspire the dread, fascination, and hatred I felt at that moment.

Many times I imagined him close. A near miss on the freeway, a small altercation on the ATM line, any such incident immediately became a potential encounter with ultimate evil in my mind. One time, while shopping in the bulk market with Mary and baby Dyson, I got into a squabble with a ferrety assistant manager over the mispricing of a head of lettuce. I didn't like his body language, the way he sneered when he talked. "Don't come any closer, you goddamn murderer," I shouted, ramming my shopping cart into the startled man's knee. "I've killed you twice!" I seethed. "I'll do it again!" It was all Mary could do to get me out of the store before the police came.

"Sorry, I don't know what comes over me . . . I just begin to see red and . . . I don't know . . ." I apologized when we got back into the car.

Mary looked at me. "Would it be better if we left Feltside, Dean? We could leave the state. Even go to another country." How I loved Mary then. I scream about having murdered people at some point in my mysterious past, and she thinks only of how we can escape to Peru. I never knew whether or not she believed that story about me conveniently contracting amnesia after the plane crash; the subject simply did not come up. She didn't care who I was, where I'd come from, only that I was here, with her, now. If I had to run, she wouldn't ask why, only where to.

"Leave Feltside?" I returned, feigning nonchalance, "and give up donuts at the Poppin' Pie? Forget it." There was no point in telling her the truth: That there was nowhere to run, that Arana's sway recognized no border or boundary in time or space. He'd get you, wherever you were, so why take the trouble to move?

And now, Arana was here, I decided, no more than twenty feet from me, inside my beloved shop. I gripped the hammer tighter. "Okay, you fuck," I said, thrusting myself through the doorway. "Here I come."

He was an elderly gentleman, probably in his late seventies, silver-maned and magisterial, with piercing gray eyes and a white bushy mustache. In his blue blazer and tan woolen slacks he might have passed for a slightly updated version of the banker on the Monopoly board. A patient, almost beguiling smile on his face, he sat in the oversized mahogany lounger I'd recently completed.

"Are you Mr. Taylor?" he asked.

"You know I am."

"Excuse me?" The old man turned sideways, adjusting his hearing aid. "Sorry, I don't hear as well as I might."

"Yes. I'm Mr. Taylor," I said, raising my voice.

"So you're the man who made this chair?"

I nodded warily. The chair, which had gone through several prototypes and false starts, was my favorite creation, but also my most troublesome. I was determined to create a wooden chair that would provide all the comfort and relaxation afforded by an overstuffed lounger, to surround the sitter with the rough-hewn feel of nature, yet be easy on the backside.

"Then this is the Taylor Chair," the old man said, with sonorous declaration.

"The Taylor Chair . . ." I rolled the words over in my mouth, keeping my eyes on the invader. As I might have expected from an Arana surrogate, there was a wintry edge to the old man, as if he'd seen no small amount of cruelty in his time, dished out at least as much. His eyes, however, relayed another message: an admiration. The stranger was looking at me with a sort of crusty affection, a grudging but unmistakable pride.

"I've waited a long time to sit in such an excellent chair, Mr. Taylor," the man said, standing up and advancing toward me with a stately dignity. Reflexively, I tightened my grip on the hammer; if need be I would slam the ballpeen down onto the old man's skull. When he was right in front of me, I just couldn't do it. I couldn't move a muscle. The old man put forth his hand to shake, penetrating the space between us.

"Thank you for letting me sit in your chair, Mr. Taylor," the man said, his sincerity unmistakable. I extended my hand to meet his. Our palms collided. It was the kind of handshake that clinches a deal irrevocably. "Thank you for coming to sit in it," I said.

Then the man leaned over, kissed me on the cheek, turned around, and walked out. He was gone so quickly it seemed as if he'd never been there in the first place. Immediately I knew: This man, whom just moments before I'd been ready to kill, was my own father, returned from the dead to make amends.

I was at the height of my Taylor Powell fame when we'd seen each other last. The cancer was already eating away at him, not that he would admit it. For him, the imminence of Death was a humiliation. Especially with me being so big. As I said before, he was under the impression that I screwed his second and third wives, which was only half true. "You would have screwed your own mother if she'd been alive when your balls grew big enough," he spat at me on that last day. I didn't argue; what was there to argue about? He hated me and I hated him. That's how we left it.

When he finally died, I cruised his funeral in a limo with Jimmy Dime. I told the driver to buzz through, quick, not to stop. I just wanted to make sure he was dead. For once Jimmy actually seemed offended. "Hey, he's still your dad, Taylor," he said, peering through the tinted window as the gravediggers lowered the casket. "You can't change that."

"That's just it," I replied, bitterly. "He's dead. They're out there throwing dirt on him. And he's still my dad. If I live to be a thousand, he'll still be my dad." With that, I told the limo to burn rubber out of that boneyard, the squeal of the tires a howl of pain in the crisp autumn air.

Still my dad . . . still my dad . . . Feeling a bit woozy, I took a seat in the wooden creation the man I imagined to be my father had dubbed the Taylor Chair. There was an immutability in the so-called ties that bind, I mulled. The guy was still a fuck; he never accepted me for myself. Indeed, I had to change into a wholly other person before he came to make peace. But he did come. He came to kiss me and say he was proud to have a son who made such an excellent chair.

He was still my dad, I was still his son. Between fathers and sons, likely there will always come a moment when the father, no matter how gracelessly he does it, will tell a son he's sorry. Fathers, after all, have so much to be sorry about. That noted, it remains for the son to accept the apology, to set the terms of reconciliation. And the son's forgiveness, should it ever be granted, can be a long time coming.

9.

By the time he was six, with his jet-black hair, perfect blue eyes, and signature square jaw, the mere sight of Dyson was enough to make doleful mall ladies lose control of their shopping carts, send their coupons fluttering. "What a lovely child," they'd say, reaching to squeeze the boy's arm, stroke his cheek. "He's like a little movie star. He'll break a lot of hearts."

"Yeah, sure thing," I'd mutter and continue on, pushing faster toward the checkout counter.

They could play as innocent as they wanted, but I knew what those women wanted from my son. I could smell it, under those polyester shifts and housecoats, between their thighs, aerobicized and not. They were wet. Wet and getting wetter.

What was it Vincent Parry said? "It's such a gamble when you get a face." Well, this was one very long shot, one any Mendelian tout would have been hard-pressed to parlay. I thought I'd seen the end of Taylor Powell, a.k.a. the Face. I didn't take into account the persistence of the gene.

"People are always staring at me, Dad," Dyson cried as we left the supermarket, his voice strangely deep-timbered for someone so young.

"That's because they like the way you look, son," I said, doing my best to offer fatherly comfort.

"I don't want to look like this," Dyson replied.

"But honey, people look like what they look like," I said, loading the groceries into the back of the station wagon. "What would you rather look like?"

Dyson peered up at me with those killer blues, pursed his

plush lips, conveyed that faintly melancholy trope of inner pain: all of which used to be gangbusters for Taylor Powell. "I want to look like you, Dad. That's what I want to look like."

"Why'd you want to look like brokendown old me," I attempted to joke, my heart pounding. "You're a very handsome young man. There's advantages in that. Someday you might like it."

"I won't ever like it," Dyson said, with a cold fury six-year-olds are not supposed to possess. "I hate it. I hate it more than anything."

The most troubling early manifestation of what a growing battery of child psychologists would come to call Dyson's "aggravated identity issues" cropped up relatively innocently. A precocious young artist, the boy quickly developed a representational style most notable for its exclusions. Something was always obscured: a bus whose driver was somehow missing, a mountaintop veiled by fog.

It was Dyson's pictures of people, however, that were most unsettling. As opposed to the rudimentary stick figures favored by most children his age, Dyson's people were well proportioned and full of expressive body language. He was partial to crowds, often sketching throngs at ballparks, or on trains. Realism predominated, except for the people's faces. They didn't have any. The heads were there, but the faces were blank.

"This is lovely," Mary said one afternoon as she examined one of Dyson's more recent creations.

"But there are things you can't see, right, Mom?" Dyson replied conspiratorially.

"Yes," Mary answered calmly. "This man doesn't have any eyes and nose."

"He doesn't have a face at all. None of them do."

"Did you forget to put the faces in, dear?"

"No, I didn't forget. They don't have any. They've been stolen," Dyson replied.

Masks became Dyson's obsession. At Halloween, whether he was a pirate or tiger, Frankenstein or Dracula, he wouldn't take off his costume until at least November 15, leading to many petulant phone calls from his teachers. It wasn't until the wrestling business, however, that I became concerned.

Although strong and well coordinated, Dyson was profoundly uninterested in playing sports of any kind. This indifference extended to watching athletics, precluding any ballpark, father-son bonding experiences. He was, however, a huge fan of TV wrestling, specifically Mexican grapplers, most of whom featured gaudy disguises. Of these, his favorite was Muchos Máscaras, El Hombre Secreto, whose numerous masks were, according to squared circle canard, handsewn by his own father, a humble tailor who lived in a mud hut on a far-off Oaxaca mountaintop.

"His masks are handsewn by his own father, a humble tailor who lives in a mud hut on a far-off Oaxaca mountaintop," Dyson explained to me one early Saturday evening as the bombast of Championship Wrestling's theme music filled the living room. "El Hombre Secreto travels to see his father before every fight, to get a new mask. They give him extra power, to overcome and vanquish."

This was to be a big night: El Hombre Secreto, long slighted by the vicious fixers of the sport, was finally being accorded his rightful opportunity to wrestle the Creeper, a 375-pound ex-footballer, for the Intercontinental crown. Champion mainly due to mindless brute strength and cheating, the hated Creeper had sworn to unveil the never-seen face of El Hombre Secreto. "I'll slice off that beaner's mask with my Bowie knife, so everyone can see what an ugly wetback he is," the Creeper bragged.

The bout proved to be a wrenching struggle, more emblematic of a clash of Titans and Olympians than a rigged carny show set in a minor-league basketball auditorium. El Hombre Secreto, quick and scientific, eventually gained the advantage and seemed on the verge of triumph when the Creeper hit the Mexican on the head with a bridge chair, knocking him cold.

It was then, as the Creeper pulled the Bowie knife from his boot, that Dyson, who'd been transfixed by the match, yelled out. "Cut it off!" he shouted. "Rip it off his face!"

I turned to my son with surprise. The walls of his room were covered with pictures of Muchos Máscaras, El Hombre Secreto. Yet now, with the wrestler at the brink of defeat and humiliation, his mask about to be torn from his face by the vulgar Creeper, Dyson turned against his sleek-limbed hero. "Slice that thing off!" he exhorted, the shocking bloodlust of the mob in his pre-teen voice. "Show his face! Show his goddamned face!"

Dyson's expectation soon turned to a wail of dismay: For beneath the mask was another mask, an even more rococo covering. "No!" Dyson yelled.

Enraged, the Creeper began hacking away at the second, Quetzalcoatl-styled mask, only to discover still another below that. This tickled the crowd at the arena, but not Dyson. He was clearly in torment, only perking up as the Creeper began cutting away what appeared to be the last layer of El Hombre Secreto's colorful shrouds. "At last," Dyson said.

However, just as the gloating Creeper began peeling off the final mask, a small, elderly, Mayan-looking man was on the scene. Attired in shabby peasant garb, the wizened gentleman began tugging at Creeper. It was El Hombre Secreto's father, descended from the far-off Oaxaca mountaintop, to help his fallen son. This seemed a wonderful turn of events to me. Not Dyson. "Go away!" he screamed. "Go away, you old . . . piece of shit!"

Dyson grew only more agitated as El Hombre Secreto made a miraculous return to consciousness, just in time see the Creeper pick up the humble tailor and throw him out of the ring. Incensed, the Mexican went into a frenzy, stomped the Creeper into the canvas, thereby winning the fight and the championship. As El Hombre Secreto pranced about, his unrevealed face newly covered with one of his father's freshly sewn masks, Dyson put his foot through the bass drum of the little jazz kit I'd bought him.

"Calm down," I said. "It's only a stupid TV show. These aren't real fights."

"Maybe it's not real to you!" Dyson screamed, running toward the television, pushing it onto the floor.

After that, Dyson's violent outbursts grew more frequent. One day I came home to find him locked in his room, smashing things. "He's breaking the mirrors and the windows, too," Mary sobbed. "He says his face is not his face; he says he's not really our son, that we bought him from some other family."

What a nightmare. My own son was locked in the most terrible emotional torment, yet I couldn't reveal to him his identity, or my own. I'd sworn to keep these things secret. "It's just a phase," I told Mary hurriedly. "He'll grow out of it."

I turned back to the locked door. "Dyson . . . please," I said feebly. "I can help you. You've got to believe that. I know how you feel."

"Liar! How can you know how I feel?" came the anguished, guttural reply, summoned from a dark, deep place that should not be visited by children. This was followed by another, louder, shattering crash.

"Seven years bad luck," I said, with inane jocularity.

"Seven and seven is . . ." There was an unsettling, almost demonic tone to Dyson's words as I heard his desk lamp crash against the full-length mirror I'd hung on the inside of his bedroom door. "And seven more."

"Dyson!" I screamed. "Open this damn door!"

"Not until you show me the paper!"

"Stop saying that! There is no paper. You're not adopted!" I slammed into the door with my shoulder, ripping it from its brass hinges. Dyson lay on the floor, face down, his arms and legs thrashing about his pretty tropical blue shag carpet, the sun glinting off the shards of broken mirror. From the look of it, he could have been swimming vigorously through a Caribbean sea. Except for the blood soaking through his T-shirt.

I bent down beside him as he continued to flail about on the rug. "Stop, honey, please," I implored, rubbing the back of his neck. Eventually, he lay motionless, allowing me to remove most of the shards embedded in his skin. I could see my own reflection in these jagged slivers, just as Dyson had seen his, a hundred jigsaw puzzle pictures of the person he knew, some-how, was not him.

The EMTs arrived in the same souped-up ambulance Dyson had often admired as it passed, lights flashing, sirens yowling. Demonstrating the heedlessly efficient insouciance of their trade, the medics were unimpressed by Dyson's wounds. "It's mostly surface stuff," one worker remarked, as he loaded my bleeding boy into the ambulance. As if the surface was nothing to worry about.

I sat beside Dyson as the ambulance sped along to the hospi-tal. They'd given him something, and he slept. Even here, amid the oxygen tanks and hazard flares, Dyson looked beautiful, and not simply because he was my son and all sons look beautiful to their fathers, or should. Dyson *was* beautiful, and beauty—sup-posedly skin deep—endured. Beauty fought as tenaciously for survival as did the doughtiest of specimens; it created its own logic. How else to explain the reprise, in Dyson, of the face I'd thrown away. How else to explain that even though Dyson's en-tire upper body was slashed and gouged, his face, the supposed offending part, was untouched?

I found hope in that. I could picture Dyson holding a blade an inch from his face, searching for the appropriate place and mo-ment to disfigure himself, to sully the beauty that was his. I saw him being unable to make the fatal incision, not out of fear or in-decision, but rather because he understood the inviolability of beauty and the grave responsibility that had fallen to him as the bearer of its sublime banner.

Sitting in the back of the hurtling ambulance, I was seized with an unprecedented sense of immortality. I wondered if a day might come when Dyson would appreciate my surreptitious legacy. I bent over and kissed Dyson's face, my face. "It's going to be all right, son. I know it."

It was at that moment Dyson opened his marvelous blue eyes, those same orbs that had hypnotized so many. "It's not going to be all right, Dad," Dyson said, through drug-hazed pain and ha-tred. "It's only going to get worse. *Worse and worse.*"

10.

That night Mary took a drink, the first since we'd been married. She was plowed before I got back from the hospital, where Dyson spent the night. "Maybe he is adopted," Mary said, as she sat up in bed, a liquor stain spread across her satin underwear much as the blood had soaked Dyson's clothes. "I showed him his birth certificate and he said something like that can easily be forged."

"Dammit, Mary!" I said, grabbing her by the shoulders. "Don't let this happen."

She was certain that Dyson's distress somehow proved, yet again, her unfitness for motherhood. "He's so unhappy. Why should he be so unhappy?"

It was an ungenerous impulse, but I could have smacked her right then. Couldn't she see what was right in front of her face? I'd been dropping hints for days, tuning in that shitty Taylor Powell festival they were running on the cable station to commemorate the twelfth anniversary of my supposed death. "Think he's good looking?" I said, casually, as we sat in bed watching *That Roman Winter*, the weepy meller in which I whipped about the cobblestone byways of the Eternal City on a Vespa, a shiftless gigolo disseminating my particular talents to rich but fraying matrons.

"Who?" Mary asked, putting down the book she'd been reading. She'd never been much for TV.

"Taylor Powell," I said. "You know, the movie star. He's dead."

Clad in briefs, my former incarnation reclined on silk sheets, kissing Veronica Wilder—ole Lady V., she'd been one hell of an

Ophelia in her day, Juliet, too. She was pushing fifty-five when we got together, and even if her hair was a tad patchy in spots, she retained that dusky voice, those wingy cheekbones, and a pair of gams, however lined with varicose veins, that wouldn't quit. The Fleet Street tabs hounded us every minute because she was married to some rich lord supposedly given to challenging people to duels, prompting Jimmy Dime to offer to be my second, as long as the shoot-out wasn't scheduled for too early in the morning.

"Taylor, Taylor, tinker, spy," Lady Veronica had said with much theatricality as she rubbed my dick between her bony hands. "To me, you are every man. You are my father and you are my son, which is so wonderful because I've always wanted to fuck them both."

"He's very handsome," Mary said, studying the erstwhile me. "But he's not my type . . ." Then she went back to reading her book.

Not her type. Really. How could she miss it? How could she look at the face of Taylor Powell and not see Dyson? It was maddening. All she had to do was say: "He reminds me of somebody? . . . but who? . . . Oh, my God . . ." Then the blanks could have been very easily filled in. Parry and Josias made me swear not to tell anyone my secret; but they laid down no contingency for someone arriving at my identity by chance. All Mary had to do was guess, then truth would sear through the festering climate of lies that had smothered our once paradisiacal lives.

Mary didn't guess. Probably she wouldn't have believed it even if I'd come right out and told her. How could any mother accept such knowledge, about her husband, her son? Even if Mary did guess my true identity, she'd have to deny it to herself, suppress the fact. Just to keep sane.

So I dropped the matter. Mary was the love of my life. To her, I was the man who fell out of the sky, weightless, without baggage. That was how it should stay.

As for Dyson, however, he said it would get worse and it did. Worse and worse.

"He was in here again," Mary told me one evening. Circles under her eyes from lack of sleep, she indicated the scrapbook on the night table. "I hid it in the closet, but he found it, again."

I opened the album. Scrawled across the first page of plastic photo holders, in Dyson's looping, almost girlish hand, were the words, "Where are you?" It was Dyson's current fixation: the fact that there were no photographs of me around the house, or as far as he could tell, anywhere.

"There're pictures of everyone else," Dyson would say, turning the pages of the photo book. "Here's a baby picture of Mom. But none of you, no pictures of you at all."

The staring was the worst of it: Dyson's cold, unwavering gaze seldom left me, forever scrutinizing, probing, like a cancer-inducing X-ray. One of the galls of parenthood is to hear the same phrases employed by the previous generation slip from your own mouth: hated old chestnuts like "Maybe," the ubiquitous "We'll see," and "Because I said so!" Now, however, I heard myself bellowing at Dyson "Stop looking at me with those eyes!"—the very phrase my own father shouted when he returned from screwing one of his married-lady insurance clients. My father, of course, was referring to my dead mom's eyes. In my case the bleat hit a little closer to home.

"Come on, Dad, you a vampire or something? I just want to know how come there're pictures of everyone but you," Dyson said, still looking at the family album.

"I don't like to have my picture taken, it's as simple as that," I replied, attempting nonchalance as I hovered over the sink, washing the dishes from that evening's dinner. "We live in a world where everyone is saying 'look at me,' making fools of themselves just to be caught for a second by the camera at a football game—as if that's the only proof of being alive. Photography was only invented a hundred years ago. How did people validate their existence before they could stop off at the Fotomat? You know what they say in the jungle: Let someone take your picture and they'll steal your soul."

"We're not in the jungle now, are we, Dad?" Dyson mocked

with his now practiced sarcasm. "We're in Feltside. How come you told that cop you lost your driver's license? You didn't want to show him your picture, right?"

He had me there. I had thrown away my driver's license exactly to avoid showing pictures of myself to people like the nosy cop who'd stopped us the other night for having a burned-out taillight. I didn't want anyone seeing a picture of me. As with Sergeant Tarpley and Josias's uncle before, even the quickest glance at my photographic image would elicit strange behavior. Bank tellers hyperventilated. Sulky supermarket cashiers peering at check-cashing cards fainted. None of them ever failed to cry. Therein, I often thought, was another thing I had in common with my unhappy son: We both had faces that controlled our lives but neither one of us knew exactly why.

"Maybe you're a fugitive from the law," Dyson speculated. "Why else wouldn't you want anyone to know who you are?"

"That's using your noodle, Sherlock Holmes," I answered, scrubbing the soapy plates in the sink. "Let's go over to the post office and see if we can find a picture of me on the wall."

"Yeah. Murder. Interstate flight." The notion seemed to thrill Dyson. "They're tightening the noose on the fugitive," the boy intoned, as if sportscasting a manhunt. "He's feeling the pressure, it's just a matter of time before he cracks."

Then, unfurling a maliciously toothy smile the likes of which the Face never knew when it belonged to me, Dyson tilted his head back. "They're gonna get you, Dad," he taunted. "Sooner or later, they'll get you."

I didn't ask who the "they" of Dyson's scenario might be. Busying myself washing dishes, I turned the hot water on full blast, losing myself in the cascading torrent and enveloping steam.

Dyson's campaign of psychological terror continued. "Seen the paper, Dad?" he'd ask, innocently. I'd look through, hoping that perhaps, this time, the boy had no other motive but to hand his father the evening tabloid. But then, there it'd be, a nondescript wire-service piece buried deep in the second section under a headline along the lines of: STRANGE CEREMONIAL DEATH PUZZLES POLICE. This particular story was about a young Zuni Indian who'd been found dead along the roadside with a *kachina* mask cemented onto his head. According to the tribal police, the young man had taken part in a night ritual, falling asleep sometime before dawn. Then, as "a practical joke gone wrong," the paper said, "unknown individuals" had poured cement into the *kachina* earhole, bonding the fetish onto the young man's head, asphyxiating him in the process.

The assault went on. One evening I came home to find Mary and Dyson watching a tape, *Revenge of the Supermodels.* "It's about a society based on looks," Dyson said blithely, offering me a chair by the TV. "Except it's backwards. The ugly people are in charge and they're really rotten. They won't let the pretty people practice their religion or use makeup. She's the leader of the Pretties. Isn't she great?"

It was Jennifer Cantrell, in her first and, as it turned out, last screen role. Looking fantastic in a crotch-cutter leotard with bearskin trim lending a sexy cavewoman effect, Jennifer stood on a rock, readying her supermodel troops for battle against the Uglies. "We have to show them that beauty is not skin-deep, but that we are lovely inside as well," Jennifer said, her voice more wooden than a grove of oak. Saint Joan she was not, but what a pair of ta-tas.

"Pretty cool, huh, Dad?" Dyson said.

"Cool," I nodded.

The worst of it was the night I came home to find Mary nearly comatose. She'd been bedeviled by a series of cluster headaches and apparently had taken too many pain pills. It took a full five minutes to rouse her. "He took Shawn's picture," she said, when she could finally talk. The picture of Mary's dead son was missing from the scrapbook's plastic pouch.

"Did you tell Dyson about Shawn?" I asked.

Mary was shellshocked. "No . . . I mean, yes. Sort of . . . We were looking through the scrapbook together and he pointed to Shawn. He wanted to know who he was. 'Some boy I used to know,' I said. I didn't tell him. I didn't tell him a thing . . .

"Yet somehow . . . he knew. 'That boy's dead, isn't he?' he asked. I told him he was. 'You loved him, didn't you, Mom?' he asked. I told him I did." Mary broke off into sobs.

I loathed Dyson then. Stealing a dead boy's image from his grieving mother seemed an unspeakable act of emotional terrorism. Enraged, I started out of the bedroom. "I'm gonna kill that kid!" I growled.

"Stop!" Mary wailed. "Isn't one dead son enough?"

I crumpled onto the bed beside my weeping wife. Again I cursed myself. Hell had descended on our home and I, along with my face—my two faces—was the cause of it.

That night my sleep was racked by terrible dreams. I was back in the jungle, with Vincent Parry standing over me, performing the surgery that turned me into Dean Taylor. Only I was watching the procedure from the point of view of a third person, as if I were sitting in the bleachers of an operating theater. Parry had drawn a thick black line around the extreme edges of my former face, inserted a small blade into the skin, and was now cutting along the tracing. He cut until he'd gone all the way around. Then he lifted up my old face, placed it on the open palm of his right hand.

There was a wistfulness to the plastic surgeon as he stood there looking down at my severed face. Then, with a flick of the wrist, the doctor flipped the face from his hand, sending it, dripping blood, through the dank air. I watched the arc of my former face's flight, the dim light flashing through empty eye sockets. It disappeared over the metal lip of a trash can, making a faint plop as it hit bottom.

I awoke with a start. Shaken, I wondered if it was really Dyson who hated me. Perhaps it wasn't him at all, but my old face, returned from the trash bin into which it had been thrown, to haunt me.

11.

In spite of these problems, I felt hopeful as we left Feltside for a trip to New York several months later. Mary had long dreamed of visiting the great metropolis and even Dyson seemed excited about the prospect of sightseeing in the big town.

It was the Taylor Chair, as it was now officially called in the fancy brochure Mary had printed up, that made the family vacation possible. When I first opened my carpentry shop, I was determined to create only one-of-a-kind objets d'art, each piece totally unique. However, despite some success at selling individual items at the Delkspot Swap Meet, I soon recognized the financial impracticality of such a plan; I needed to be able to reproduce my designs. It was soon after that mysterious visit from the elderly gentleman I took to be a manifestation of my departed father that I decided the Taylor Chair, as the old man called it, might be the ticket. The concept of an ergonomically sound, wooden chair that could be customized to fit the individual spinal curvature had proved a nationwide winner, especially after an article in the *Washington Post* quoted a noted senator saying that after fifty years of regarding the sitting position as an attack on human physiology, he finally "felt at home" in the Taylor Chair.

"Quack chiropractors be damned!" the senator said. "Your spine never had such a friend as the Taylor Chair." After that, orders went through the roof.

As I pondered the many ways the success of the Taylor Chair had changed our lives, I looked through the plane window to the brawny clutter of Manhattan Island. The massive structures below could be roughly separated into two categories, I thought. There were the older stone towers, with the points on top. In these one felt the grand skyward soar of aspiration, as if their designers not only sought the attention of Heaven but felt that their bold Promethean achievement was worthy of such scrutiny. Then there were the newer structures, arranged like desultory dominoes across the breadth of the grid, their roofs as flat as the defeated affect of the men and women who'd conceived and built them, people resigned to a world of reduced expectation. I took the liberty of allying myself with the soaring American optimism of those who pointed steeples toward the Eye of God. In this affiliation I found hope for the world in general and my family in particular. However large our problems seemed, we were healthy and together, on the verge of a new adventure.

It was soon after returning from a visit to the Statue of Liberty that we were approached by a grizzled, multichinned man wearing an orange reflective vest. "Free tickets," the man croaked, fanning ducats between his knobbed fingers. "Free tickets to *That's Who I Am!*"

There seemed no reason not to accept. *That's Who I Am!*, a top-rated game show, was a favorite in our house. The concept was familiar but not uneducational: A first-person account of an incident in the life of a historical figure or current celebrity was read by Ty DeBoll, the heavily coiffed, bombastic host. It was not enough for the contestant to simply know the correct answer; an exaggerated emotional display, preferably punctuated by a Rocky-esque hand-over-head pump and the shout of "That's who I am, Ty D!" was equally important. This obligatory coda was key to the show's popularity and was always greeted with woofing cheers from the live studio audience.

From the moment we took our seats in the ex-Broadway house, however, it was obvious that something was amiss. Less than fifteen minutes before the scheduled taping, Ty DeBoll, his shiny face half made-up, his shirt unbuttoned, was on the stage, verbally assaulting a stolid man who appeared to be the show's producer.

"We're not calling off the show. No way!" DeBoll shrieked, in a cracking falsetto. "No fucking way!" It soon was announced that the limousine carrying the prospective challengers to Denise Newbill, the current champion, had been sideswiped by a cement truck in Herald Square. The limo had crashed through a window at Macy's and burst into a fireball, instantly killing the slated contestants.

"Live TV's sure got its surprises, heh, heh," DeBoll, now fully powdered and in proper Botany 500 attire, said a few moments later. "We're short some challengers . . . so, who'd like to come on up and play . . . *That's Who I Am!*?"

The task of recruiting a challenger for Denise Newbill's crown fell to Missy Fowler, *That's Who I Am!*'s resident bimbo. Sexbomb favorite of supermarket tabloids that never tired of reporting her miscarriages and kindness to animals, Missy, platinum hair piled on her head, Beefeater style, cut a cartoonish figure as she maneuvered her Mae West–lite body through the catcalling audience.

It was only as she bumped and ground down our aisle that I remembered seeing Missy before. Except her name wasn't Missy then, it was Karen, Karen Kralaw, except that in high school they called her Kunty Karen Kralaw. "You know, KKK," she said dolefully, one night almost twenty years ago.

Not yet sixteen, a one-hundred-pound junior whore and as sweet a cupcake as you'd ever want to see in a cum-spattered thigh-high satin dress, Karen was blowing Jimmy Dime in the "master suite" of a disgusting Nevada-border whorehouse, doing her slurpy best. Poor kid, she'd been at it about an hour, jaws aching, getting nowhere. That was pretty much par for the course since Jimmy, ever fearful of the ole pre-ejack, had OD'd on those Sta-Hard pills. It got so he rarely ever came anymore, leading him to declare, "I got bluer balls than B. B. King." He'd get some hooker to suck him for hours while he caught up on his reading or simply stared off, which he claimed was "super for my TM." This time, however, Jimmy came. Like wham, all over Karen, an ultra-pneumatic spew.

"Oh," the youngster said in wonder, jism dripping from her chin. "I never knew it could be like this."

Jimmy, the asshole, he didn't even look up. "Hey Taylor," he said, engrossed in the *Racing Form*, "I really like this Lukas horse in the sixth." Don't ask me why I snapped, I'd seen a lot worse. There was something about Karen Kralaw, how young she was, and her notion that transcendence could be found in the splat of apathetic spermatozoa, that made me ashamed for my entire sex, including myself. I guess I hit Jimmy D. pretty hard, because blood was everywhere. "Shit, Taylor!" he yowled. "What the fuck was that for?"

I took her out of there, past the yammering Chinese madam. We drove out to the mobile home where she lived. I resolved to sit down with her parents and respectfully tell them Karen was a good girl and they should take better care of her. However, once her old man stuck his twelve-gauge shotgun out the trailer window and set his dogs on us, I abandoned that tack. Karen and I wound up in bed, of course, which was the only other place I could think of taking her. I rocked her slow and fine, let her cry the night away, her every tear another hideous memory. I guess I got a little carried away, in a parental sort of way, because the next morning I gave her two thousand dollars and the name of a good all-girl junior college in Tacoma where I knew the head-mistress. A couple of years with her head stuck in a book would do her good, I thought. Last I'd heard she'd dropped out to join a convent, which sounded like overdoing it a bit, but to each her own.

The convent thing must not have worked out. "How 'bout you big fella," the former Karen, now Missy, mock-purred, deploy-ing her torpedo-like breast augmentation in my general direc-tion. "Want to give it a whirl?"

"Whirl?"

"Play *That's Who I Am!*" She batted her whisk-broom lashes.

"Not me . . . I'm shy."

"Too bad," Missy said humidly. She was taking aim at a yahoo wearing a Miller beer T-shirt in the next row when she stopped in her tracks. Pivoting on spiky heels, Missy turned back to me. A muscle near her eyebrow twitched, creating fault lines in her lavishly applied TV makeup. "Do I know you from somewhere?"

"Don't think so." By this time, I'd more or less gotten used to people stopping in their tracks to insist they knew me "from somewhere." But I'd never encountered someone who actually *did* know me, however briefly.

"You sure? . . . You sure we've never . . ." It was awful. The exaggerated brass of Missy Fowler was falling away, piece by piece, to the sad little Karen Kralaw below.

"No . . . I have no . . ." I felt sweat trickle down the back of my neck. It had never taken this long before; invariably people gave up the notion that they knew me almost immediately.

"I do . . . I know you," Missy continued. It was only then that I realized Missy was no longer looking at me, but rather was staring at Dyson, who, under the intense studio lights, looked more like Taylor Powell than ever before.

"Hi," Dyson said, flashing that smile I'd made famous. "Oh," Missy Fowler said, before she fainted, falling directly into my arms. With this there was a crash of music and the amplified voice of Ty DeBoll. *"Looks like Missy got her man!"* The TV host jabbed a finger at me. "Come on up! Come on up and play . . . play . . . *That's Who I Am!"*

There was no escape. The audience, immediately falling into a *woof, woof* chant, wanted me. Ty DeBoll wanted me. Missy Fowler, still out cold, her puffy body a dead weight in my arms, obviously wanted me. "Go ahead, Dad," Dyson said, under his breath, a clipped whisper amid the shouting of the crowd. "Play . . . play *That's Who I Am!"*

A moment later I was standing behind a podium bearing a panel spelling out: DEAN. "Dean!" Ty DeBoll shouted. "A carpenter, just like our Lord . . . a carpenter from Feltside!"

Peering at me across five or six feet of highly-charged TV air was Denise, the longest-reigning champion in the history of the show. Dark, petite, with a mouth full of tapered little teeth, Denise had her tax-auditor-game face on. I offered my hand, but she only squinted malevolently.

Denise's strategy was to blow me out of the water from the jump. Wagering heavily, she went with the "Modern Political Geniuses" category, one of her best. "All right, for five thousand dollars," Ty DeBoll brayed, affecting a thick central European accent, "here's your quote.

"'To be a great statesman, a peacemaker, you must create war and then stop that war, declare peace as you declared war. This goes doubly for genocide. To be seen as a member of a victim group is intolerable for a statesman. If genocide has been practiced against you, you must perpetrate genocide on others. This is why as the supreme diplomatic leader of the Free World, I chose to revisit the Nazi holocaust upon several million faceless Vietnamese and Cambodians. To ignore the screams of those unfortunates even as I arose to accept the Nobel Peace Prize, a prize given by men who looked so much like Nazis, was, to me, the paramount moment of personal triumph.'

"Okay, contestants!" Ty DeBoll shouted, returning to his normal Californian accent. *"Who am I?"*

Of course, I knew the answer. Who wouldn't? But timing was everything on *That's Who I Am!* and Denise was cat quick. She slammed down her buzzer before I could even twitch. "I'm Henry Kissinger," Denise whooped in her fraudulent little-girl voice. Then, thrusting her arms in the air in mock triumph, the mousy woman exalted, *"I'm Henry Kissinger . . . That's who I am, Ty D!"*

Denise was $23,000 ahead before I managed my first score. Stifling a yawn, Ty DeBoll went into a vague drawl, "'So I got a headache and they says, okay, take the day off. Next day I say I'm feeling a heck of a lot better. I'm ready to go on out there, but they says, take 'nother day off, you don't look so hot. That's 1921. 1922, same story. 1923, 1924, too. I'm the starting first baseman for this club and they got me on the bench, year after year. So it went. Finally, 1939 they say, hey you, you ain't sick, get out there . . . Called me a goddamn malingerer. Shee-it. I might have had a headache, but least no doctor ever named no disease after me.'"

Down I slammed.

"Dean!"

" . . . Um . . . Wally Pipp."

Dead silence enveloped the studio. Everyone was staring at me as if I'd committed a heinous crime. Realizing my offense, I unfurled the biggest and phoniest smile I could muster. "I'm Wally Pipp . . ." I boomed with good-guy numbskullery. *"I'm Wally Pipp . . . That's who I am, Ty D!"*

From there on, it was a dogfight. Immediate favorite of the studio audience, I gained confidence with every question, reeling off several winners in a row. Denise, however, proved a tenacious champion; she fought back, identifying William of Orange, P. D. Ouspensky, and Iggy Pop.

It came down to "Buzzer Off/Sudden Death." A pair of questions would be asked in each round, if one contestant answered correctly while the other did not, all the money and prizes would be his. $193,000, an unprecedented sum in *That's Who I Am!* history, was on the table. Money like that meant expanding the shop, a worldwide-distribution system for the Taylor Chair. It meant college for Dyson.

Sudden death rules dictated each competitor select the topic for the opposing player. Noting that Denise had failed to identify two separate quotes from Honorius I in the "Bad Popes" category, I opted for "Recently Discovered Secret Files of the Saints."

"Are you ready, Denise?" Ty DeBoll asked breathlessly, his congenitally cynical nature somewhat stripped away by the drama of the moment. "All right, here we go.

"'Faith is Love, but also Fear. So, we now come to understand that the divinity of our Lord, Jesus Christ, stems not only from the creationist point of view, but rather the evolutionary as well. Fear and power are naturally selected, so too belief. In the earliest times, men, thinking themselves weak, prayed to effigies of the strongest animals, bears, lions, and the like. Mastery over these beasts, symbolized by Yahweh's consolidation of the Deity under the abstract banner of monotheism, was but a half a loaf. As men came to dominate the Heavens and Earth, an affirmation of that triumph was needed. The revolt against Yahweh, the cruel and unknowable Father, by the Son was inevitable. Herein is the triumph of Christ, and of Christianity. This is a God who shows his face. Man's face. And in His Face, we see ourselves.'"

My heart sank. *That's Who I Am!* was obviously just another rigged quiz show. How else to explain handing Denise such a cinch question at this critical juncture? Denise wasn't slamming down, however. She knitted her beetlish brow, forced a cramped grin. Denise was toast, I knew. I've always known how women look when they're about to bullshit you. Only a lucky guess would save her now.

"Five seconds, Denise," Ty DeBoll said urgently.

"I'm Saint Thomas," Denise chirped with hysteric faux enthusiasm, *"I'm Saint THOMAS . . . That's who I am, Ty D!"*

DeBoll's head hung, followed by a unison groan from the studio audience. "I'm sorry, Denise . . . the correct answer is: *'I'm Saint PAUL . . . That's who I am, Ty D!'"*

The contest was now mine to win: $193,000 for answering a single question. A nail-biting delirium seized the studio, but I felt cool and collected, confident. Denise, as was her right, chose my category for the question that would put me over the top. "Dead Movie Stars," she said.

"Dead Movie Stars!" DeBoll repeated portentously. "Are you ready, Dean?"

I never said I was ready, but the guy began reading anyway.

"'Call me anything you want to call me,'" DeBoll quoted, the words already causing tightness in my throat. "'Because I don't care what you call me. All that mattered to you was how hip she was supposed to be. Slept with Belmondo, Godard, half the Black Panther Party, a hundred black guys with AK-47s. All those stories . . . What do you want me to say? She was as nice as anyone. Nicer. You want me to say we screwed? Okay, we screwed. It was what she wanted, what I wanted . . .'"

It wasn't word for word, not even close, more of a bunch of conversations spliced together, but what was I going to do about that now?

"'They say I held up shooting for two weeks after she killed herself, like that was some kind of crime. I'm a human being, I was upset. I didn't try to change the script. All I said was "I've read *War and Peace* and *The Brothers Karamazov*" wasn't as good a line as "I've read *War and Peace* and HALF *The Brothers Karamazov*." And you know what? It's not. Mine's better. How was I supposed to know the director had a weak ticker? A hundred pictures, he drops dead on mine and that's supposed to be my fault? So go screw yourself . . . screw all of you.'"

If I'd been in a quiz-show glass booth, the sort they scrapped after Eichmann's performance made them inappropriate, the walls would have closed in on me until I was shrinkwrapped. The decades-old headlines flipped in front of my eyes: DEATH STALKS POWELL PICTURE. DID DON JUAN SHARE SUICIDE BED? We were playing mental patients—"Loons in Love," they called the picture on the set—and she just lost it. Supposed to cut her wrists for fake and doing it for real. Goddamn method actors. And all the tech boys too drunk to see she was bleeding to death.

Ty DeBoll drew a deep breath. "Okay, Dean, for all the marbles—clearies and the pearlies and just plain spinners— *who am I?*"

I sought a focus object, a solitary image upon which to concentrate. I chose a stack of bills, tens and twenties, a few hundreds maybe. $193,000 makes a substantial pile. Try as I might, though, I couldn't fasten on the money. Instead, I looked past the blare of the stagelights, out to the studio audience. There had to be at least five hundred people out there, each of them with their own face, their own particular arrangement of features wholly unique to them. Now, however, the faces bled together, seeping into one another until they merged to one great mouth, a dark, sucking tunnel ready to swallow me up.

"Ten seconds, Dean," Ty DeBoll said, his voice a barbarously clanging metronome building speed. "Five . . ."

I wanted to say it, push the words over my quivering lips. There were only nine of them: *I'm Taylor Powell . . . That's who I am, Ty D!* Nine words, barely a dozen syllables. What would be the ramification of uttering such a small segment of the language, a gaggle of sound that to non-native speakers would be so much indistinct glossolalia? For one thing, Missy Fowler, recovered from her swoon, would kiss me. She kissed every male champion, crunching her silicon-stressed bustline into the winner's chest, the copping of a quick feel offered as a perk of victory. There was that. That and the $193,000.

I closed my eyes, seemingly deep in thought. The quiz-show guys loved that. Big suspense. I looked into the audience, tried to lose myself in the blur of humanity. But now that dark had coalesced into a single face. Dyson's face. The one I once wore. Shining through the murk like a diamond, he sat there, smiling, waiting. "Come on, Dad," Dyson mouthed, "answer the man's question."

"No," was all I said.

"What was that, Dean? Speak up . . . loud and clear. Tell us, *who are you?*"

My jaw locked. No words came forth, nor would they. I couldn't break my promise. $193,000 was a lot of money, but not that much.

"Last chance, Dean!"

An audio chainsaw chewed through my head, and I was momentarily blinded. My time was up, the buzzer had sounded, the houselights put on. "So sorry, Dean," Ty DeBoll mewled as if his own mother had been shot dead, his commiseration surfing atop the audience's rolling wave of *"ohhhhh."*

As for the remaining events of my sojourn as a contestant on *That's Who I Am!,* I am a bit sketchy.

I do recall Denise Newbill answering the question I missed, hearing her shout, *"I'm Taylor Powell . . . That's who I am, Ty D!"* and watching her pump her spiny little arms in the air. The fact that Denise would win $193,000 by declaring to be me while I lost through the denial of such self struck me as a small but significant moment in the history of late twentieth century identity issues. Mostly, however, I remember seeing Dyson in the audience, something clicking inside his beautiful head.

I remember, too, following him through dazed eyes, as he got up from his seat and walked out of the theater, even before Ty DeBoll had thanked everyone and invited them back for another edition of *That's Who I Am!*

12.

By the time I appeared carrying the Hoover vacuum and Oster-izer blender some functionary (not Missy Fowler) handed me as "consolation prizes," Mary was in a panic. Dyson had disap-peared in the crowd. A quick check of the hotel room revealed that the boy had gone back there, taken his backpack, and, ac-cording to the desk clerk, gone out the revolving door, laughing "kind of giddy like."

"Oh, he's probably just walking around the big town, look-ing in windows, buying dirty magazines," I said to Mary, attempting to lighten the situation. Dyson had always been an independent sort, I rationalized, it made sense he would want to be alone in such an exciting environment. When he got back we could yell at him for scaring us so, but for now we should treat it as if we were simply loosening the parental leash a bit.

"That's right," Mary agreed, when she managed to stop pacing the hotel room. "A child should be allowed some space." She re-called walking away from her squalid rural home, hitchhiking to Knoxville. "Knoxville's not New York, of course," Mary said with constrained cheeriness. "I liked the idea that I would be somewhere and no one on earth, not my mother, not my father, not anybody, had the foggiest where I was at that moment, it re-ally made me feel grown-up."

"There you go," I put in, trying to sound upbeat.

"But I knew the truth," Mary went on, morosely. "It wasn't that no one knew where I was, it was that no one *cared* where I was. I knew pretending to be grown-up only meant I'd moved closer to that part of life where every waking moment could be lived in alienated loneliness."

"Would you knock it off?" I snapped. "Take it from me, it's different for boys, they *want* to be alone. Some ritual-of-the-hunt thing. Dyson's going to be fine."

As midnight passed with no sign of Dyson, however, I decided to go to the police, ending up in the "tourist services" section of the scruffy NYPD Midtown North Station. After a lengthy wait on a knife-gouged wooden bench, Detective Krantz, a shirt-sleeved, balding man who identified himself as a "visitor liaison officer," led me through a maze of desks to a small fluorescent-lit room, the walls of which were plastered with air-bubbled I♥NY bumper stickers.

"This facility is maintained by the City of New York to cater to the anxieties of our valued guests," Krantz droned with the nasal autopilotness employed by men of his ilk for reading Miranda rights to derelicts they'd just beaten senseless in a subway stairwell.

"My son is missing. He disappeared from the hotel room," I told Krantz, handing him Dyson's most recent class picture.

"Nice looking kid," Krantz said, examining the photo. "He looks like that actor. You know the one—"

"His mother is out of her mind with worry . . ."

Krantz knitted his brow and snapped his fingers. "What's the name of that actor . . ." Craning his thickish neck, he yelled to a cop in the adjoining cubicle. "Hey, Kevin, what's the name of that actor . . . you know, the dead one."

"Which dead one?" replied Krantz's brother officer.

"You know that one . . . the one who you always think might be a fag except he isn't a fag," Krantz said, handing the second cop Dyson's photo. "This kid looks like him."

The two cops puzzled over the picture. The name of the actor Dyson resembled was on the tips of their tongues, but they couldn't quite remember who he was. Then Krantz took my statement, said missing persons was pretty booked up but they'd keep a lookout. "Just sit tight, we'll be in touch."

We spent the next few days alternately walking the streets and hovering over the hotel phone. Mary ran into a woman in the elevator who, although quite fuzzy on the details, had spoken at great length about large criminal rings operating in the Times Square area that had been known to shanghai attractive young males and press them into sexual servitude up and down the Eastern Seaboard. "They call them chicken hawks, and you know how handsome Dyson is," Mary said, relating the incident.

It wasn't until the next day that Loma Tarr called. She lived across the street from us in Feltside and was Mary's best friend in church choir. "I saw the light on in your house," Loma related. "At first I thought someone was robbing the place. But then, there was Dyson, standing by the screen door, drinking a bottle of pop."

"Drinking a bottle of pop by the screen door? Oh, my God!" I felt lightheaded, bowled over by a massive wave of relief. Loma said Dyson had found his way to the bus terminal, and using money he'd saved over the years, taken the Greyhound down to Feltside.

It didn't exactly compute, Dyson always got nauseous on buses, but I didn't care: He was okay; not drowned in the river, not prisoner of some sex-crazed crack kingpin. "Could you put him on, Loma. We'd really like to talk to him."

There was a pause on the other end. "Well, Dean," Loma said, her voice growing pinchier, the way it did when she ordered her real estate agent husband, the despondent Bill Tarr, to clean up the palm fronds in the yard or to get her a drink. "Dyson's kind of busy now. That's why he asked if I'd call."

"Busy? What do you mean he's busy? Put him on, Loma."

Again Loma hesitated, not her usual mode. In her mid-forties, crag-faced and nicotine-fingered, rail-thin in avocado Capri pants, she ran the beauty parlor down on Regal Street with a brusque jes'-folks manner, sculpting thickly sprayed man-catcher ringlets onto the heads of half the women in town.

"Loma's a dyke, you know," I used to tell Mary.

"That's quite a thing to say, Dean Taylor!" Mary would respond indignantly. "If you ever came to church and heard her sing, you'd know she was full of the Spirit."

Then we'd squabble, just a bit, me saying that being a dyke and full of the Spirit were not mutually exclusive. Rather, it was a kind of sadness I sensed in Loma, even as she wisecracked through a backyard barbeque, that gave me the feeling that she wasn't getting what she needed.

Loma, always so quick with a pithy down-homeness, now seemed unsure of herself. "I can't . . . I mean, he's not here . . . He's building something over in your backyard, said he wanted it to be a surprise for you folks. Why don't you just get on that airplane and come on back?"

I was already steaming when I hung up. "He scares us out of our minds and then he's too busy to come to the phone! Who does he think he is?"

"Oh, Dean," Mary said, gently taking my hand. "He's safe and sound. Isn't that really the most important thing?"

He met us at the airport the next day. He was standing at the gate in the blue gabardine suit Mary bought him on his thirteenth birthday, a plush bunch of red roses in his hand. "Mom!" he shouted and hugged Mary. It wasn't a boy's hug, or even a son's hug. He kissed her, not on the mouth, but close.

"I'm sorry," Dyson said to Mary, his eyes wide with contrition. "I didn't mean to make you fret. I'd *never* want to do anything to make you upset. It's just that . . . I dunno . . . I felt like it was time for me to . . ."

"To do what, dear?" Mary asked expectantly.

"*Do* something. Break away a little. Be *myself.*"

Dyson turned to me now. His smile was dazzling. "You understand, don't you, Dad?"

"Right." I understood perfectly well. There was no way of knowing everything that had transpired in the week since Dyson left the taping of *That's Who I Am!* but I was certain of one thing.

He'd gotten laid.

Crossing the line into the realm of women, loving them, admiring them, committing your member to their loins, prick straining across empty space to expectant vagina, much as the finger Michelangelo drew on the chapel ceiling reached toward that of the Creator—this is the sacred journey of the male, the singular Epic of a man's life, a journey that no degree of idiot macho debasement can defile. There is a line, and Dyson had crossed it. It was in the way he stood, the way he talked; it was as plain as day, at least to me. I always could tell. I'd drive by a gaggle of high school students and immediately know which ones got it and which didn't, know if they'd gotten it *good.* Dyson had gotten it good. His body language spoke volumes. Usually wrapped tighter than a tourniquet, his shoulders tucked in so severely that they almost met in the middle of his chest, Dyson now evidenced a loose-slung freedom befitting a yogi adept.

My mind reeled back nearly four decades. I thought of Betty Lou Stiles, with her hawk nose and pimples strewn across her cheeks like a Milky Way of sores. She was nineteen back then, a virgin, and resigned to always being such. She thought no man would ever want her, she was too ugly, too shy. Even if she lived to be a hundred, it would only get worse.

I'd seen her a few times before. Her parents were fairly wealthy and my father was trying to sell them insurance up the wazoo. At least that's what he said; I knew he was banging the lady of the house. I watched Betty Lou from the back of the car that wintry day. In her huge overcoat she appeared to be a moving blotch as she trudged up the walkway to the house, only to stop after opening the door. Likely she heard my father and her mother inside then, because she started crying. It was something to cry about: coming home to find the insurance guy fucking your mother. Then she took a breath and pushed through the door and I knew, this was the way it had always been, the way it always would be, for her.

That's when I decided Betty Lou Stiles would be the one. If it was okay with her, that is. Which, of course, it was, as beautiful as I was. I was a few days short of my fourteenth birthday, but that didn't matter, the physical and empathic properties of the man who would become known as God's Gift to Women being fully intact from the start.

I saved Betty Lou Stiles, as I would so many others over the years. Three weeks after we made love, she moved out of her house. She went to St. Louis, where she got a good job, married, and raised a very lovely family, a picture of which she enclosed with the Christmas card she sent me every year until my supposed demise.

I wish I could have told my father about Betty Lou, how great it felt, how we fucked and then just embraced, so grateful that we'd found each other, and no one else, with which to share this moment. But I didn't tell Dad. I was afraid he'd just mock me out, in that imperious way of his, for fucking Betty Lou when there were so many other better-looking babes around.

That's what slayed me, standing there in the airport, watching Dyson: the ruined continuities between fathers and sons, and how hard it all is. I thought fondly of Jimmy Dime, how he'd take it on himself to get each one of his sons from various marriages and nonmarriages laid. "Rite of poontang passage, a bar mitzvah-va-va-vooom," Jimmy chortled, wheeling his Corniche down La Cienega, looking for what he described as "a father-and-son package."

"Family that bangs together, hangs together," Jimmy said, misting up a tad. "It's good that you're there that first time. I mean, he's your kid, your flesh and blood, you gotta be there when he dips the wick *el primero tiempo*. That's a bond for life. If you have a son of your own, Taylor, then you'll understand what I mean."

Who'd been Dyson's Betty Lou Stiles? I wondered. Was it that pert blond with the black velvet hairband seated beside him at the *That's Who I Am!* taping? Clear green eyes, creamy skin, budding breasts tight against plaid jumper: She'd given him a look when we sat down. Or possibly the tarted-up hat-check girl at the hotel coffee shop. Randy old bat, she just couldn't get enough of Dyson's bottomless blues. How difficult would it have been for her to have ducked into the elevator with the boy as he returned from the show, to slip her painted fingers into his dungarees?

It could have been anyone, really. Dyson had the Face. The Face got you what you wanted, as I well knew.

Pulling into the driveway of our home, I noticed the construction right away. It was hard to miss. Dyson had already blocked out a ten-foot-square foundation in the backyard. "What are you doing here," I asked.

"Building a house," he said, tersely.

"This is kind of a big doghouse," I said, in reference to my long-standing promise to get Dyson his own pet, should his allergies ever clear up. "You planning on having a whole pack in here?"

"It's not a doghouse, it's my house," Dyson said, evenly. "I'm going to live out here. My old room was too small."

"Is that so? Who gave you permission for that?"

Dyson tweaked his plush lips into a half smile. "Mom."

I could feel myself flushing. "Your mother said it was all right for you to move out of our house?"

"That's right. If you don't believe me, ask her."

"Don't worry, I will." Feeling that I could, at any moment, haul off and strike my son, I wheeled away. As I went, Dyson called after me.

"You know, you were right, Dad," he said, casually.

"Right about what?"

"My face. You said I might get to like it. And I'm starting to. I really am."

Mary confirmed Dyson's statement. She had told him it would be all right to build a house for himself in the backyard. "What could I do, Dean," my wife said. "He's my son. He tells me he's going to leave home. That he can't stand another moment. At least this way, he stays with us."

I stood at the second-story window, watching Dyson work on his house. It was a bigger structure than I first thought, it was taking up half the backyard, built exactly on the spot where I'd planned to make a free-standing trellis for Mary's climbing roses. Down below Dyson was nailing together the oak box he planned to use for the floor of the structure. There was a discipline and precision to his work, I noted with a mixture of pride and foreboding. Many times I'd invited Dyson to come to the shop, to help with the Taylor Chairs, or just to do his own thing. He was never interested. I couldn't even get him to saw a piece of wood in half. Now, out of nowhere, he embarks on this huge project, goes about it with the élan of a natural. What manner of genetic weirdness was at work, that he should inherit not only Taylor Powell's looks but Dean Taylor's touch as well?

"Why didn't I know anything about this house?" I asked Mary. "We should have sat down, discussed it."

Mary ran her fingers through her graying hair. "Oh, Dean, it's no use denying it. The boy hates you. *Why* is beyond me, and Lord knows you don't deserve it, but it's true. You two can't even spend a civil moment." Mary gave me a haunted look. "Dean, please, don't make me choose between the two of you."

I didn't. Dyson could have his house if that's what he wanted. If he cared to consult me for carpentry advice, I'd supply it. Not that this was likely, or even smart. The sort of architectural design in which Dyson was engaged had never been my forte. Indeed, the commercial success of the Taylor Chair aside, as I continued on in my carpentry career, the limitations of my creative ability became appallingly apparent. Many of my pieces now looked more like ratty driftwood sculptures due to be marked down at a barn sale than the "fantasies in wood" I once imagined them. Dyson, at age fourteen, was already a better carpenter than Dean Taylor could ever be.

The hits just keep on coming, I thought, lying awake at night listening to Dyson hammer, the boy now often continuing to work well past midnight.

Just that afternoon, with the temperature past ninety-five, I'd seen Loma Tarr stride across the yard and hand Dyson a Coke. The two didn't speak, but Dyson nodded respectfully to the older woman, as a soldier on a battlefield acknowledges the kindness of a nurse bringing water. Loma gently touched the boy's arm, watched him smack a few nails, and then left without a word. There was an uprightness to her stride I'd never seen before, and I knew: Loma Tarr was Dyson's Betty Lou Stiles.

I should have known. If I'd still been Taylor Powell, I *would* have known, right away. No wonder I'd assumed Loma was a dyke. Someone like Dean Taylor would think that. You see a woman bossing everyone around and, if you're Dean, her pain is beyond your primitive comprehension. You call her a dyke, exclude her, marginalize her suffering. Taylor Powell wouldn't have done that.

Loma Tarr needed it. Someone to touch her, feel her. She was a job for the Face. Dyson could see that right off.

"Dean? Are you up?" I heard Mary ask. She'd been talking in her sleep, letting out these tiny yips, then a nice long series of purred moans, the soft sounds providing counterpoint to the crash of Dyson's hammer.

"Yeah, I am." I was really glad to hear her voice. She always slept in the nude and her body, even if somewhat less streamlined than before, still proved ultimately seductive to me. I had quite a rod on.

"Oh . . . Dean. I had the most wonderful dream," she said, managing a crooked smile.

"Yeah?" I rubbed the edge of her jaw, running a fingertip over the outline of her neck. Soon I'd get to her breasts.

"I guess it was the hammering," she said, with a happy grogginess, unaware of my aroused state. "I dreamed he was making an ark. A great, big ark. A giant boat to float away from this troubled world, even as Noah sailed above the flood waters. Two of every creature, a single pair of each from which every future generation will spring forth. It was the glorious menagerie of Life, Dean. And you know what the best part was? Dyson, our own beautiful son, was at the helm."

"Dyson."

"Isn't that a wonderful dream, Dean?"

"Fantastic." I rolled over. "Well, better get some sleep. I've got a lot of orders to fill tomorrow."

13.

It was about two weeks later that I returned from the shop to find Reverend Watkins sitting in the living room. I hadn't seen the man since that morning in Pardosville when Mary brought me to his church without walls.

"Brother Dean," the reverend boomed in his deep-timbered voice, clapping his dark catcher's-mitt-sized hand upon mine. "I happened to be in this vicinity, so I thought to stop in. I hope it is no inconvenience."

"Not at all, Reverend. It's a tonic, just to see you." The Man of God had added several inches to his already ample girth and lost much of his hair, but he was as upright as ever, his huge smile indicating the vast reservoir of compassion behind the stern exterior. "Please stay for dinner."

"Oh, he already is," Mary chimed in. "Why else would I be making these sweet-potato pies?"

"Sweet-potato pie? Lordy!" Reverend Watkins piped, a tad too brightly. "Are you a sweet-potato-pie man, Dean?"

"Isn't everyone?" I glanced first at the vaguely uneasy preacher, then at Mary. "You didn't just happen to drop in, did you, Reverend?"

The reverend raised his moon-shaped eyes. "No, Dean, I did not," he said flatly.

"I asked him to come," Mary said, soberly. "I thought he might be able to help us."

Mary was worried about me. My mood had turned progressively darker since our return from New York. I was spending almost all my time in the shop, coming home only to sleep. I claimed to have no choice in the matter, new orders for the Taylor Chair coming in at an unprecedented rate. Mary was after me to hire a couple of the better carpenters in town to help me with the back orders, but I refused.

"The Chair is my creation, it's me, Dean Taylor," I said, in defense of the long hours. More and more I found it was only when I was in the shop, making Taylor Chairs, that I felt safe. When I was anyplace else, especially the building I'd once so lovingly called home, I felt adrift, a target.

I was nervous, suspicious, and short-tempered. Mary and I fought constantly. One evening, during a petty dispute I'd actually slapped her across the face. Even before the hideous sound of the blow had dissipated, we were both in tears. Sex cured nothing. One night Mary brought out her Casio and started playing "Peace in the Valley." I'd told her to stop, that I didn't want my cherished memories of our early days together sullied by the desultory present.

"I don't know what's happening to me," I told her that night, a malarial-like sweat covering my body. "It's like there's something inside me, something terrible . . . *evil even* . . . eating away, burrowing up to the surface, contaminating everything good, everything we have."

"Evil?" The word shook Mary as no other. "Oh, Dean." She reached out for me, to hold me, as she always had. I pulled away. I was ceasing to trust Mary, which was the worst thing of all.

I supposed she'd told most of this to Reverend Watkins. They often spoke on the phone, Mary continuing to regard the formidable sin fighter as a dominant spiritual influence. "Would you do us the honor of saying grace over our table, Reverend," Mary asked, as we sat down to dinner.

"The honor is mine," the preacher nodded, smiling as he surveyed the beautifully set table, hand-dipped candles from the flea market casting a warm light on the copious portions of collards, smothered pork chops, and dirty rice. He asked, "Isn't someone missing?"

That was when it started up again. The hammering. The incessant banging. The awful *whomp, whomp, whomp*. The thumping that was on the verge of driving me insane. "Dyson's building . . . *er* . . . a house in the backyard," Mary said.

"Yes," the reverend replied. "You mentioned this to me on the phone. Certainly he'll stop now and come to dinner."

Dyson was out there with an electric saw now, the shriek of the blade almost deafening. "Goddamnit!" I slammed my fist onto the table, sending the plates clattering. "I'll go get that kid and drag him in here right now."

"Dean, please don't," Mary pleaded. "Why don't we eat in peace?" I grunted and sat back down. After that we ate quickly, a meal devoid of conviviality, save Reverend Watkins's incessantly annoying flattery regarding Mary's cooking. Dyson hammered the entire time. It was over peach cobbler and coffee that Reverend Watkins told how he and Mary came to meet.

"It was at an AA meeting," he began. "There were many people there, many kinds of people. Black, white, rich, and poor. Drink—the leveler—had forged our bond. I could tell that Sister Grant and myself shared a more dreadful union . . . and this was so: We'd both been responsible for the death of our own God-given child."

Reverend Watkins bowed his head, his spacious tones filled with boundless regret. "Ronald was his name, a lovely two-year-old boy . . . not that I would have known, then . . . Throughout the blessed days of his life, I'd never once heard the cries of my own flesh and blood. Indeed, I didn't even hear the sound of his bones breaking beneath the wheels of that Chevrolet I so carelessly threw into reverse simply because I was too drunk to walk to the liquor store to get another bottle . . . I didn't hear his cry then, Dean, but I have heard it every night since: the terrible cry of what I did to him, through negligence and paucity of the spirit."

Watkins reached across the table to clasp Mary's hand. "When Sister Mary told me about Shawn and how he died, I understood immediately. Shawn's cry also went unheard . . . only to be heard a million times over . . . Shawn's cries blend with Ronald's, two little dead boys, crying for someone to hear . . . It is because of them that I became a preacher. Once a man hears such a cry, he has no choice but to respond, to shout with all his breath: 'Here! Here I am.'"

Watkins reached out for my hand, so the three of us might be linked. "Hear your son's cry, Dean. And perhaps he'll hear yours."

"Please, Dean," Mary said, in the form of an amen.

I looked first at Mary, and then Reverend Watkins, an unexpected and inexplicable resentment welling up inside me. It was too bad these two ex-boozers killed their kids, but where'd they get off including me as a potential member of their sad little clique?

"Listen, Reverend," I said sharply, removing my hand from the preacher's grasp. "I'm sure you mean well, but I don't see what this has to do with me. Dyson and I have had our problems, but these things happen in all families. What kind of a man do you think I am? What kind of father?"

Mary looked at me quizzically. "Dean, please, I know you're upset, but please listen to Reverend Watkins. He knows—"

"Knows what?" I snapped back. "He doesn't have the first clue about me and how I feel. That's the trouble with these so-called preachers, thinking they know squat about anything beyond the vapid claptrap they spew out every Sunday. Who does he think he is, coming over here with these horror stories—"

"Dean Taylor! I can't believe my ears!" Mary's face turned red. I'd never seen her so angry. "Reverend Watkins drove up here at his own expense to help you, and you treat him like this!"

I pulled out a twenty-dollar bill and tossed it on the table. "Here's some gas money, because the reverend is leaving. Right now."

Mary turned to Watkins. "Reverend, please forgive Dean, he has been under so much stress of late—"

The preacher held up his hand. "Mary . . . I take no offense. In the Lord's work, one learns not to stand on ceremony."

"Then don't let me rush you!" I shouted, handing the Reverend Watkins his coat. As crazy as I felt then, I might have actually tried pushing him out the door if the phone hadn't rung.

"Hello," I spat, grabbing the kitchen phone on the fourth ring.

"Mr. Dean Taylor?" a come-hither Brit-inflected woman's voice asked. "Please hold for Tim Renard, thank you."

What kind of shit was this, I wondered. Even aluminum-siding salesmen had cunty-sounding secretaries these days. I was about to slam down the receiver when this overactive, adenoidal sound came through the line.

"Dean! God, you can't believe the hassle we had getting to you. Those quiz-show people are total nerds. Absolutely nowhere. First they can't find your number, then they won't give it out. I guess that's why they're doing TV. Small screen, small mind."

Living in Feltside all these years, it had been a while since I'd heard anyone speak that fast. The voice reeked of skittish self-esteem. "Who did you say this was?"

The sharpness in my voice rattled the caller. "Tim. Tim Renard. Didn't the secretary tell you? Tim Renard of Tamberland and Greive."

Tamberland and Greive? The combination of names struck a distant chime: my old talent agency, back when I was Taylor Powell. Made them a fortune of ten percent in my day, the fuckers. "What can I do for you, Tim?"

"That's more of a two-way question, Dean. I was thinking about what I can do for you. Let me explain myself. One of the many hats I wear here at the agency is to look for new talent, and the other day your tape came across my desk. It's interesting, Dean, very interesting."

"My tape?"

"Your *That's Who I Am!* tape, Dean," Renard replied with a gagging laugh. I could hear the up-from-the-mail-room flop sweat in Renard's voice. His "secretary" was obviously some other lowball like himself, playing the part as a favor that would no doubt be called in before long, because that's how these people worked.

"It's an awesome tape, Dean. You know, we get a lot of submissions here, and most of them, well, they suck. But yours . . . I dunno, I'm looking at it and I'm thinking, this guy, this Dean Taylor, you, Dean, well, he's got a nice face, it's nothing extraordinary. In fact, it's like what you might call *ordinary*. Like anybody's. Like *everybody's* maybe. You know: like everyone, and no one."

I swallowed hard. "Everyone and no one . . ."

"Everyone and no one: Yeah, that's right. I don't mean to be insulting when I say that, it's a face that looks familiar and then it doesn't. That's the beauty of it." Renard's patter halted now. There was a moment of dead air, followed by what sounded like a whimper.

"Dean, I won't shit you. I wouldn't have called you unless I pushed the VCR button by mistake. The PAUSE button. The one that makes the still picture, you know." Renard was drawing quick, shallow breaths. He sounded on the verge of hyperventilation. "I'm looking at it *right now!* I'm looking at it now . . . Dean!"

Suddenly, I felt woozy and had to grab the edge of the kitchen counter to keep from falling over. "You're looking at my face . . ."

"Yes, a still of it." Renard was weeping now.

I sat down. "What do you see? Tell me!"

"It's like . . . I'm looking at myself . . . and everyone else, at the same time . . . like I'm there, and you're there, and they're all there . . . in you. Damn! It's so intense."

There was a period of silence, during which Renard must have gotten it together to shut off the VCR, because his jerkoff patter returned. "Sorry, Dean, but I guess you can see how special your work is to me. I thought maybe we could sit down together, nothing formal you know, to talk about our plans for you."

"Plans for me?"

"Yes . . . your future."

"My future."

Renard took a deep breath. "Sure thing. I've gotten with Larry Demic on this. He's the president here."

Larry Demic! That fruit was the head of the agency now? He

used to be a liplock jockey on the Paramount backlot. Jimmy Dime used to let Demic do him behind the caterer truck just to show he had "equal opportunity dingus, dude."

"You showed that tape to Larry Demic?"

"Well, he hasn't actually *seen* it," Renard squeaked. "He will, though . . . he definitely will. His assistant is a personal friend of mine and he said he would . . ."

I breathed easier. Clearly there wasn't a chance in hell Larry Demic would look at anything coming from a nobody like Tim Renard. "Just who *have* you shown the tape to, Tim?"

"What?"

"Who'd you show the fucking tape to?"

Renard's voice was very small now. "No one . . . not yet. I tried to get my roommate to look at it but he was studying for a test and . . ."

"You've got some heavy-duty sense of entitlement for a bottom-feeding cap-sniffer, don't you, Tim baby? You've got no right to show that tape to anyone, you understand? If you do, I'm going to sue your squirrelly little ass. Better still, I'll just kick it. Kick your ass from here to next week. You get it?"

"But . . . Dean . . . your work, it's so . . . beautiful . . ." Renard was weeping again.

"Hey, Timbo, do yourself a favor. Go fuck yourself before Larry Demic gets around to it. He'll leave treadmarks, for sure."

Which is when Renard hung up, and I almost passed out. Maybe I shouldn't have gone off on the poor schmuck like that but I couldn't have him showing that tape around town. What was it about my current face—the still image of it, at least—that affected people so dramatically? I still didn't know, still didn't want to know.

I staggered out the front door, in hopes that the night air might revive me. The Reverend Watkins was out there, in his car, pulling away from the curb, departing for the long drive back to Pardosville. He still drove that same Chevrolet in which he'd run over his son. Immediately, I was overcome with shame.

"Reverend," I said, tottering after the Man of God. "Please forgive me, I don't know what got into me." The preacher never heard me, the sound of his malfunctioning muffler blotting out my entreaties. He turned the corner and was gone.

I stood there a moment, the offshore breeze on my face. Then, shattering the silence, the hammering started up again. Dyson was banging away, building his house. He stayed at it almost constantly now, ten and fifteen hours at a time. Asked what he was doing, all he'd say was, "Improvements." Apparently, he'd decided to put on a second story. The structure was now at least twenty feet tall. If he kept going at this rate, soon his house would be bigger than mine.

14.

The dark gray puppy's name was "Doke," mostly because the mutt had a brother named "Okie." That made the pair of them "Okie Doke," a "positive kind of thing," according to the dog seller, a lapsed Pentecostalist, fifth in a line of Remmerswald dirt farmers, with a sideline in used hubcaps and suspiciously pedigreed Akitas.

"One I would of chose," the farmer said, when I picked up the slightly rheumy-looking, but sweet-faced animal. "Don't forget to get that distemper shot, hear?"

Remmerswald was a good thirty-five miles inland, and even though I had several appointments that afternoon, I was in no hurry to get back to town. Only trouble awaited me there, a seemingly insurmountable loom of dismay that made me feel like a Lilliputian bound by a swarming army of Gullivers. Out here, however, cruising the swamplands, George Jones on the box—steel belts humming on the asphalt—I exercised every American's birthright to illusory unfetteredness. Finally, I felt I could think straight.

As I drove, something Reverend Watkins had said at dinner came back to me. "Always remember, Dean," the preacher intoned. "Everything happens for a reason, there are no accidents, no such thing as chance."

"Tell me then, Reverend," I asked, then. "What happens when things happen for the wrong reason? Like, when God's pissed, or fucks up?" It was a mean image I had then, a picture of the Deity as a hunching coward, the sky as nothing more than a one-way mirror for Him to spy through as he fingered the next victim for His irrational, spasmodic Wrath.

Watkins, however, had been resolutely unoffended. Smiling with melancholy empathy, the preacher said, "Dean, I am a Man of God, but I am also a man. I know what it is to shake an angry fist heavenward. I have lived too long in this world to expect perfection, even from Him. This is the purpose of Faith: To shield us not only from our own excesses but also from His. We must show our unshaken Faith, so as to help the Creator, to make Him all we need Him to be."

"Great," I'd replied. "God screws up, and it's up to us to bail Him out."

Now, however, motoring through the scruffy savannah, I appreciated the scope of Watkins's compassion. God knew His World was flawed, and this failure led Him to despair. It was up to us to help God help Himself, so He might help us. As we prayed for His Grace, He likewise prayed for ours. This was the true bond between man and God. In a world filled with Evil there was little other choice since we were all in this mess together.

That's why I got the dog. A boy should have a dog, I thought. Just the other day, I'd been telling Dyson about the little dog my father got for me.

"His name was Farlow, after one of my father's men. And he was so little when I got him," I told Dyson with unrestrained sentimentality, "the runt of the litter, barely had his eyes open. I used to nurse him from a baster, cuddled him at night."

"I want something that bites," Dyson interrupted.

"A pit bull?" I asked, mildly.

"Nah, they're mean, but they're small. Akitas are mean and big."

So, four hundred dollars poorer, I was bringing this murderer dog, this product of fifty snarly generations, home to my strange son, who hated me. It was the least I could do. When a boy wants a dog, if you're his dad you get it for him. Should my last words, "I love you, son," escape as a wheeze through a jagged hole ripped in my windpipe by the Akita, then, at least I'd know I tried.

"What do you think about that, Doke?" I asked the puppy. "Think you'll kill me one day?" Doke sighed contentedly. "I didn't think so. Good boy," I said as I turned up the radio and stepped on the gas.

It was the thin smudge in the sky I noticed first, then the unmistakable smell of burnt wood and sharp chemicals. By the time I crossed the railway tracks, I knew what had happened.

The fire must have started in the early morning, probably even before I left town, because it was all but out by the time I arrived on the scene. A lone fireman in a red slicker and yellow boots remained, playing an orange hose over the field of steaming ash.

I got out of the truck and immediately threw up, splattering my pant legs and shoes. As I dropped to my knees, I heard a faint, high-pitched cry of pain. Then someone was yelling at me. After which, I got pushed, knocked face-first onto the vomit-splashed, blackened earth. I could feel the ground's heat on my midsection.

"What the—" I looked up. It was the fireman, rage on his large, soot-smeared face. He was holding Doke in his arms. The dog had balled himself up tight and was whimpering.

"Didn't you see your puppy jump out of the pickup?" the fireman yelled. "Now the bottom of his paws are all burned up."

Even though the events had occurred only moments before, they replayed in my mind as an antique kinescope. I had staggered from the truck, leaving the door open. Doke scampered out, joyfully kicking his legs behind him the way puppies do. "Look at me," the dog seemed to say, "I'm so glad you took me instead of those others."

Except then he must have stepped on an ember, mahogany likely, hardwoods burning longer, hotter. Puzzlement invaded the little dog's face; no doubt it was the first time he'd ever felt pain like that. He jumped again, reddish cinders flying up in his wake. Then he started to yelp.

"This is my shop," I told the looming fireman, whose name, O'Dell, was written in reflective letters on his bright slicker.

Immediately O'Dell's anger fled. He pushed up the brim of his huge black fire hat. "This the first you see of it?"

I nodded. "I was out of town, getting that dog for my son." It was hard to talk, my throat felt parched.

"Oh shit," the fireman said, helping me to my feet, knocking the black-flecked vomit from my jeans with his oversized, insulated glove. He picked up a charred piece of a Taylor Chair. "These are beautiful things, man," O'Dell said slowly, according me a moment of genuine masculine respect. "Soulful things."

The outraged fury of moments ago returned to the fireman's face. "I hate fire. It just eats away and kills things." Then, moving quickly, fiercely, O'Dell threw the piece of burned Taylor Chair onto the scorched ground, raising a cloud of ashy dust. Something irretrievable was being lost, I understood. Dean Taylor, the Dean Taylor I knew, at least, was in that cloud, which was now scattering into the early-spring sky.

When I turned back, O'Dell was staring at me. By now I could follow the well-worn thought processes, the synapsial journey from the fireman's brain to his mouth: Didn't he know me from somewhere? The Dean Taylor I created for myself might be fleeting on the wind, but this other Dean, this specter everyone seemed to see when they looked at my face, was still around. Faces are like that, out of your control.

"Do I know you from somewhere?" O'Dell asked.

"Don't think so."

"Sorry. I see a lot of people on this job." Then O'Dell said we better get going, pulling off his glove and unashamedly taking my hand, as a big brother or even a father might. "Let's get you out of here."

When I finally got home, Mary was waiting for me at the door, wearing that tight blue top I always liked. "Oh, Dean . . . what a terrible thing . . ." She led me to the couch, sat me down.

The house smelled wonderful, especially after the stench of the fire. Mary had picked several of her most beautiful purple roses from the garden, put them in my favorite vase. When I sat down on the couch, she touched the inside of my thigh, high up. Again, I knew why I loved her, why I always would. And maybe, if we could have made love right then and there, a savage, hard-pumping danger fuck, the way we both preferred, it would have been fine. After all, fire is a potentiality any carpenter accepts. A stray cinder can quickly incite an inferno. If I'd been able to throw Mary down onto the shag rug right then, our groins locked, likely the two of us would have been able to get up an hour or two later and proclaim the blaze an Act of God, an event to accept, even celebrate.

But this wasn't to be. I could tell we weren't alone, a notion confirmed by the sound of a flushing toilet. A moment later, a large, florid man emerged from the downstairs bathroom, zipping the fly of his too small trousers, a visible pee stain to the left of his crotch.

"Al Delavante, Title and Life," the man said, by way of blunt introduction. "I know you've had a rotten day, Mr. Taylor, but it's company policy to begin the discovery process in arson-probable fires immediately."

" 'Arson-probable'? Are you saying the fire at my shop was set on purpose?"

Delavante's smile was small, clipped, vicious. "Let's just say, as of now we've got a pretty strong indication of deliberacy and premeditation. What happened to your clothes?"

"I fell in a puddle of puke," I answered with truthful animosity.

"Never rains that it doesn't pour, huh?" Delavante replied flatly, shuffling his papers as the hammering started up again. Delavante turned toward the sound.

"My son," I offered. "He's building his own house in the backyard."

"Dyson."

"Yes, you know him?"

"My son knows him." Delavante spit this out as if his child's association with Dyson somehow soiled his entire, no doubt genetically marginal, family tree. "Got thrown out of Feltside, didn't he?"

"Suspended. He got suspended, not thrown out."

It was all I could do to keep from punching Delavante. Where'd he get off making a comment like that? Screw those prissy rednecks at Feltside High, too. Dyson was probably the smartest kid in the history of the dubious institution, 1540 on his boards, doing college-level math in the ninth grade. So what if he "incited an adolescent sexual frenzy in ancient history class" as that pus-brain guidance counselor claimed during his sickly prurient inquiries as to Dyson's "odd power over teenage girls."

I knew why Delavante was ticked. His lumpen son Zack had been captain of the football team, the highest-rated linebacker in the state, until Dyson turned his girlfriend's head. The boy started missing practices, messing up in games, eventually quitting the team. After a while, he barely came out of his room. Cost Delavante big, too, that major college scholarship down the drain.

"Like father, like son," Delavante remarked.

"What's that supposed to mean?"

"No offense," Delavante said, holding up his palms. "Only that he's taking after you, building stuff, doing carpentry." With that, the insurance man jammed his stubby fingers into a large Ziploc bag marked EVIDENCE and pulled out several wads of crumpled newspaper. "They're soaked with gasoline. Wind must have taken some of it; we found several clumps around the perimeter."

The gas smell blotted out the scent of Mary's roses, making me momentarily lightheaded. Delavante straightened out several of the reeking wads. "There's something funny here . . . these newspapers are old. In fact, they're from sixteen years ago. Exactly sixteen years, actually. April seventeenth."

He handed me a few of the singed broadsheets. One was the front of the *Houston Chronicle,* another the *St. Louis Post-Dispatch,* a third the *Baltimore Sun.* Delavante was correct. Each paper was from exactly sixteen years before. Sixteen years, to the day, since the supposed death of the man once known as Taylor Powell. Sixteen years to the day that I'd been supposedly burned alive in Jimmy Dime's Learjet.

"Anything here that rings a bell, Mr. Taylor? One of the stories perhaps?"

"The Lakers won," I noted, indicating the flag on the front page of the *L.A. Times.* It came back now, the way Jimmy Dime fixed it with those star-struck guys in the control tower at LAX on that fateful night. The plan: to bang inside the Learjet, then land the plane on one of those outlying strips, closest to the Inglewood Forum. A limo was to pick us up, drive us over in time for a few pregame snorts with the team. Then we'd sit courtside, and after the expected victory, get down bigtime with a bevy of waitresses trucked in from the nearest Hooters.

"I guess that was the day those actors got killed," Delavante mused, his abrasive edge somewhat blunted. "My wife was all busted up. She was really a big fan of that Taylor Powell. I remember her saying she couldn't believe it, that beautiful face burned to a crisp. I told her to pipe down, it's stupid to cry over some jerk actor. She said I didn't understand."

"The men don't know, but the little girls understand," I mumbled.

"What?"

"Nothing."

"Fire starters are funny," Delavante said, with the overused sigh of the professional. "It's cat and mouse between us and them. Cat and mouse." The insurance man pointed to a couple of stories near the bottom of a newspaper page, one about an Oriental gangland rubout, another detailing a major stock swindle that ruined a downtown bank. "Any particular significance for you in any of these, like maybe you knew some of these people involved?"

"No," I said, barely glancing at the articles.

"Look again," Delavante said, his manner stiffening once more. "There's a nice settlement at stake here, Mr. Taylor. I'd like to be able to say you cooperated fully with my investigation."

"I don't want your damn money."

Delavante looked at me with ultimate suspicion. He was a man paid to sift through lies, yet now, presented with the unalloyed truth, he instinctually reacted to it as if it were another, bigger lie.

"What the hell are you trying to pull, Taylor? You're not interested in settling your claim?"

"That's exactly what I said. Now get the fuck out of my house."

15.

It was payback, nothing more, or less. He'd burned my shop, I'd burn his house. A simple exchange. Nothing beyond that was ever intended.

I had to wait until dark. Dyson often hammered away late into the evening, but he always slept in the room where he'd grown up, in "his" bed. Just to make sure, however, I double-checked, padding into his room as I'd done so many times when he was little and all I wanted was to watch him breathe. There he was all right, his long, thin body covered by the lovely comforter Mary made for his tenth birthday. He looked so innocent there, I was tempted to bend over, give him a kiss, but stopped myself. I couldn't risk waking the boy.

The night was perfect, windless and not too hot. Containment to the target building was key. I wanted a fast, clean burn. It wasn't until I touched my kerosene-drenched torch to the cherrywood shingling and the flames shot upward that I saw him there, through the tiny porthole-shaped window on the second story.

"Help! Help!" Dyson yelled. I looked in horror. The boy hadn't been in his own bed. He'd merely shoved pillows under Mary's comforter to make it appear that way. He'd been out in his house the entire time.

"Jump!" I yelled. "I'll catch you!" But Dyson did not move, choosing instead to remain inside the burning structure.

"Save me!" He screamed again, louder now. "Save me! I'm being burned alive! *By my own father!*"

He was smirking at me, that oh-too-familiar smirk. Once it

had made me millions, now it twisted in the intensifying heat, seemingly melting before my eyes. "Come on, Dad," Dyson purred seductively through the gathering flames. "It's getting hot in here. You going to save me or not?"

"You little shit."

The fire was getting to the beams, huge spears of flame ripping through the peaked roof. A great roar went up, like a rocket's blast, the house seeming to shift on its foundation. Up in the window, Dyson was actually beginning to look afraid. I'd be lying if I said I didn't take at least a second to savor my son's fear. In my demented state of mind, I felt Dyson had that much coming.

He was crying for real now. It wasn't the panicked shrieks of someone trapped in a consuming blaze, but rather that same mournful whimper that always chilled me when Dyson was a baby. He didn't cry like other children; his was not a defiant statement of discomfort, or frustration at an inexpressible emotion. Dyson's cry struck me as the sob of a grieving old man, a lament of a life almost gone by, not one at its outset.

I looked at my son again, framed by that fiery window. When that face was mine, and I cried, my father did not come running. Disgraced and envious, he hated me for having the most beautiful face in the world. Just as Dyson, an innocent, now hated himself for the same reason. That face, Taylor Powell's face, it was like a bad card, a malediction to be passed on to whomever might be defenseless enough to be tricked into receiving it. There was terror in that beautiful face, an unspeakable loneliness that Dyson, my son, knew from the beginning.

I'd given Dyson his face, and it was up to me to take the curse from it. I smashed down the door with my shoulder, made my way into the smoke-choked structure. He was unconscious before I reached him. A cedar rafter almost fell on us as I raised him into my arms. Inside the burning hulk, I couldn't help but admire the talent of the edifice's author. That Dyson could fill this monument of his hatred with such homey elegance filled my heart with pride. The tears in my eyes evaporated immediately in the heat, but they were real.

With Dyson in my arms, I crashed through the fire engulfing the first-floor doorway and landed on the backyard lawn. Mary was out there, her palms pressed against her head, the garden hose squirting wildly at her feet. She took one look at Dyson's motionless body resting in my arms and let out a shriek. "He's dead!"

"No! He's alive!"

If Mary heard me, it didn't register. "It's happened again . . . it's like Shawn . . . again."

She stumbled forward, dressed only in a sheer nightgown. "I've let it happen again," she wailed. "I can't protect my children . . . I murder them all." She was walking right into the flames. She was going to kill herself.

"No! It was me! I set the fire!"

"You?" She turned but it was too late. The hem of her nightgown ignited. She barely seemed to notice. "Dean . . . you? You tried to kill our own son? How could you?"

There was no time to explain, no time to say anything. "Mary! Drop and roll!"

She made no move to save herself. She was enveloped in flames by the time I'd lain Dyson down and dove toward her, knocking her to the ground. Over and over we went, our bellies pressed together more tightly than during any lovemaking. In the swirl of red blaze and the black night, the only constant in my field of vision was Mary's face. For her part, she stared back at me with equal intensity. It was like that first morning when we woke up together in storm-ravaged Pardosville.

"Your face . . . is the only face . . ." she'd said then, in words that pledged eternal love. That was when, after five thousand starlets, I knew I loved her. Her and her alone. What she saw in my face now horrified her.

Finally we stopped rolling. She got on her feet. She was naked, her lustrous skin resplendent in the light of the fire. She wasn't burned as badly as I'd feared. Still, I had to get water on her. Drench her body. "Stay there! Don't move."

She didn't listen. She got up and went to the now-conscious Dyson. They embraced.

"Mary . . . are you all right?" I shouted from the other side of the yard.

She didn't answer my question. "Go away," she said. "I never want to see your face again."

She and Dyson turned, began to walk away, hand in hand, their bodies illuminated by the raging fire. I called after them but only Dyson turned back.

I had expected a leer of triumph, but that wasn't the case. The heartbreaking fear and sadness I'd seen in the burning window just moments before had been replaced by a shocking void. I'd never seen my former face so vacant, so uninhabited, so dramatically disconnected. It would be wrong to call it the face of a dead man. More like the face of a man who never was.

As I watched my naked wife and son disappear from view, I felt a knifing pain running up my leg. The little dog Doke had been gnawing on my ankle for some time. The bone was already through the skin.

C O L L I E R

1.

When the world's gone wrong, it gets to the shelters first. They're closer to the bottom, the slime bubbles up quicker through the floorboards. The Hugh Street Armory is the bottom of the bottom. In here someone always has a knife or a gun, and they always want to use it, usually on the person closest to them. That makes bed assignments kind of a crapshoot because you can't always tell, just by looking, who the real wackos are. Yesterday, an ex-librarian, some meek Burgess Meredith type, stole a funnel from the kitchen, jammed it into the eye socket of the guy sleeping three beds down, and pissed into it.

Me, I was only trying to keep my head down. I kept a few of the gasoline-soaked clippings Dyson used to burn down my shop neatly folded in my frayed knapsack. Whenever it got real heavy at Hugh Street—midnight screaming, big blades flashing, arterial blood spurting—I'd pull out the papers, bury myself in reports of my own death.

Every word was true, I told myself: I was crushed flat as a tortilla out there on the desert floor: me and Jimmy Dime, like Buddy Holly and Ritchie Valens before us, great talents nipped in the bud of our semiprime—the day the movies died, bye, bye, American Pie. As for the rest of it—the jungle craziness with Vincent Parry, my life with Mary and Dyson—I had no clue. Something I ate before the plane crashed, probably. One long, strange dream. Or don't dead people dream?

Not that it would matter, soon everyone was going to be dead, according to the TV. Fifty years of cold war, living under hammer of the Bomb, panics over microbes and plagues, and then this rock comes flying out of the black. Supposed to end life as we know it.

News of the "death comet" appeared only a couple of days after I left Feltside. It was an "unprecedented astronomical event," scientists said, the way the thing seemed to appear out of nowhere, like a hardpacked snowball aimed for the planet's heart. How'd they miss it, you wonder. The *Farmer's Almanac* knows if it's going to snow on a Tuesday nine years from now, so how does an asteroid bigger than the one that wiped out the dinosaurs escape Mount Palomar? Like, wow: where'd the heck that come from?

Yesterday, the news had a guy from Cal Tech predicting a sixty-seven percent likelihood of earthstrike. Another station reported that MIT had raised the possibility to eighty-one percent, up from fifty-nine percent a week ago. CNN was coming in low at fifty-five percent, but that's ratings suicide so that number's bound to rise.

The doomsday comet is putting psychological pressure on the boys here at Hugh Street. The place has gone stone shelterskelter. Last week four guys were hacked to death with kitchen utensils, their parts tossed into a vat of stew like in a Greek play, not that any of the hungry seemed terribly put out. The Tuesday Night Massacre they called it, to differentiate it from what happened last Friday, which I won't even go into. They sent a chaplain over from the mission to say the Twenty-third Psalm over the bodies. He was up to "I will fear no evil: for thou art with me; thy rod and thy staff" when someone blew his head off with an M-16. The detached head managed the words "comfort me" even as it flew across the room, which I took as a powerful testament to the reflex of Faith.

I was calling myself John Lee Pettimore at the time, don't ask me why, except that I heard the name in a song one night on a trucker's radio. Before that I'd been Bobby Layne, Bert Russell, Gordy Wasson, and a dozen others, multiple identities being useful when the state's handing out rations. I went through jobs, all menial, as fast as names. It had been a year since Mary turned me out, a year I'd spent sinking and sinking, to get to where I was now, which was nowhere.

It was pretty quiet by Hugh Street standards the night the attendants dumped that guy onto the cot next to mine. The way he lay there so still, I figured it was just another of those administrative screwups: The man was dead, ticketed for a drawer downtown. It wasn't until his teeth began to chatter that I realized he was alive.

The Armory, a cavernous place built as a fortress to repel Civil War draft rioters, was freezing. Rats lived in the heat ducts and no one could remember the last time the boiler worked, not that it would have helped much. Wind howled through the crashed-out windows and it was no big thing to wake up covered with snow.

"I'm so cold," the new arrival moaned, his face still pressed against the bare cot. "Do you have a blanket?"

"I've got *my* blanket."

"I need a blanket," he said plaintively.

I got a better look at him now. He was likely in his mid-twenties but looked younger. A matted shock of hayseed blonde hair stood away from his narrow, pallid face. There was a creepy newness to the boy's countenance, as if it had just been picked off the shelf, more the product of a quick sketch than any sort of longterm biology. His eyes especially, gray and flat like buffalo nickels, revealed little; he might as well have been wearing chrome contact lenses. I could tell, even though he was curled into a ball for warmth, he was skinny and very tall, at least six and a half feet. His clothes, familiar city-issue cheap chinos and denim shirt, were at least three sizes too small, revealing pole-like wrists and ankles, which added to the fellow's eerie procrustean aspect.

I pulled out one of the blankets I'd stuffed into a hole in my mattress. It was something everyone did. When a guy died, you snatched his blanket, otherwise the security guys would get it and try to sell it back to you. On Hugh Street, blankets were currency. "Here."

"Thank you, sir," the boy said appreciatively, still shivering.

As in most gatherings of outlaws where violence hovers as a highly likely contingency, Hugh Street etiquette warned against the asking of unnecessary questions. But this boy appeared so harmless, so lost, so terribly pale, that I was seized with an almost paternal sense of responsibility toward him. He wasn't like the other hardcase losers who populated the place. "You sure you're okay?" I asked.

"Not so great, tell the truth," he croaked, allowing that his name was Stan—Stan Valentine—from "down South." He didn't remember exactly how he got to Hugh Street, except that someone hit him on the head in the bus station, stole his money and clothes. "Woke up buck naked, stuffed into a Dumpster like an old car seat," Stan said, with a soft drawl.

"That's a bitch. It's colder this year than any in the past ten, they said so on the radio," I offered.

"Maybe it's got to do with that comet," Stan replied, continuing to wrap my blanket about his thin body. "Supposed to block out the sun."

"They say all kinds of shit on the TV. Crap about dust scattering over the world, so we'll choke like brontosaurs."

"You don't believe it?"

"I don't believe it or not believe it. The truth is, I don't really care."

Stan seemed alarmed by this. "It could destroy the earth, and life on it . . . that'd be terrible."

"Big fucking deal. Comets are hitting planets all the time. It's an astronomical fact. Earth's just another stupid boulder out in space, let it take its chances like the rest."

"But we live here, doesn't that make a difference?" Stan said, shivering once more.

"Yeah, we *live* here," I brayed. "Fuck it, I say."

"This is the only planet we got, don't you think we ought to try to defend it?"

"How are you going to defend it? Shoot atomic bombs into

space like these Pentagon morons say, pollute the entire universe? That'll be great."

Stan stared at me soberly. "A-bombs won't help. Not with this comet. No way."

The boy's sudden declarative tone made me wary. "Oh, this comet is different than every other comet? You have inside celestial information or something?"

Stan shrugged. "All I was thinking was: If somehow the comet could be stopped, wouldn't you try to do it, if you could?"

"You talking to me, in particular?"

Stan shrugged again. "You . . . anybody. It was just a thought."

"Listen, man," I exhaled. "I'm just a bum in a flophouse. Nobody at all, less than nobody. Right now I'm a pretty tired bum. Way too tired to stop any comets, tonight at least. Why don't you put your head down and go to sleep, okay, dude?"

"Sure thing," Stan said. "Thanks for the blanket. Sorry to trouble you." The boy rolled over. "Well, sleep tight, don't let the bedbugs bite, that's what my granny always said."

I'd just about dozed off when Stan bolted upright in bed. "What's today? What day is today?"

"I dunno. Tuesday?"

"What date?"

"Couldn't tell you. March something."

"March? Are you sure? I was supposed to be at school on February twenty-seventh!"

The boy was beginning to get on my nerves. "Don't worry about it. Just go over to the place tomorrow, big deal if you miss a couple of days."

Stan grew more distraught. "No, that's no good. It's already over, that's what it said in the brochure, 'No allowances for late arrivals.' "

"What kind of school only goes for one day?"

"Barber school," Stan said, shaking his long narrow head.

"You came all the way up here on a bus to go to barber school for one day? What kind of shit is that?"

"It's not school exactly, it's to take the test," Stan despaired. "It's a correspondence school. They sell you a dummy and a hundred hairpieces. Costs five hundred dollars, plus the mailers. You send them your haircuts and they grade 'em. But you got to come up here to test on a real human being."

He let out a small wail. "It took me two years working at the filling station to save up for the course. I lived on Coke and corn flakes, and now I come up here and go get myself mugged on a bus . . . I'll never be qualified. I'll never be *anybody* . . . You're right, mister. It doesn't matter if that damn comet crushes us all. Nothing matters anyway. We might as well just yield to all the Evil in the world."

I looked up. "What about all the Evil in the world?"

"Nothing. Just an expression."

The boy looked at me blankly for a minute, then started to get up. "Damnit, I might as well go home right now. Daddy's gonna mock me. He said I was a sissy for wanting to cut hair to begin with. Here, mister, here's the blanket you gave me, you've been kind."

I felt a need to buoy the boy's spirits. "Listen, if you think you can cut hair, you can cut it. You don't need some stupid diploma from a correspondence school to tell you if you're good or not."

Stan's pallid face brightened. It was just such an expression I'd so often hoped to see from Dyson: An acknowledgment that words I spoke might actually offer him a kind of succor, a love he could accept. "You think so?"

"Absolutely."

"You're right," he said, with newfound confidence. "I know I can do it, as good as anyone."

"There you go."

"I got an idea," Stan said enthusiastically. "I could give *you* the haircut. That's what I'm supposed to do, *cut the hair of a human being under the watchful supervision of judging authorities*. It doesn't say *which* authorities. You're right, we'll know if I can cut or not, you and me."

"I don't need a haircut."

"But you've been so nice to me and all. If I give you the haircut then it won't be like the trip was for nothing. I won't mess up, I swear."

"I said I don't need a haircut."

"Yes, you do. Shave, too." There was a confidence to Stan's tone now that cut through the dreary deep freeze of the Hugh Street air. "You can't even see your face. It's totally covered up."

It was true. I'd caught a glimpse of myself in a mirror only days before, during the fumigation process prior to my admission to the Hugh Street shelter. My hair hung past my shoulders; I'd grown a full beard. The face Vincent Parry made for me, Dean Taylor's face, was covered by a hirsute mask.

I hadn't noticed the growth at first. Facial hair had never been a concern of mine. As Taylor Powell my beard was just thick enough to attract women who appreciated a rough-hewn veneer. Dean Taylor never shaved. Not once. It seemed that Vincent Parry's alchemy had banned whiskers from my face; my chin and cheeks were as smooth as porcelain.

Mary never mentioned my lack of bristles. For Dyson, however, it became an issue. "Dad," he asked running his hand over my face one day when he was about seven, "how come you don't look sharp and feel sharp, like the men on TV, they get twenty-seven shaves out of a single blade."

"Twenty-seven shaves out of a single blade? Don't those guys have any sense of personal hygiene?"

"Dad, you don't shave at all. Does that mean you're not a man?"

I put my hand around my boy's shoulder, drew him near me. "Son, things like shaving don't make you a man."

"What does?" Dyson asked.

"That's for every man to find out for himself. Because every man is different."

"But when . . . when do you know if you're a man or not?"

It was a big question and I sagely rallied to the task. "Well, son. There's a single moment, or a series of moments, when a man confronts his destiny. This doesn't happen for everyone and maybe that's just as well, because the world can only stand a certain number of men of destiny. This is why sports were invented. Some men, however, have no choice but to accept their destiny. At that point he becomes a man. Or doesn't."

Dyson looked puzzled. "You mean, like when they lead you out into the jungle with nothing but a stick and you've got to find your way back to the village and there's tigers all around, or like when they throw you in a pit, or cut up your dick with sharp stones?"

"Those are primitive peoples. They have their backward rituals. In modern times, rites of passage are more symbolic. You know, you might read from a holy book of some sort."

"Reading from some dumb book? How does that make you a man?" Dyson shook his head. "I'd rather shave."

My beard began to grow only after I almost killed Dyson. Within days after leaving Feltside my follicles sprouted with Whitmanesque profuseness. To say I let myself go would be an understatement. Hair grew all over me; I guess it made sense. Vincent Parry may have created Dean Taylor but Mary's love maintained his existence. Once she told me she never wanted to see my face again, it was as if my face no longer wished to be seen by anyone. The shaggy mane covering my head seemed a suitable mark of Cain.

Now, however, this strange Stan sat next to me, scraping his scissor blades together, telling me he wanted to cut off all that hairy remorse.

"Sorry, Stan," I said, attempting to ward off the sudden fear flooding my veins. "I only get my hair cut at Saks. Mr. Leroy, transsexual genius of the shears, he's my personal coif trainer, know what I mean?" I rolled over. "Gotta get some shut-eye, when the barometric pressure's low, you never know what time they'll start screaming in the morning."

I thought that'd be the end of it, but then I could feel him pushing closer. He was whispering now, his voice no longer that of a desperate young man, but rather something older, deeper, weirder. It was a voice I knew.

"Once salvation pitched up from the earth itself," the man who called himself Stan said. "People could drink the blood of the land, eat its flesh, and then love and memory would be restored. Evil would be repelled. The earth cannot help us anymore. It is a hollow thing, gasping for air. Now, for better or worse, freedom resides on the surface. In the mirror, in what one can see in his own face.

"For every man there comes a moment when he must confront the task for which he was created. That time has come for you, Mr. Dean Taylor."

"Josias . . ." I turned around. I could see his eyes now, gray blind and gluey, his timeless Indian face in place of the one worn by a young barber-school student. "Come," he said. "This won't take long. When we're done, it'll be a new you. A new everyone. A new everyone and no one."

2.

He cut my hair in the shelter mess hall, at a bridge table, under fluorescent lights. He had everything with him in a canvas sack: buzz-clippers, comb, can of Barbasol. Then he took out a strop and began sharpening the edge of an antique razor. The razor looked as if it were made of solid gold and was studded with human teeth. On the handle, an inlay spelled out MARZO 22.

He'd stolen the razor when he was just a little boy, before he understood who he was, the power he had, the destiny that lay before him. He had walked through the jungle for more than a week to get to the giant house on the river. When he arrived, *Los Muchachos*, who'd murdered his mother and father, were sleeping drunkenly on the bright green lawn. He stopped to look at them in their bloody shirts, their machetes strapped across their bellies: He'd never seen a lawn before, nature beaten back like that.

Inside the mansion were more wondrous things, objects from every corner of the globe. He saw a rug from Persia on a smooth planked floor, a telegraph, an electric lamp, and a wooden box that sang a sort of music he never knew. He looked inside the box and watched a black plate turning. On every wall were pictures in frames. He saw his first photograph. But that wasn't what he had come for. He came to kill a man, and like the henchmen outside, that man lay sleeping before him.

"He was on a giant bed, wearing a cream silk dressing gown, surrounded by pillows of pink and green. The curtains were lace and blowing in the breeze. I'd never seen such a place. The razor was on a table beside the bed, resting on the lip of a washing bowl. It was open, he'd just used it. There was a tiny speck of dried blood on the blade. I picked it up, intending to slit his throat. The bed was so big—as big as the whole house where I was born—I couldn't reach him from the edge. I was only eight years old. I had to climb into bed with him.

"I watched him there: Arana, the murderer, asleep. I saw his windpipe, prominent in his throat. He was not the happy ogre I'd expected. I assumed he loved killing, that he lived for nothing more. This was the face of Evil, I thought: It enjoyed itself, went about its work in perfect bliss. In sleep, Arana seemed only melancholy, as if he knew his purpose on earth was a grim one. I edged closer, sinking into his soft, huge bed. I could feel the warmth of his body beside me. Perhaps it was the enormity of the task before me, but suddenly I felt tired, too. I could have gone to sleep right then, snuggled beside him, as I'd done so many times before with my own father.

"But I knew why I'd come, what I was to do. I understood killing a man, even a sleeping man, would not be easy. I was only a child of eight, but I did not feel that I would fail. I felt the strength of every man he had killed—thousands!—rushing through me. I raised the razor. I would cut through his throat like butter. He would be dead . . . what happened when *Los Muchachos* caught me did not matter.

"He woke up at the last moment. Whether I could have struck more quickly doesn't matter anymore. He looked at me with re-gret, as if he lamented the fact that the two of us were forced to meet in such conditions. I let my guard down, for as I said, his sadness moved me. Then, without warning, he spit at me. His saliva landed on my forehead, eating away at my skin. Dissolv-ing it on contact. The spittle ran down into my eyes, and I was blinded.

" 'I can't be killed . . . you should know that,' Arana said. 'Now you will see only my face for the rest of your life.' Then, rising up, he shouted that an intruder was in the house. 'He is here!' Arana shouted, over and over. I could hear *Los Muchachos* running down the marble hallway.

"I jumped through the window onto the beautiful lawn below. It was like the most marvelous carpet on my bare feet. *Los Muchachos* were searching for me, calling out to each other. They could not find me. They ran right by me without knowing. At any moment I expected them to seize me, to slaughter me as they had my parents. But they did not. It was as if my blindness had made me invisible to them.

"I ran back into the jungle. The path was very clear to me even though I saw nothing, only a universe of darkness with Arana's face, his sad and terrible face, at the center. He was right. His face would always be before me. In my blindness I would see him always. He could not be killed. I knew then, the voices of *Los Muchachos* fading behind me, that I was like him . . . I would live forever, just as he would."

He flicked the foam from the razor, finished shaving me. I rubbed my hand across my cheek, felt its smoothness. "Stan" would have certainly passed his test: A cleaner shave had never been given. "It is good that your face was able to rest beneath this hair," Josias said. "Sleep, deep and not unlike death, is necessary, before a great undertaking."

"What am I supposed to do?" I asked.

"To look," Josias said, holding up a silver-framed mirror in front of my face. It was Arana's mirror, the same one Parry had me look into back in the jungle. "You must see yourself, and everyone else."

Then, as he had back in the jungle, Josias pressed his giant hand against my face, his fingertips digging into my forehead, his huge palm flattening my nose. It felt terribly hot, as if all my features were on fire.

"Good luck, Dean Taylor," Josias said. Then I was out cold.

3.

I woke up as the predawn light filtered through the steel grid of the mess hall windows. Josias was gone. The only people around were the breakfast crew, mixing plastic garbage cans full of steaming oatmeal with four-foot-long sticks. Moments later a few insomniac Hugh Street residents filed in, listlessly pushing their bowls forward to be filled with mush. Sometimes the kitchen boys hit the bowl, sometimes the oatmeal plopped to the floor.

As always, the television was on. It'd been on while Josias cut my hair and shaved my face. It'd been on as I slept. A cable station had gone "all comet, all the time." The apocalypse, it seemed, would be televised. Odds of earthstrike were holding steady at eighty to twenty in favor of collision, the perky morning anchorlady said. Nothing new on that front.

The focus of debate had shifted to the where and when of impact. A staid German astronomer, appearing on the *Countdown to Nothingness Hour,* said there was "no chance" the comet would make the earth's atmosphere any time in the next two hundred years. His findings were hooted down by the studio audience. More popular was the view espoused by a fly-haired Hungarian who maintained the collision could occur in as little as fifty years. "If not in our lifetimes," the scientist shouted excitedly, "well within that of our children, and certainly our grandchildren, should there be any." This was greeted with raucous applause.

One result of "comet mania," the TV reported, was the worldwide drop in birth rates. The phenomenon, called "population subzero," left maternity wards in Europe deserted. Throughout Africa, midwives sat idle. Apartment space in Shanghai was going begging. "People have decided they cannot bring children into a condemned world," a high-placed party official theorized.

I thought of Mary, and Dyson, the child we'd brought into the world. I didn't know where they were. By the time I'd gotten the courage to call, the phone had been disconnected. I called the Tarrs next door.

"They moved," said Bill Tarr in his unvarying monotone, adding that Mary had asked him to sell our house. "It's not going to be an easy sell, what with the fire and all. Hurts marketability. I'm waiving the commission, maybe that'll be something."

"I appreciate that, Bill. They didn't happen to say where they were going?"

"No, they did not. Even if they did, I'm not supposed to tell you. I shouldn't even be talking to you." Then Bill Tarr paused. "Sorry, Dean. I always liked you, Dean."

"Same here, Bill," I returned. Not a bad guy for a terminal depressive, Bill Tarr. I wondered if Loma had told him about her and Dyson. I hoped not.

Mary and Dyson seemed to have disappeared overnight. Nobody knew where they were. "We thought he'd dropped out," a beleaguered office secretary said when I rang up Feltside High to inquire about Dyson's whereabouts. "They're dropping out every day now. They say it's no use, doing homework when the earth's bound to blow up. Can't blame 'em, can you?"

I called Reverend Watkins, but he was dead, keeled over from a heart attack right in the middle of a sermon. "Oh, Sister Mary? That nice white lady who played the organ . . ." Watkins's sister Ethella said. "Do tell her a special hello, especially in these uncertain times."

One night I called Martin Grant, Mary's former husband. It was the longest of shots, but I was desperate. His wife, Toshi, answered pleasantly and said Martin was in the yard playing touch football with the kids. She would get him. Martin Grant sounded genial, much the friendly, easygoing sort Mary had described.

His tone grew hesitant as I told him who I was and what I wanted. "Why would Mary call me?"

"I don't know . . . she hasn't contacted anyone. She didn't talk about it much, but she often thought about you. She's alone, except for our son."

"Your son?"

"Dyson, our son."

There was a pause. "Mr. Taylor. The son Mary and I had . . . well, he's dead. I don't think she'd call here." It was horrible. I'd plunged Grant back into a world of grief he'd kept at bay for years. Still, I wanted to know. "Can I ask you a question, Mr. Grant?"

"Yes?"

"Is there any way, any way at all, that you could imagine forgiving Mary for what she did?"

Grant paused. "No," he said, and hung up. That's when I stopped looking for Mary. If Martin Grant would not forgive her, I saw no reason to believe she would forgive me.

On the TV, a panel was discussing the remarkable drop-off in worldwide condom sales. In Europe purchases were down as much as seventy-five percent, with the U.S. figures not far behind. "The impending disaster affects more than the unwillingness to bring children into the world," a woman psychologist said. "It goes to the very nature of desire itself. Sexual desire is blunted by the specter of doom."

"What's that mean?" bellowed David Towes. A six-five, three-hundred-pound cottage industry of mayhem, Towes looked like Sonny Liston's bigger, meaner brother. He'd killed five different Korean grocers, burned down four synagogues, been drummed out of both the Bloods and the Crips for excessive violence. Even the edgiest cops didn't want to mess with him, especially when he was toting his trademark bloodstained two-by-four, which was always.

"That mean nobody's fucking?"

"I sure ain't getting none," answered several residents clustered around the blaring tube. Indifferent to mass suicides in

Greenland and nuclear arsenal mutinies in Central Asia, the report that dicks were not entering cunts as often as they used to threw the Hugh Street populace into a tizzy.

It was at that moment that Russian satellite cameras began transmitting the first real-time pictures of the comet back to earth. There it was, on the TV screen: a massive ice-crusted stone ball hurtling through boundless space, shadowed by a swooshing tail of sparkling debris. At first I thought it was simply the fuzzy reception, or the fact that the mess hall television was coated with layers of grime, but in the head-on view, the comet seemed to have a face.

I blinked once, then twice. There was no mistake. There was a human face on that charging rock of death. Arana's face! I had to be insane, seeing Arana's face on a comet flying through outer space. But there it was: the dark, brooding eyes, wide nose, protruding forehead. The face of the man whose cognac I drank. The face of Evil.

I moved closer to the television set. It was hot, way hotter than a normal TV. The cathode tube was like a blast furnace against my skin.

"Get the fuck out of the way," came the cries from behind me. The Hugh Street residents didn't like me blocking the set. I didn't move. Now that I'd seen Arana's face, he'd seen mine. Across untold miles of space, Arana's stare held me, drew me closer. For a moment I thought I'd be sucked right through the TV screen.

"Move, asshole!" came the yowls. But there was no breaking away. Arana and I stared at each other, joined the battle. And I knew the fight between him and me was an ancient one, going back further than the moment Vincent Parry changed my face. A lot further back.

I was glad Josias had told me of his experience in Arana's bedroom those many years before. So, when the face on the comet puckered up and spit, the saliva gushing through the TV screen, I knew to hide my eyes. I'd turned away just in time, the bile splattering onto the right side of my forehead, burning into the skin. The pain was tremendous, I could feel the vicious phlegm score into me, cancerous razor coils churning toward my brain. I tore at my face, grabbed the vileness in my fist, and cast it down. It'd leave a scar, to be sure, an unsightly gouge. But that was all right. My face, in its current configuration, had a lot of give. On the TV, Arana only smirked, and continued his relentless flight toward earth.

The other residents of the Hugh Street shelter appeared unaware of the cosmic skirmish being waged before their eyes. "Get out of the way before I shoot you out of the way," someone bellowed. Another unhappy TV viewer threw a metal plate at me, which missed and hit David Towes instead, caroming off his shaved-and-tattooed noggin.

That did it. Towes reached for the man closest to him, a crippled Russian former pickpocket, and smashed the man's head into a bowl of lukewarm mush. The Russian struggled, futilely kicking his thin legs, but Towes was too strong, too insane. The snapping of vertebrae echoed around the room. "Knock it off, Towes!" I shouted, but it was no use. Towes kept pushing until the Russian went limp, suffocated in a bowl of Quaker oats.

When he was done, a sick executioner's smile spread across his ghetto-charger mug, Towes turned toward me. "See what you made me do? A man is dead and it's your fault."

"My fault?"

"If you hadn't been blocking the screen I wouldn't have been forced to kill this poor fuck here," Towes said. "For this, you will be punished. *¡Muchachos! ¡Adelante! ¡Muchachos!*"

They were off their cots now, at least thirty of them, phalanxed left and right behind Towes, in various states of undress. Towes brandished his signature two-by-four, rhythmically rapping it into his open hand. The others gripped necks of broken bottles. They began to move forward, just as they must have so many times before in the jungles and slums of the world.

"*¡Muchachos!* He alone can stop us. He must be destroyed." His homeboy argot discarded, now an Indian-inflected Spanish slithered from Towes's lips. My sheltermates-turned-*Muchachos* made a circle around me and the television set. On the screen over my shoulder, Arana's face hurtled forward. I could feel his hot breath on my neck.

That's when I saw the razor—Arana's razor—exactly where Josias left it, the inlaid MARZO 22 catching the dim cathode light. I waited a moment for Towes to get closer and then sprang. The razor opened a slash the full length of the huge man's forehead. He grabbed at himself as I bolted by, then crashed through the heavy wooden door and down the stairs.

Out on the street, I heard Towes and the others clamoring after me, just as Josias heard the shouts of *Los Muchachos* through the underbrush as he escaped from Arana's house so long ago. But the backstreets were my jungle and I knew them well. I ran through an alleyway, past the bus station and the theaters playing X-rated movies.

Jimmy Dime always said he'd end up in theaters like this, doing porno. "I won't even be able to fuck," Jimmy would say, shaking his head. "I'll be the syphilitic bartender, watching the cuties, throwing in a joke or two. It'll be a real House-of-the-Rising-Sun scene. I'll be a father figure to the whores. Maybe they'd jack me off once or twice, for old time's sake."

Dashing past those rundown movie houses, I thought I should spill a bit of wine for my dear departed buddy. But there was no time. I had to keep running. By the time I reached the edge of the business district, I was sure I'd lost *Los Muchachos*.

4.

It was the morning rush hour. Crowds streamed out of train station doors, exited from buses. Into revolving doors they poured, to be whisked upward in stainless-steel elevators. The great blue boogie-woogie of the city, the marvelous goings and comings, the throb of commerce: Many times, as a boy, I'd sat in my father's black Dodge and been enthralled by this bustle.

Now, I knew, I was watching a hopeless charade. Class and identity issues, long since abandoned in shelters like Hugh Street in favor of more elemental pecking orders, still held sway among these oblivious individuals. With their briefcases swinging, high heels clicking, cellular phones stuck in ears, they soldiered on, desperately clinging to the illusion of their own self-importance.

One hundred feet above the massive square, the electronic news-ticker read: SCIENTISTS NOW AGREE: 70% POSSIBILITY OF EARTH-STRIKE IN TWO GENERATIONS' TIME. . . . Fools! If those so-called scientists really knew what was happening, then they'd understand earthstrike was a one hundred percent chance, and not in any fifty years either. It might be a matter of weeks, even days. There was barely enough time to dig a grave and pull the dirt in after you.

I tried to impress this fact on the lemming army of urban professionals scurrying by. "Listen, you fools," I ranted. "This isn't some dispassionate astronomical event! This is a snowball of Evil aimed at the hearts of men! This is Arana's comet!"

A lot of good that did. The city was thick with lunatics, shouting of the End. Crude anvil choruses of wooly-headed eschatology beat from every street corner. Longtime doomsayers, their day finally come, kvelled their respective knells in moth-eaten overcoats, mismatched shoes, smelling of beached eels. Dressed in my shelter duds, I fit right in. No one in their right mind would listen to a rap like mine. There was too much reflexive continuity at stake, too much denial to overcome. It was enough to make you cry.

"Here," she said, "have a Kleenex, I can't stand to see a grown man cry."

I'd been leaning against a wall, weeping. She'd gotten out of the wind to light a cigarette. Her perfume came in a dense, vaguely familiar cloud. "Thanks," I said, taking the tissue, which, I noted, was faintly smeared with lipstick. I didn't exactly recognize her right away, blown out as she was. "Don't I know you?" I asked.

She took a rueful drag on her Virginia Slim, and set her gunny sack of a purse down on the large Samsonite suitcase she'd been wheeling. "Everybody knows me. I used to be Missy Fowler, from *That's Who I Am!*, you know, the TV show."

"You're not Missy Fowler anymore?"

"No, I gave her up for Lent." She laughed derisively. "I got too fat. They got a new Missy Fowler. I'm going back to who I used to be. Karen Kralaw, that's my real name." Kunty Karen Kralaw, KKK, I could picture her bobbing head under the motel bedsheets as if it were only yesterday. She looked at me again. "You look a little familiar yourself."

"Lot of people say that." Under that avalanche of Avon, she looked as sad, as forlorn, as she had so many years before in that Nevada whorehouse. "You going home?"

"Home?" She sighed and peered up at the news scrolling by above. SCIENTISTS INDICATE THE SUN NOT LIKELY TO BE SEEN FOR YEARS AFTER IMPACT, it said. This was followed by POLL REPORTS 82% OF U.S. NOW BELIEVE PLANET SURVIVAL POSSIBILITY TO BE NIL . . . CHURCH ATTENDANCE UP . . . INDIANS WRAP UP SERIES IN FOUR . . .

"Burma shave," I said, idly. "You going home, to Tonopah?"

The once and future Karen Kralaw squinted at me quizzically. "Yeah . . . hey, how'd you know I'm from Tonopah?"

"Wild guess. God speed, Karen Kralaw."

She began to edge away, teetering off on her high heels. Crammed into her too-tight miniskirt, her butt looked like a pair of overinflated soccer balls. The *That's Who I Am!* people were right to dump her. With the seven to eight pounds the TV camera adds, she was way over limit.

Watching her go, it came to me that I had more in common with Karen/Missy than just a fleeting instant of carnality. We were both on the same journey, a voyage that began before our birth and would last well after our death, a trip stretching beyond the recorded history of nations and philosophies, a passage that predated the advent of our mutual species and one that would continue on long after our extinction.

Josias said the secret was as simple as looking. Now, after a life of being looked at, I looked. I stood at the Crossroads of the World, watching multitudes glide, trudge, and saunter past. Man, woman, black, white, young, old: Every face looked familiar. I knew them, every single one. Knew them as well as I knew myself. I knew them because I knew my own face, every aspect of it.

I saw a crook of my eyebrow there, on the face of a man selling donuts. I saw a hint of my upper lip mirrored in the mouth of a woman pushing a kid in a stroller, a kid whose nose might as well have been my nose, except for its size. On and on it went. One face after another, and in each a common bond. I was everyone, and no one. Everyone was me.

I was beginning to understand—who I was and the great task before me, work that I alone might do. Yet, with the onset of huge responsibilities came terrible dangers, and right then, charging around the corner, came *Los Muchachos.*

"Get that motherfucker," David Towes yelled, vaulting atop the green metal lid of a hotel Dumpster, pointing me out to his heinous confederates. There were dozens of *Muchachos* now, hundreds perhaps, streaming into the square, stovepipe hats on their heads, machetes raised, randomly hacking. People dove for cover, left and right. "Get him!" Towes yelled, wielding his two-by-four in my direction.

As Taylor Powell, I never could stand those actors who figured doing your own stunts proved what big balls you had. "Fuck them," Jimmy Dime used to say. "If their *cojones* were so heavy, they wouldn't be actors to begin with. Let them hang upside down from Mount Rushmore in the hot sun, I'd rather be back in the aircon trailer dealing with the *real* stunt."

Now, however, there was no choice but to swing into action. Full-out, I leaped onto the windshield of a taxi cab like a bug on the interstate. I looked through the glass at the frightened Pakistani driver, saw he had the same earlobes as I did; he squinted back, he'd seen me before, too. We were brothers across the dashboard.

"Drive!" I yelled, and he did, fast and true, until he crashed into an ambulance crossing against the light. A half dozen vehicles spun out in unison, leaving a like number of perfect rubber rings on the avenue: urban crop circles. The taxi hit a wall and blew up, sending up a pillar of fire fifteen stories high. I jammed a ten spot into the cabbie's hand as we scrambled from the flaming wreckage. "Thanks, Mac."

Then I ran. I ran for what must have been miles, toward the great spires of the bridges, toward the river, and the freedom of the sea. I ran until the sun was stark in the sky, and sweat seeped from my every pore. I ran until I got to a small cobblestone street where the only sound was a distant hum and the thud of my own feet.

It was deserted down by the docks, as if the evacuation the government planners talked about (to where? I wondered) had already occurred. Satisfied that I'd eluded *Los Muchachos* once again, I walked another block or two, looking for signs of life. Finally, around a windy corner close by the riverfront, I saw a crowd of perhaps twenty-five people gathered outside an appliance store, their eyes riveted to the stack of TVs for sale in the window.

It was a syndrome associated with the advent of the comet, both psychologists and semiologists said: people leaving the relative comfort of their homes—mansions and shitty little cottages alike—to congregate in front of common info sites. "A process reminiscent of the herding instinct seen in other social animals before great storms," said one parchy-skinned environmentalist.

To facilitate comparison shopping, each of the Sonys, Hitachis, Mitsubishis, JVCs, and RCAs arrayed in the window was playing the same show, the satellite feed showing the real-time progress of the comet toward earth. It was, after all, the only thing people wanted to see: the rich blackness of space, the twinkling of stars amid the infinite heavens, and, smack in front, the comet hurtling forward—impassive, bloodcurdling, unstoppable.

An announcer said they were about to go live to the White House. The president was going to speak. For security purposes, only the audio would be available. The picture stayed on the comet.

"In these dread times, we must pull together," the president said, his voice, so long a vessel of humdrum venality, edging toward panicked sincerity. "We must find the Common Thread that binds us to one another." It was hard to know if the people standing in front of the appliance store actually heard these words. They appeared drugged, hypnotized by the image before them. This was Arana's doing, I knew. Whether he be ten thousand miles in space, or a seemingly innocent baby rocking inside Hitler's cradle, his Evil permeated the soul.

"The Common Thread," the president repeated, desperately trying to become the man he'd taken a solemn oath to be. "This is our chance, our only chance . . . to find that bond that . . ."

Off in space, Arana smirked. As if he could be thwarted by any pep talk uttered by this pipsqueak of a public thief. Army officials barked of governments pooling technology, collaborating

on massive missiles to blow him out of the sky. That was bullshit, too, Arana knew. The rockets would fizzle on the launching
pad, victimized by shoddy workmanship, crippled by graft.
Nothing could stop him. Thousands of miles away, but gaining,
he pursed his lips and spit in contempt, his saliva winging
through measureless space. As he'd done to Josias, as he tried to
do to me, he would spit in the eyes of the planet, blind the whole
world.

"The Common Thread . . . our only chance . . ."

That was when I sensed the shift in the collective gaze of the
people in front of the appliance store. You've seen it a thousand
times. You walk past an electronics display and there you are, on
a television monitor, courtesy of a video camera in the window.
A behaviorist's bona fide hard sell: Put someone on TV and they
get so giddy they'll buy anything.

That's how I showed up on that particular Trinitron, the only
screen in the window not filled with Arana's face. I happened to
be in the right place at the right time because that camcorder
picked up a perfect headshot of me, the kicker being that this
particular unit came equipped with a stop-action feature, which
somehow, at this exact instant, activated itself.

There I was: Dean Taylor, my face, freeze-framed.

During the flush of my stardom as Taylor Powell, I'd occasionally sneak into a theater, hat pulled down low, to catch one
of my pictures with an actual paying audience. That's when I
first felt it: how much they wanted me, the insatiable ardor that
seemed to coalesce into a palpable *physical* force, bouncing off
the screen, seeking me out. Originally I thought it was my imag-
ination, a fantasy common to the widely adored. Then I began
finding bruises all over my body. But it was nothing like this.

Now, it was as if I'd been thrust, face first, into the teeth of an
impossible gale. My nose bent back toward my cheek, my lips
were crushed against my gums. I felt for my ears, fearing they
were gone. The feeling grew more intense as, one by one, those
assembled in front of the appliance store tore themselves away
from Arana's image and focused on mine.

"That . . . guy . . ." someone said with a gasp. "I know that guy." Others agreed. "Yeah, he looks so familiar, so close . . ."

As the crowd logged on to me, I did the same with them. We were together in this struggle, and recognition of this commonality was our best hope. Yet, as fervently as it had come to me, that collective attention was ripped from my grasp. Arana's impassive face was wresting them back, his hypnotic gravity strong, undeniable. He would not give up without a fight.

A fight? This would be more than a fight. Still in its early rounds, this was to be a primordial struggle, a war between the Force of Evil and whatever humanity conjures to defend itself against that implacable power. Once the battle was waged in the hearts of men and within the natural tissues of the planet itself. Except now, in a world battered to an inch thick, it was a showdown of appearances, his face against mine.

Then I saw them, two other faces in the crowd, more familiar than the rest: Mary and Dyson. They'd been there the whole time, watching the comet with the others. They looked tired, worn. Only a year had passed since our tiny family broke apart, but Mary seemed a decade older. Her hair, once so full of body, was pulled back into a lank, haphazard ponytail. Her skin, always so soft and alive, looked pasty, her cheeks blotched and ruddy. For Dyson's part, his incomparable beauty shone through, but he too seemed haggard, without sleep. The two of them had done some hard traveling, that much was clear.

How had it come to this? The three of us standing before the plate-glass window of an electronics shop at the edge of a huge, heartless city, so far from our home, so far from one another? This was not the life Mary and I had hoped for when we first moved to Feltside and stood beaming over Dyson's crib. I stared into the video camera projecting the frozen image of my face. I wanted to embrace my wife and child, beg their forgiveness. If the world were to end, at least we would perish together.

This was not possible, however. Those other people, they needed me. Or rather, they needed to see my face. They needed to keep looking at me because if they didn't there'd be nothing else to see, except Arana. I was their only chance, I knew that now.

Standing in front of that appliance shop, I glimpsed the true nature of Vincent Parry's great, tormented achievement. As he said back in the jungle, Parry had "all God's copyrights," every face, inside his head. And that's what he made me: *every* face. Every face, for every place, for every time. A face that would always change, always be up to date. A face that would forever be in motion, a constant composite of every human being alive on the planet. Only, like the hands of a clock, you couldn't see it move. Couldn't follow the endless inclusion, exclusion.

Everyone and no one. The Common Thread. That's why so many people thought they knew me: They recognized themselves in me, but then, my face ever changing, the self they saw would disappear from view. Unless you stopped it, of course. Stopped my face. Froze it long enough so everyone might see themselves in me.

"Dean."

It was Mary. The love of my life. If I could only hold her now, laugh with her, make love with her. But that was not possible. We couldn't even look at each other. Direct eye contact was out; as much as I loved my wife, now all that mattered was my face. The Face: the frozen image on the TV screen.

"Your face is a church," Mary had said one night in that fleabag Cuban motel. From the beginning, she understood. Just like she understood now, our love notwithstanding, that at this moment I couldn't belong to her, or even to myself.

Beyond that, there was Dyson. My son, my rival. Poor, tortured, brave Dyson.

There were two dozen other people standing at that window. The eldest was a seventy-six-year-old retired dentist from Ohio, in the city to visit his daughter; the youngest an eight-year-old girl from Virginia Beach, up to live with her grandmother, a fifty-six-year-old employee of the Department of Motor Vehicles. The girl was unhappy because her mother was in jail and she didn't think she'd get out before the comet hit. Through the medium of my paused face, I tried to tell her not to worry about that. I told her to keep looking, to find herself in me, find her mother, too, and then she'd know hope wasn't lost. This was the nature of my communication with the people looking through the appliance-store window. I could touch them, each and every one of them.

Except Dyson. I couldn't reach Dyson.

He was looking, like the others, but he didn't see. The cold, forlorn fact was apparent to me now. Dyson couldn't see me not only because I was his father, which was liability enough; Dyson couldn't see me for the very reason he'd always hated me. He had my face. My old face, a dead man's face.

The terrible dream came back to me now: watching Parry cut along the thick black line, lift off the face of Taylor Powell, toss it with the flick of a wrist, blood dripping, into the trash. My old mug, the Face, that was the one face Vincent Parry hadn't figured on, the one he left out.

I felt I would fall to my knees, howl in pain. I could walk this entire planet, climb the highest mountains, return to the steaming depths of Josias's jungle and never encounter a human whom I didn't know, who didn't know me. Except my own son, who stood alone in his supreme alienation, owner of the one face that didn't fit.

Amid my despair, I heard him speak. "Come on, Mom," he said, in that low, quiet voice. "Let's go."

"Yes," Mary said, taking hold of his hand. "Let's go *home*."

I watched them go. Someday, if things went right, we'd be together again. There was no time now. As I said, I had a lot of stuff to do.

5.

"Tamberland and Greive," the operator said.

"Tim Renard, please."

Renard, no more than a couple of steps out of the mail room when he called me after my appearance on *That's Who I Am!*, had moved up in the world. Due to an unprecedented rash of suicides at the agency, including my old agent Steve Clay, that dickhead cross-dressing freak, Renard was now the acting president of the company, and consequently one of the most important men in Hollywood.

He was in a meeting, of course. His secretary asked me if I wanted to leave a message. I didn't. I was at a pay phone and didn't have any more quarters. If Renard wanted to talk to me, this was his only chance. I'd wait fifteen minutes, no more.

He called back in ten. "Dean. Dean Taylor," Renard said. "Long time no talk, great of you to get back."

"Least I could do."

"What can we do you for, Deano?"

"Well, if you remember, we were talking about me coming in and getting down to business."

"Remember? You're uppermost in the old mindset, Dean man. Uppermost. When do you want to come in? How about next Monday? Let's check the ole schedule . . . Gene *Hack*-man? Fuck him. I hate these aging vets, notices as long as Dead Sea Scrolls, hanging on for dear life. Yeah. Hackman out, you in, Dean. Three-thirty good?"

"Fine."

"See ya then, big boy."

I was sorry about Hackman, a great actor, maybe I screwed a couple of his wives. But like Renard said: Fuck him. Three-thirty, Monday: That gave me only four days to get across the country, so I went to the bus station, laid my cash down, swallowed a bottle of downers, and woke up approaching the California line.

After freshening up in a YMCA stall toilet, I donned a mock silk shirt off the rack at Kmart, slapped on a $3.99 pair of Thrifty Drug sunglasses, and was ushered into Renard's tastefully appointed outer office by a woman named Charisse, a stunning, hazel-eyed, dusk-skinned Inglewood ghetto girl dressed in a south Indian sari.

"Tea, sir, while you wait?"

I nodded and Charisse returned with a perfectly steeped pot of Earl Grey. Then she began to rub my shoulders. Apparently this was part of the service; Renard liked his guests to be relaxed.

As the strong mocha fingers pressed into my taut tendons, I could not help but remember so many other Charisses, girls who grew up poor and angry in homes full of violence, betrayal, and ugliness. For those girls, the good-looking ones like Charisse, there was only the mirror, that little zone where their own beauty served as a salvation amid the squalor. Narcissism had its place, I thought.

"Is that good for you, Mr. Taylor?" Charisse asked. "Mmmm," I replied. If I was still Taylor Powell I'd have gotten to fuck Charisse, just as I'd fucked the entire previous generation of Charisses. A block-long stroll on Rodeo Drive was a surreptitious old home week. I'd spied no less than a dozen of those once favored with Taylor Powell's incomparable talents. In their forties now, they didn't look too much the worse for wear. I still loved these women, robot shoppers that they were; I'd always love them, even after they became toothless and stooped, their cunts crackly and dry. I'd love them even after my dick shriveled and baggy skin hung off my ass, when we became walking scarecrows with moles and fissures to frighten children on Halloween night. I'd love them because the twinkle would still re-side in our eyes, fond memories of so much blissful in-and-out. Thinking of it now, the recollection seemed sexier than the original act. It made me understand what people were missing, trying to stay young all the time.

A rude buzzer interrupted my reverie. Acting on this signal, Charisse halted her ministrations, and her manner suddenly becoming brusque, she led me to a much smaller office. "Mr. Renard prefers you wait in here. You'll be called," Charisse said, with the insouciance of a security guard, as she slammed the steel door behind me.

From the luxury of the reception area, this inner office, six foot square and windowless, was notably spartan. Painted an industrial green, in the style of a Karachi dental parlor.

I was not alone. On the hard wooden bench across from me, sitting with a straight-backed military correctness, was a man who looked to be in his late sixties. Fastidiously, if somewhat eccentrically attired in maroon leisure suit and tan shoes, the man's swarthy, weather-beaten face featured a snow white, twirl-ended mustache that imparted an impish Kris Kringle aspect that was unsettlingly undercut by a pair of chillingly clear blue eyes. A large shiny red box topped with a frilly pink bow rested in his lap; it seemed to be a child's birthday present.

After sitting in silence for some time, the man beckoned me closer. He spoke with an accent, a guttural French, his voice, seemingly ruined by disease, was barely audible. "Have you been waiting a very long time?" he asked.

"Not so long."

"Do you have an appointment?"

I nodded.

"Then you will be seen. Everyone with an appointment is seen." The old man shifted in his seat. "I have no appointment. I have been here three months."

"Three months!"

"Yes. In the beginning, I would come every morning and leave at night," the old man said as he looked around furtively, as if afraid his conversation was being monitored. Then, indicating a tiny bedroll secreted under his chair, he whispered, "Now I sleep here, in this little room."

"You sleep here?"

"Please, not so loud. It is not allowed, to sleep here. Every night I must hide from janitors. That black woman, Charisse, she watches me every moment. She waits for me to slip up, any excuse to call the guard, to have me taken away. This is because I do not have an appointment. He sees no one without an appointment. It is a rule which cannot be broken."

"That's criminal. Renard can't do this to people."

The old man held up his hand. "Please, do not blame him. He is a very important man. Besides, it is my choice. I could have an appointment if I asked for one. Then I would be seen. But I will not ask. It is not the place of a father to ask for an appointment to see his own son."

The man gathered himself with much formality, stood, and bowed. "I am Henri Renard. Timothy is my son."

"Pleased to meet you, Mr. Renard. How can—"

"How can any son act in such a fashion to his father?" the elder Renard interrupted. "Is that your question? The answer is that every son acts this way. Do you have a son, my friend?"

"Yes, I do."

"Then you understand why I do not leave. The father is prisoner to the son. You have a son, so I don't have to tell you this." The man sighed once more. "My son is a very important man, now. Gentlemen such as yourself travel great distances to speak with him. What am I? An old, sick man."

He dug into his pocket, drew out a torn black-and-white photograph. "This was me as I once was. Forty years ago, in Algeria." The picture showed the elder Renard, muscles bulging, in the uniform of the French Foreign Legion. He was standing at stiff attention, an endless expanse of sand behind him.

"On the very day this picture was taken my regiment captured several Arabs, terrorists all. We buried them up to their necks and shoved sugared rocks in their mouths. Their cries were music to our ears as the scorpions struck again and again."

"That's terrible."

"Yes, but necessary. In war, much is necessary. In war a man must act as a man." Wistful, the old man placed the photo back into his wallet. "These are things which are not understood in this country. Here a man is said to be tough because he controls money. Because he can shout on a telephone."

He bent over, motioned me closer, indicating that he wanted to whisper. "They say my son is very tough. A tough negotiator, hard as nails. I read all this in the newspapers, how tough my son is. I know better." Renard's father was grabbing my arm now, squeezing it hard.

"Hey." It was not the grip of a frail old man, but of a torturer, the gleeful sadist.

"May I ask a favor of you? You have an appointment. You will be seen. Can you tell my son I've brought his Fluffy?"

He opened the shiny box on his lap, bade me to look at the stuffed animal inside. It was a grayish toy rabbit with pink matted ears and button eyes peering out with silly delight. "My son slept with it every night," the elder Renard said. "Even after hair grew around his balls, he'd sleep with it. His mother said he needed it. Now that he is so important, I return it to him. When you are called, tell him I have his Fluffy."

Charisse opened the steel door. "Mr. Taylor, Mr. Renard will see you now."

Tim Renard sat behind a twenty-foot-long, boomerang-shaped desk. He was much thinner than his father and far pinker. His head was strangely long and slender, like a side view of a Ritz cracker box. His smallish eyes were set on the extreme edges of his narrow head, giving him a grouperlike aspect. Still, he looked familiar. As if I'd known him all my life.

"Great of you to come over on such short notice, Dean," Renard said, barely peering up from his computer screen. "So what can a li'l ole bottle-sniffing cap-feeder like me do for you?"

I'd actually called Renard a bottom-feeding cap-sniffer when he rang me on the phone after my *That's Who I Am!* performance, but I was too filled with pity for the nervous little executive to correct him. Poor sap, sitting behind his big stupid desk like it meant something. He'd obviously kept a list of every single person who had ever humiliated him during his stint as a "nobody." This explained my ability to get an appointment so quickly: It was payback.

"Which is it, Dean? Want me to make you a star? Or should I just piss on you?"

"Interesting options, Tim, but I already am a star."

Renard looked at me for the first time. "Come again, Deano?"

"I said I am a star, Timster. I'm the biggest star out there."

Renard chuckled. "That's rich. A laugh and a half. I hate to break it to you, Dean. You were on a dumb game show for twenty minutes and you didn't even fucking win. You lost. That's some kickass résumé. You're not even a blip on the screen."

"I *am* the screen. I'm the only face anyone wants to look at."

Renard's laughter came a tad more anxiously. He was looking at me harder now, no doubt seeing what I saw in him: our kinship. The bond between us. "Oh, something I don't know, something I missed in the trades?" he said with poorly feigned nonchalance. "Some hidden credits, perhaps?"

You could have called it a stroke of luck, but more likely it was due to anal corporate organizational fixation: Even though I'd arrived in town via Trailways, I was still a *client*. My name appeared in the book, so someone, likely Charisse, had pulled the Dean Taylor file, slim as it was. The tape of my stint on *That's Who I Am!* was resting on top of Renard's in box. I picked it up.

"If I want to watch reruns, Dean, I'll set up a screening of *It's a Wonderful Life*," Renard said, trying to be cool.

"But this is my only credit, Timbo. The only one I need." I shoved the tape into the VCR sitting on the cabinet on the far wall of the office.

The TV was already on, silently playing the network's continuing comet coverage. Violence was escalating. Albanian mutineers were advancing on Tiranë. They'd taken their commanders hostage, but when asked for their ransom demands, couldn't think of a single thing they wanted more than killing the officers, which they did. The network showed a few garden-variety atrocities before switching to the satellite coverage of the comet's approach. As if looking at an ever-developing picture, I could see greater definition in Arana's face now, his eyes dark pools. He was getting closer, closer all the time.

I snapped off the live feed, popped the tape into the VCR, and fast-forwarded to the climactic sequence: $193,000 on the table, all mine if, like Rumpelstiltskin, I'd only say my name. I hit PAUSE. A nice head-and-shoulders shot it was, too: Dean Taylor, frozen in the frame.

A single glimpse of my telegenically braked face was enough. Renard was immediately rapt. "Sorry . . . I don't know why it affects me like this . . . It's just so . . . so totally . . . *total* . . . I've never seen talent like that before." Renard appeared near shock. I put my hand gently on his back. Sweat had seeped through his twenty-five-hundred-dollar suit.

"It's not about talent, Tim," I said. "Talent's got nothing to do with it."

Renard blew his nose with a honk. He couldn't take his eyes off my stock-still image. "Then what is it?"

"I don't even know myself. I am merely its instrument. I do know we've got to sell the shit out of it." With that I stepped between Renard and the TV screen, breaking the hypnotic connection.

"Listen up, because I'm only going to make this offer once. I need someone I can absolutely trust. I'll give you twenty-five percent of everything."

"Twenty-five percent of what?"

"Twenty-five percent of me. Twenty-five percent of the biggest star this town will ever see."

Renard was regrouping, attempting to reestablish his status as the man behind the desk. "Offers like this don't come along every day, Dean. What exactly do I have to do to ground-floor myself on this windfall."

"Quit your job. Work for me exclusively. Be my manager."

Renard laughed. "You want me to give up the presidency of

the biggest agency in Hollywood to work for you? Just like that?"

"Only chance you have." I turned off the VCR. Regular programming returned, Arana's face charging ahead. "Only chance we all have."

"You're psycho."

"Am I?" I turned the VCR back on, froze my image again.

Spellbound once more, Renard sought to deny the attraction of my face. The man was in obvious pain. "All my life I've been trying to . . . be someone . . . not to be a schmuck, a loser . . . and now I have it. I'm big. Nobody won't take my call. I won't give that up. I won't." Renard was shaking now, desperately trying to turn away from my frozen image in the TV screen. "Get out of here, Dean. *Get out!*"

"Sure thing, Tim," I said casually as I got up. "I guess I was wrong. You really are too big for a shit job like this. You're a fucking colossus."

I turned to leave. Then, over my shoulder I said, "Oh, by the way, your father's outside. He's got Fluffy with him. He wanted me to tell you that." It was a mean thing to do, but I had no choice.

Renard's hand dropped to his mousepad. "He's still out there?"

"Three months now," I answered. "He's got a little bedroll tucked under the chair. He sleeps in that room. He told me about the sugared rocks, Tim. The ones he shoved in the Arabs' mouths. He told me about the scorpions."

Renard bit his lip. His office was big. Bigger than big, befitting an individual with his fingertip on the means of production. Renard could greenlight pictures, that made him godlike, a pharaoh. Now he looked like a trapped little boy, a prisoner in his own throne room.

"Why doesn't he go away?" Renard said, shakily.

I felt Renard's pain as if it were my own. But I couldn't stop now. "Because they never go away, they're always out there, waiting." Again I turned to leave. "Too bad we couldn't get together on this, Tim. See you sometime. And, good luck."

I was almost out the door when Renard called after me.

"Okay. But I want thirty percent, forty percent if you gross over a hundred million dollars in the first year."

"You drive a hard bargain but that's the sort of fellow I want on my team. I can live with those numbers. But no lawyers. This is man to man."

"Man to man?"

"Because we're both men, Tim," I said. "Free men."

6.

There was only one thing to do now: get on a bus and go home.

A few days later, around midnight, I was in Feltside. The house was a mess. Some drunken teenager had plowed a stolen Plymouth Duster through the fence. No wonder Bill Tarr couldn't sell the place. The town hadn't even bothered to tow away the rusting junker; a rampage of kudzu crowded through the shattered windshield. In the back, barely visible amid the undergrowth, were the charred floorboards of Dyson's house.

Several of the porch stairs, always in need of repair, splintered under my feet as I walked up to the spot Mary and I had enjoyed so many warm evenings. The front door was ajar and I pushed it open. The stench of mildew and urine wafted out.

The living room furniture was trashed, the legs yanked off chairs, an axe embedded in the arm of the shredded sofa. A roving band of squatters had obviously moved in, satanists of some sort, judging from the faux demon-seed invocations scrawled on the walls. Beer bottles were scattered over the floor, smears of fecal matter on the rugs. This, in the place I'd once called home.

I was still standing at the doorway when I heard the Casio's quavering tremolo slip through the murk.

I went toward the music, those shimmering chords forging a passageway through the chopped-up furniture and sodden rugs. "Peace in the Valley": I remembered the first time I'd heard Mary play the tune, that morning in Pardosville, inside Reverend Watkins's roofless church. The recollection buoyed me. As the Spirit still dwelled in that ruined tabernacle, love, which once ruled in this house, might do so again.

The music was coming from behind our bedroom door. I was halfway up the pitch-dark stairs when the singing started. "There'll be peace in the valley, for me, someday . . ." Until that very moment I'd never heard Dyson sing. He simply refused. Whenever the Tarrs came over for a round of hymns, he'd lock himself in his room. At church, the boy sat closemouthed. Now, no longer a boy, Dyson's voice swelled from my old bedroom: It was a voice like no other, desolate and forlorn, fearfully clear, a sound that could break as many hearts as his face might steal.

Mary joined in, her reedy alto mixing sweetly with Dyson's baritone. "And the lion will lie down by the lamb,/The host from the wild will be led by a child . . ." The fierce melancholy of their harmony anchored me to my spot. Mary bore down, her passion bursting through the Jap-transistored limitations of her instrument, driving the piece home. Partly out of fear, but more from respect, I kept myself from opening the door to the bedroom. I would let them finish. "And I'll be changed, changed from this creature that I am."

I swung open the door.

In years gone by it had always bothered me when Dyson came into our bed late at night. He'd pad into our room after midnight, snuggle up to Mary—never me—and proceed to toss and turn in uneasy sleep. "It was one thing when he was three or four," I complained to Mary. "He's eleven. When is this going to stop?"

"Oh, Dean," Mary replied. "Give the boy a chance, it's so very hard to grow up."

Now, Dyson was back in our bed. The two of them lay together, cuddling as they always did. Mary stood up. She was wearing a clingy nightgown I'd bought for her during our New York vacation. The gown was worn now, its hem frayed, but her whole aspect, especially with her hair frizzed by the humidity, remained for me the consummate turn-on.

As Dyson sat up in the tousled bed, I immediately noticed several changes. Wearing only a pair of briefs, the first sprigs of what would become a manly mat had begun to cover his chest.

His shoulders, once girlish and sloping, had assumed a more squarish and muscular aspect similar to my own. Now that I looked at it, his face, the Face, appeared to be filled in as well. Indeed, he was ahead of schedule. I didn't get that famously faint chin dimple until my late teens. His eyes had already acquired the subliminal wrinkling that only comes with a mysterious primal wounding, that deep-dish shit that really gets you over with chicks. There could be no doubt that Dyson, not yet sixteen, was already the handsomest man in the country. He looked more like me than I ever had.

I stood there a moment, looking at the two of them in that rumpled bed where I'd spent so many blissful nights. My wife, my son: Damn. Sometimes it's better not to ask. There is an ineffability to the forces of attraction; if anybody knew that, it was me.

"Dean," Mary said. "You're home at last."

"Yep," I replied. "Here I am."

When Mary moved over to make room for me in the bed, there wasn't anything else to do but to stretch out with them, providing the final element to a most beleaguered, yet unique triangle. Mary, in the middle, took both Dyson's hand and mine, pressing them both to her chest.

The three of us were lying there in silent contemplation when we heard the stomp of boots rush up the porch and into the house. A moment later, fifteen cops decked out in riot gear burst into the bedroom.

"Well, look at this cozy pervert scene," a smallish, rodentlike cop screamed through his bulletproof visor. He waved his automatic rifle at us. "Okay, sickos, off that bed and up against the wall!"

They weren't local cops. Their badges identified them as SPE-CIAL DEPUTIES, part of the presidential task force "Project Common Thread" organized by the government "to combat the wholesale unraveling of the social fabric" fostered by the approach of the comet. Charged with protecting life and limb, these guys were out of control. Reports of their excesses—rape and murder included—were rampant up and down the coast.

The rodent looked to be in charge. Named Koonce, he gave the three of us a once over, then squeezed Mary's left breast hard enough to make her scream in pain. "Not bad," he said.

Enraged, I jumped at Koonce, only to be met by a rifle butt across the forehead. "What's the matter?" the cop sneered, licking his thin lips. "We're strangers in this town, how about a little hospitality?"

"Leave my mother alone, you pig," Dyson said. An instant later, his foot was in Koonce's groin. He looked good doing it, too. One fearless quick kick, followed by a forearm smash to the cop's jaw, sending his yellowed teeth flying. The rest of the cops reflexively converged on Dyson, knocking him to the water-logged shag carpet.

"You don't look so bad yourself pretty boy," Koonce seethed, back on his feet. He kicked Dyson in the spine, doubling him up, then, with a single clawlike swipe, ripped off the boy's under-wear. "Not bad at all. Turn over, let's see that pretty little ass, boy. He has a pretty little ass, doesn't he, *Muchachos*?"

The word hung in the air, not that hearing it was such a tremendous surprise. As his henchmen tied Mary and Dyson to chairs, Koonce walked over to me. "So good to see you again, Dean," he said, with a sneer.

"Fuck you."

"Just what I had in mind," Koonce snickered, as his men pinned me to the bed. "We're going to put on a little show. Fun for the whole family."

There were about fifty cops now, each with his fly unzipped, a hideous hard-on poking through his pants. They were arrayed in two single-file lines that snaked out of the bedroom door and down the stairs. The front of one line faced the chair where Dyson was tied; the second stood before Mary. It was pretty obvious what was going to happen next. Two men were positioned on either side of my wife and child, both pressing knives against their necks. Should either Mary or Dyson bite down, even gag when swallowing, these men had instructions to cut off their heads. "And you know what, Dean?" Koonce leered. "Even that ain't going to stop us. You ain't really lived until you've fucked a decapitated head."

There was nothing I could do. Koonce instructed his minions to kill both Mary and Dyson if I made the smallest move. So I sat there and watched. Saw them do what they did. There was a robotic routine to the procedure, a rote mechanism that made me think these weren't humans at all, but zombies in Arana's service.

They were nicer to Mary, almost polite. They'd pat her on the head, tenderly touch her cheek when they were finished. As for Dyson, though, they were brutal. They were ugly men, the foulness of their hearts leeching through their hide, swelling to boils and carbuncles. They hated Dyson's beauty; one after another, they'd smash their fists into his face. Dyson sat there and took it.

When I yelled for them to stop, they hit me, knocked me out. In the blackness I found myself sleeping in Mary's car again, on that first night. We made love, then, beautiful and tender, the perfection of that moment forever unsullied even by the events currently transpiring. When it was morning, I woke up and she was watching me.

"Your face is moving," she said. "What happens when it stops?"

"Maybe I die," I said, basking in the sweaty glow of sex.

"Maybe the world dies," she said. "Dies and is reborn."

"Don't you think anything ever dies without being reborn?"

"No. That's the way things work."

Anyways, that's what gave me the idea. Vincent Parry had made my face to be everyone and no one, to forever change as life itself changed. Every life and death and rebirth was registered on my face. This was how I was wired, my connection to the world. Right now my own particular little part of the world was being destroyed most horrifically by Arana and his *Muchachos*. My only choice was to grind that world to a halt.

As for the physics of what happened next, don't ask. I will however, in the spirit of full disclosure, reveal my thinking on the matter; that is, since my face's perpetual movement was tied to the planetary ebb and flow, it made sense that the reverse might also be so. That: My face was not merely a mirror of existence, but rather an active partner. That: My face might actually take the lead position in such a relationship, capable of instituting, as well as reflecting, change. In other words, if I could stop my face, then the world would stop.

It was worth a try. So what if my head blew up? It was about to get cut off anyhow. It was a tricky sort of thing, stopping the world, but all I needed was the smallest interruption, just enough time to break the trend of what was happening in my bedroom.

So I stopped it. I focused every bit of energy that had ever flowed through me or would ever flow through me. I marshaled every real, true feeling I'd ever experienced, the good and the bad, the stupid and the sane, and merged them together into a single force. My whole head got hot, a cauldron to parboil my brains. My vision blurred and it was hard to breathe. But I stopped it. I stopped my face.

Then everything that had been fluid grew solid, stuck to its place. Those foul *Muchachos,* their warty dicks out; Koonce, in midsneer; even Mary, her eyes rolling up in her head, became statues.

Nothing moved except Dyson and me. It made sense, really, Dyson's face being the only one in the world that wasn't part of mine. The boy bit down, hard, on the bulging prick of the huge, immobilized cop in front of him, pushed the bleeding man aside, and walked over to me.

"You all right, Dad?" Dyson asked. He hadn't spoken to me so tenderly in years.

"Never better, son." The g-force of an untold number of reentries was pressing against my face. "How do I look?"

Dyson smiled. "Kind of stressed. Kind of purple. Kind of funny."

I couldn't talk anymore, my lips were turning inside out.

Dyson took my hand. "I get it now, Dad. The whole thing."

I wanted to take him in my arms, hold onto him the way I did when he was a baby. But my forehead was seized up, my eyebrows felt like they were peeling off. It didn't matter. He knew what I meant.

"I love you, Dad," Dyson said. "Whatever happens."

Suddenly, Dyson's face was tight with awe and terror the likes of which I'd never seen before. "Look at that," he shouted, pointing toward the bedroom window.

"Shit." It was incredible. Arana's comet was no longer ten million miles away, a streak across the blank of space. Now, with time and space suspended, the comet was hovering right outside my Feltside bedroom window.

Arana. His huge, bile-filled Latinate face, right there, leering and snorting, swearing vengeance, spoiling for the real showdown. The sound was deafening, the thunder of a thousand tornadoes.

"Hey, Arana," I shouted through the curtained window. "Come a little closer."

The monster moved ahead, his hideous cave of a mouth opening to reveal the measureless depths within. The stench of his breath was enough to strip paint.

"Closer," I said, calmly, coyly. After all, I knew how to be seductive.

"Dad, are you sure . . ." Dyson held my hand, tighter now.

"Come on, don't be shy," I coaxed the malevolent comet, keeping watch on Arana's foul, bilious face. I didn't think he'd actually do what I said, but Evil's kind of dumb when you get down to it, stupidity simply another aspect of its hatefulness.

"Closer. I got something special for you." Arana sailed into position. And I spit, a perfect lunger complete with ironic comet-like trailer, right into the murderer's eye.

"Aghhhh!" Arana growled and shuddered, the comet's gravity shaking the house down to its foundation. It was as if every Newtonian rule was suspended; the world turned upside down, the hinges and moorings of whatever held things in place ripped away. For a second I thought Arana had triumphed, that he'd managed to dekilter the universe. But it was only my face. It was moving again, and the world with it. Reacting instinctively, I ducked as a gunshot exploded behind me.

Loma Tarr stood in the doorway. She'd blown Sergeant Koonce's head off with a shotgun. The cop's still-zapping nerve endings twitched his torso into an eerie breakdance before it crumpled to the blood-splattered rug.

"Just calm down lady," the other cops pleaded.

"You calm down," Loma shouted back, pointing the gun their way. "Lemme see your hands!"

"Sure, sure . . ." the cops said. They were in no mood to squabble. Their leader gone, they seemed unsure of their agenda. The zombie violence that informed their every act just moments ago had vanished. They seemed more like little boys dressed up to play soldier, not *Muchachos* at all. With the comet's force field receding, at least for the moment, these impressionable souls, like so many Germans before them, were wondering what had gotten into them.

"Why you boys want to come around here bothering honest homeowners," Loma Tarr said, advancing.

"Homeowners?" several cops exclaimed with surprise. "Why didn't you say that in the beginning! Damn. We've got this house down on the foreclosure list, but there must be some mistake. If you say they're homeowners, that's good enough for us. We're working for the people, not the banks. Ain't that right, fellas?" The deputies shouted their unanimous assent. "Right."

A cop walked over to Dyson and Mary. "Ma'am . . . son . . . what can I say? Nothing but, we apologize. People should be decent to each other." The cop looked around the room. "This place is pretty trashed out. We'll get a crew out here, have the house looking ship-shape in no time, take care of that little problem at the bank, too." He never noticed his prick was still hanging out of his pants.

When they were gone, Bill Tarr, standing beside Loma, said, "Dean, there's a phone call for you."

"Phone call?"

"Back at the house. Imagine calling so late, scared me half to death. The man insisted you were here. Said it was important. That's why we came over in the first place and saw what was up."

"Good thing you did, too," Mary said. "You're pretty handy with that shotgun, all right, Loma."

"Never shot one before in my life. Come over here, son," Loma said to Dyson. Blood was seeping from his formerly perfect nose. It was broken, for sure, listing seriously to the left.

"Damn shame," Loma said, tracing the ruined line of Dyson's nose as she handed him a Kleenex. "Used to be such a pretty thing."

7.

When I picked up the phone, Tim Renard said he had good news. He'd set up four screen tests, all on sure green-light pictures. "This is a total score. I sailed right past the casting directors, right to the heads of production," Renard said hurriedly. "Ron Zah, Dickie Tannawheel, Shirl Bloch, and Dawn Vurley. They'll all see you."

"Crack of Dawn Vurley?"

It just slipped out, another of Jimmy Dime's pet vulgarities. He used to bang the high-powered Ms. Vurley just to use that tired old "I've seen the crack of" joke.

"We have to move fast," Renard said sharply, noting that arranging the tests had more or less exhausted every chit he'd managed to accumulate during his meteoric rise to the top of the Hollywood world. "This doesn't work and I won't be able to give myself away with a set of dishes."

"Can't do it until next Thursday, Timster."

The exec swallowed. "But everything's set for this week. Do you have any idea what's involved with changing a date like this?"

"Change it, Tim," I interrupted. "I've got a lot of work to do around my house."

"Work around your house? Dean, I don't think you get it. These people are big."

"I get it. I'm just trying to figure out a good time for them to come."

"Come? Come where?"

"Here. Feltside. Nice little burg in a brittle neo–Grant Wood kind of way, they'll love it. We can do the test in my garage. I'll set up some floodlights, they got them over at the hardware store."

"You must be kidding."

"Why should I kid? Oh, and Timmy? No limos. We've got an egalitarian town here; people don't put on airs. These assholes are going to have to drive themselves, all the way from L.A., in rented Subarus, over back roads. Let them experience the nature of the quest."

Stupefied, Renard laughed. "Why tell them the address at all? Why not make it a scavenger hunt, with clues written in soap on mirrors in abandoned service stations, and on backward tapes played through the drive-through boxes of fast-food joints."

"Now you're getting into the spirit."

"But where's the trail end? On top of a mesa in Hopi Indian country? How about if you're an anchorite, chained to a rock?"

"No. It's got to be here. My home."

"Righto," Renard agreed, giddily. "That's better. Little suburban backyard, Weber grill, garden gnomes, plastic woven chairs, flagstone patio, freeway hum in the background, smell of a backed-up septic tank: the saint in his postmodernist environs. You want them to mow your lawn when they get there?"

"It could use it. I'll sharpen the blades. It'll be like the Peace Corps for them."

Renard paused now. A renewed gravity came into his voice. "There're two things, Dean."

"Yeah, Timbo?"

"One, you got to have a new name. Dean Taylor just doesn't cut it. It's too Clintish, sharp, and unforgiving. We need something homey, more user-friendly, something to settle into."

"How about Collier Stone?" It was a secret homage to Jimmy Dime. He used the moniker while banging certain Deep South society babes. "Collier Stone, that's my real name," he'd lie in that awful fake drawl. "Before the Jew studio made me change it." Being able to whistle a little Dixie was essential to success in the whips-and-chain scene, Jimmy claimed. "Those Mobile girls," he'd say, "they're the only ones who know how to tie a proper tourniquet."

"Collier Stone . . ." Tim Renard rolled the syllables luxuriantly about on his tongue.

"Not bad. Southern, but not southern fried. I like it. Collier Stone . . . *that's who you are!*"

I had to wait for Renard to stop chortling. "What was that other thing, Tim?"

"Other thing? Oh, yeah. The Subarus won't play. I'm going to put these people on a Learjet, with a full wet bar. Trust me on this."

"Have it your own way. The landing strip's off behind the dump."

8.

Of everything that happened over the next couple of years, some you know, some you don't.

One thing that's for sure, when comparing my two separate tinseltown careers, I was a heck of a lot huger as Collier Stone than I had ever been as Taylor Powell.

Not that acting talent had anything to do with it. I never was much of an Olivier, I don't have to tell you. I just play myself, which is the easiest or the hardest thing for an actor to do, depending on the person and the degree of self-knowledge involved. Mostly, it's how you pick the parts. As Collier Stone, that was easy; there was only one role he was born—or rather made—to play.

All the critics agreed. They said my one-man performance as the shipwrecked sailor in *Hand on the Tiller: Story of One Man's Journey Home* was a tour de force, the greatest acting achievement they'd ever seen. In unison, they noted the "strange hypnotic effect" of my face, which turned the "otherwise unpromising specter of watching a man float aimlessly in an open boat for two hours into perhaps the most compelling movie experience of all time."

But you knew that. You saw the picture, most everyone did. It's the biggest grossing film ever, ten times over. The incredible thing is how no one ever notices that the action stops for an instant every time there's a close-up of my face. Maybe a couple of projectionists could tell, if they looked at the film, frame by frame. Except those guys are like cops, always in the donut shop.

Besides, even if people do see my face stop, nobody can remember it happening. They get swept up and forget.

I think about those moments, how it affects people to see themselves in me. I try to trace the process of it: every face in the world poured into the ultimate melting pot until the perfect composite emerges. I still have difficulty accommodating that Ur-Face as my own: Dean Taylor's face, then Collier Stone's. Kind of solipsistic, I guess, thinking about your face as much as I have over the years. But it's a solipsistic age. That's how we got in this mess to begin with. All I know is, I'm happy it worked out.

Dyson was the first to note the comet's incipient demise. He spied it through the telescope I had bought him for his twelfth birthday. "It's wobbling on its axis, Dad," he said, as we scanned the skies from our lawn in Feltside a couple of weeks after *Tiller* hit the theaters.

"I don't think so, son," I replied. "It's too soon." I figured the psychic confrontation between Collier Stone's face and the malignant onrush of Arana's comet would be a long, drawn-out struggle. Millions, hundreds of millions of people would have to see *Hand on the Tiller* before the cumulative effect of their common insight created an impregnable atmospheric shield of Spirit that Arana would not be able to penetrate.

"No, Dad," Dyson yelled. "I can see it shimmy. See for yourself."

Through the lens I could see that Dyson was right. Arana's comet had begun to waver and shake. Its once-blinding glare was flickering, like a loose fluorescent ring in a tenement kitchen. "Far out," I marveled.

What a sweet little father-and-son science project it was for Dyson and me, peering through the forty-dollar telescope, charting Arana's comet's increasingly erratic path on our homemade sky map. We worked well together, reveling in exactly the sort of activity we'd missed out on during the years when hatred and distrust ruled between us.

"It's too unstable. I think it's going to blow up," Dyson concluded. "You beat it, Dad. You beat Arana."

I put my hand on Dyson's shoulder. "It wasn't just me," I said sincerely. "It was us together. The two of us and everyone else."

We were ahead of the astronomical curve. It wasn't until a month later that the big observatories, with their massive optical capacity, began arguing over which had been the first to "discover" the "sudden decay" in the comet's trajectory. "This is the craziest comet ever," said a famous skywatcher. "It came out of nothingness and to nothingness it returns."

A couple days later the television had the definitive pictures. The world watched the comet breaking up, diffuse its mendacious mass to a harmless but spectacular meteor shower, a rain of shooting stars to accompany the midsummer night's hump of randy teenage lovers on grassy hillsides.

Amid the sanctimonious punditry and hysteric religiosity following the "sparing" of the earth, no connection was made between the end of Arana's comet and *Hand on the Tiller* grossing one billion dollars within a month of its release. Not a single heroic chronicle of the battle of the faces, mine against his, appeared. That was just as well, I thought, as I sat inside the quiet darkness of Frankenstein's head.

Tim Renard couldn't believe it when I told him I'd chosen the old Karloff vehicle for the follow-up to *Hand on the Tiller*. "You're the most recognizable face in the world and you want to cover yourself up with fifty pounds of makeup?" Renard had shouted in exasperation. "We've got six hundred million in pre-sales for *Tiller Two*."

"There ain't gonna be no sequel."

"They're going to sue you."

Was that typical or what? You save the damn world and they want to sue you. "Let them sue, Timster. I'm Frankenstein and that's it."

"Are you all right in there, Mr. Stone? You can breathe?" It was Ray Suarez. An excitable Brazilian, he was the top makeup artist in the business, according to *Monster Face Monthly*. Suarez had already done six previous Frankensteins, with a couple of *Munsters* reunions thrown in, but vowed this would be his masterpiece. Through several layers of latex and papier-mâché I could hear Suarez lecturing his assistants, explaining his grandiose vision of the character.

"The face of Frankenstein is the unholy thing produced when man seeks to seize the power of Creation!" Suarez pontificated.

"Gee, Ray," came the unimpressed reply. "Is that like only God can make a tree?"

"Lowlife! Without me you are pancaking *Oprah* guests!"

"Say it, don't spray it. You're drooling, Ray, it's melting the papier-mâché."

"Oh, shit." This was followed by a further flurry of garbled cursing and sniping, none of which, thankfully, was any concern of mine. Perhaps on the outside Frankenstein's head was the terrifying product of a flawed meld of science and nature. Inside, however, it was a dark and peaceful place. A safe zone. In there I couldn't see anyone and no one could see me. Dreams were possible. Indeed, Frankenstein's head seemed the perfect refuge in which to review my current situation. To figure out what to do next.

"Let's leave," I'd said to Mary only a week before. "Sneak away in the middle of the night. Disappear to a place where no one knows us. Then we'll be free again."

"That would be wonderful, Dean," Mary said, wistfully. "Someday, maybe." God, it was killing me: Mary's smile, her sweet acceptance. She knew there was no escape, no place in the world where we could run to, where things would be as they were before. Like Taylor Powell before me, as Collier Stone I was, once again, the most famous face in the world. I was everyone and no one. If someone knew themselves, they knew me. How could I disappear?

That was the glory and the horror: being common property, the knowledge that I belonged to everyone, not just my wife, child, and those few people I'd found myself able to stomach over the years. A scummy junta leader in Burma, a sheepherder in Tajikistan, a commuter in Jersey, all of them had as strong a claim on me as my family. Mary understood that. She was the one who said we might as well take the house the studio rented us for the duration of the Frankenstein shoot. Now that I was a big star, dowdy ole Feltside wasn't for us anymore, she said sadly; when I walked into the hardware store, or sat down at the coffee shop, I'd just make everyone uncomfortable.

"This house is nice, we can make it cozy. You'll see, Dean," Mary said of the thirty-five-room rented mansion in the Hills. The place once belonged to Roland Tusk, the producer. I'd been there before, of course, screwed Tusk's wife on the pool table. I can't remember if he wanted to watch or not. "Sure," I told Mary, "real cozy."

Mary held me then, kissed me hard. "Don't worry, Dean, please don't worry." I was worried, though. That kiss worried me. Once Mary's kiss had been for me and me alone. Our kiss. It could not be decoded or reproduced: It was a classified kiss. Now, however, I'd come to regard my years as Dean Taylor as a weird aberration, a quick thaw between ice ages. As Taylor Powell, my every kiss was public, a kind of community property held between me and the women of the world. As Collier Stone, it was worse. Nothing, kisses included, could ever be private again. I'd come full circle: come back to this hideous sprawling city, shackled by a celebrity beyond reckoning. What a joke.

It was in the midst of this despair that I heard Vincent Parry's voice once more, a rising thrum inside Frankenstein's head. *"The butterfly . . . the beautiful butterfly . . . returned to the cocoon . . . from where he might emerge again . . . as something beyond beautiful . . ."*

I heard him as clearly as if I were back in the jungle. Vincent Parry: my maker. My Doctor Frankenstein. I was his masterpiece, yet he never lived to see the results of his handiwork. Parry had talked of butterflies and then blown his brains out. Twenty years later, my face wrapped in a very different kind of mask, the memory was still horrifying.

This time, however, the suicide made sense to me. Vincent

Parry had once been a frivolous man, a nose snipper and tummy tucker. A talented, senseless fool. Then, from Josias likely, he learned of the singular purpose for which he'd been put on this earth. A responsibility that he discharged when he met me. And when he was done, there was nothing left for him to do.

"The butterfly . . . the butterfly . . ." I heard Parry's words one last time, followed by silence. Good-bye, good doctor, the victory, fleeting as it is likely to be, belongs to you. I was merely the tool. A tool whose usefulness was likewise fulfilled.

"It's such a gamble when you get a face . . ."

"Did you say something, Mr. Stone?" It was Ray Suarez, yelling through the layers of my cocoon.

"Yeah," I said, through Frankenstein's face. "Where's the men's room? I gotta take a piss."

9.

As Collier Stone, it would have been a mob scene. As Taylor Powell, I couldn't have beaten them off with a switch. As Frankenstein, making my escape from the studio was a piece of cake. The gate guard barely looked up from his wrestling magazine as I clumped by in my size 16s. Ditto as I stumbled along the frontage road of the freeway, the late-afternoon sun glinting off the stainless-steel bolts in my neck. No one cared.

Once the quixotic missing link between man and God, Frankenstein was now just another easy-to-ignore nutbag hitchhiker. Half of L.A. must have passed me before some ZZ Top–style biker stopped on the Burbank off-ramp. "Where to, Frank?" he asked.

"Home," I said. "No place but home."

Home. I'd decided to kill myself inside that stupid mansion I currently called home. At least the dump was secluded as hell. That made it perfect. If my life could never be private, at least my death would be.

I was going to poison myself, no muss no fuss, no bullet in the mouth, no body swinging from a rope in the aircon breeze; the last thing I wanted was to leave my wife and child with one of those indelibly nasty images vengeful suicides serve up to punish those who live on after them.

I'd take pills, a whole handful. Conjure up a state sweet and torpid, like a heavy day in New Orleans. Maybe my liver would look like Dresden, but on the surface, where it really counted, I'd be smiling. And why shouldn't I? Mine was a happy death. I'd come and I'd done. Had my time and it was through. I'd saved the world, which was accomplishment enough for one lifetime.

When Mary found me, I wanted her to think I'd simply fallen asleep in bed. I wanted her to come over to stroke my forehead, the way she always did. That's when she'd know. The smile would tell her I hadn't suffered. Then she'd smile, too, because she'd know it was for the best. There was no need to leave a note. Everything would be in our life together.

But I had to get this damn head off first. I couldn't let Mary find me looking like Frankenstein. That would ruin everything. I pulled, tugged, and tore. None of it worked; the head clung. "Fuck!"

Time was running out. Mary had managed to locate the only quilting bee in the L.A. area, over in Pasadena, where, she said, "all the little old ladies are." She usually returned by six. If I planned on being dead by then I'd have to hurry. In a frenzy, I bashed the Frankenstein head against the bathroom sink, trying to crack it open like Humpty Dumpty, but only succeeded in nearly knocking myself silly.

I'd have to slice the thing off, I decided, rummaging through the medicine chest for something sufficiently sharp. Mary's nail scissors wouldn't do. The only thing in the medicine chest with a big enough edge was the razor. Arana's razor—the one Josias left for me in the shelter after he cut my hair.

How many necks had Arana slashed with this gleaming blade, I wondered, as I gently inserted its edge above Frankenstein's eye, careful not to pierce my skin. I just about had the stupid head off when I heard someone stirring behind me. If Mary had returned early my entire plan would be wrecked. But it wasn't Mary.

It was funny, because in the shadows on the other side of the doorway, I thought it was Josias. That made me laugh. "Weird you're here now," I started to say, breezily. "Because you're blind and I'm Frankenstein and that's just what happens in *Bride of Franken*—" It wasn't Josias either.

It was a much shorter individual, a hunch-shouldered, dingy-faced man with plastered-down salt-and-pepper hair and a pencil-line mustache. He was holding a revolver in his left hand.

I figured he was some breaking-and-entering geek. "Why don't you just take the silver and split," I said impatiently. "I'll throw in the TV and sound equipment if you make it snappy. I'm kind of busy here."

"You think I am a robber? You patronize me this way?"

"No need to get all huffy about it."

"I only come for what is owed me. Have you forgotten your debt, Mr. Stone? Or should I call you, *Mr. Taylor?*"

I looked up, studied the man. There was something familiar about him, but I couldn't place it. He walked closer now, dragging his right leg behind him.

"You truly don't remember me?" There was a faint hurt in his voice.

"Can't say as I do."

His eyes slitted. "You owe me a thousand dollars."

"A thousand dollars? For what?"

"Once, long ago, I took your picture."

Now I got it. Emilio. Josias's uncle. A thousand dollars. For the passport. That sick little studio. The smell of semen and beer.

"That's right . . . you took the picture . . . the first picture of me." Present circumstances notwithstanding, I was overcome by nostalgia. It was like five minutes ago. Emilio looking at the smudgy Polaroid . . . that strange double take, the one that would repeat itself more than a billion times over, or however many tickets *Hand on the Tiller* had sold right up to that moment. Emilio, this little crab of a man, had been the first to see it, the first to see the face that would save the world.

"A thousand bucks is a lot for a passport picture. But a deal's a deal. Let me get the checkbook." Anything to get the creepy little man out of the house before Mary got home.

"It is more now. More money," he barked.

"Interest. Yeah. Can't argue with that. You're entitled. I'm really sorry about not sending you the bread, I'm not usually like that. I even pay my parking tickets." I opened a drawer, took out a wad of bills. "Look, if you don't want a check, I have cash. How about five thousand? Seven? I got seven. That do it?"

Emilio shook his head. "Twenty. Twenty million."

"Twenty million? On a thousand? The mob doesn't even charge vig like that."

Emilio pushed the gun toward me. His face clenched. "You will pay. You will pay or I will tell everyone who you really are, Mr. Powell."

"Who?"

"Don't play me for a fool, *Mr. Taylor Powell.* I've known this from the beginning. I have family in the village as well, people who served that doctor. Parry. They told me who you were. An actor from America. Very handsome. Taylor Powell, *el hombre muy guapo* . . . that's what the women say."

Emilio craned his neck unflatteringly. He was an ugly man. An ugly, vicious little man. I'd met many like him over the years, men who hated me for being beautiful, men whose very ugliness made them mean. Or was it the meanness that made them ugly?

"Taylor Powell, *muy guapo, muy sabroso.*" Emilio's foul impersonation of a fawning female was followed by a brutal slam of his hand against the tabletop. Light glinted off his gold tooth. "So you are handsome and I am ugly. I have always been ugly. I can accept being ugly." He moved forward now, the gun barrel pushing through the Pine Sol–fresh mansion air. "Then, after so many years, I hear these same women, once young and beautiful, now old crows, their bellies fat from children, tits sagging, ugly like me. They come out of the movie theater talking of a vision. They have seen a man in a movie who makes them feel young again. A man that is like Christ to them. Every day more and more people are waiting on line at the movie to see this man.

"And who is this Holy man? Collier Stone. The same man whose picture I took so long ago. The man whose passport said Dean Taylor. The one who once was Taylor Powell. You,"

Emilio's mouth twisted in hatred, "you think you can have everything, be the most beautiful and the most Holy, well, you cannot!"

There was no use arguing. Even if I'd given him the twenty million he'd never be satisfied. "You know, if you're going to shoot, shoot. Blast away. It's not how I planned it but I never figured to see another sunrise anyhow."

Obviously unprepared for this response, Emilio squinted without comprehension. "I will tell your secret, Taylor Powell. The secret you have kept hidden all these years."

Once I would have died before I allowed myself to break the promise I made to Vincent Parry and Josias. But now everything was done and I was going to die anyway. "Secret?" I shrugged. "What secret? Tell whoever you want. Take ads on TV. I don't give a fuck."

Emilio's unprepossessing features shifted in frustration. "You are very rich!" he screamed. "You will pay!" His wretched little revolver trained on my midsection, Emilio reached his other hand into a canvas sack, drawing out a mason jar half filled with a dark yellow liquid.

"You will pay me or I will throw this acid in your face!"

I watched the contents of the jar slosh about. Emilio might have been bluffing; the bottle could have been filled with tea, or bourbon. But I didn't think so. It was acid all right, sulfuric likely.

"I am not joking! Give me the money!"

There was no other way it could end. My fantasies about a weightless tumble through a Coleridge-like web of opiate feathers to a smiling death were nothing more than that: an illusion. My escape from this life would not be without considerable pain and smoke. Metaphorically speaking, however, I could not complain. Emilio, whether he knew it or not, had provided that exact right way for me to go. I just wanted to get it over with.

"You want money?" I shouted. "Rob a bank. I won't give you a nickel. Not a fucking penny."

"You're leaving me no choice!"

"Screw you, gimp."

It was automatic from there, Emilio reacting reflexively. After a life of insults he just couldn't abide one more. In one quick motion, he ripped the cover off the jar and the acid sailed forth in a solid, arching rope. As the corrosive liquid reached its apex I noted the change in Emilio's demeanor. I knew the look well, having seen it on the faces of so many people over the years: They squint a bit and then start to say how they're not exactly sure, but "don't I know you from somewhere?"

So there was a bit of sadness there, Emilio realizing, only too late, that he'd thrown acid into a face that was as much his as the unfortunate mug stretched across the contours of his own skull. That would be his problem from now on, not mine.

Indeed, it was all working out quite nicely, except for Mary's arrival in the bedroom an instant before the acid spattered across my features. God, she looked great. Those Rodeo Drive fashions fit her fabulously. I assumed they were only for people with full-body jobs. But Mary was radiant in a sage green shift with a blood red scarf.

"Lookin' good, hon. Really love you." If I had it to do over again, these would have been my last words, but I never got the chance. I never got the chance to say anything.

The acid had already burned through that uppermost sediment of myself, which had once been Dean Taylor and the world now knew as Collier Stone. It sizzled into the lower realms, dissolving what was left of Taylor Powell, raged through the tissue and sinew supplied by my so-hated dad, my so-loved mom, bubbling to the forgotten faces of ten thousand unknown relatives, a hundred thousand hairy-foreheaded primates and more, backward through the countless faces of time, plunging ever downward in the swirling, bottomless cauldron that was me.

10.

I was a butterfly again. Returned, once again, to my cocoon.

I held on to the image, through the numerous operations, the pain and the subsequent months of healing: the butterfly. That same monarch my friends and I had chased with nets through yet unbuilt subdivisions of north Jersey.

"The butterfly . . . the butterfly . . ."

Mary and Dyson did it all. They got me out of the house alive, rushed me to the hospital, flew me out of the country, found the way south. Money came in handy to be sure, greased any number of sticky spots. But Mary has always insisted that everyone who helped—from the ambulance driver to the customs guys, ambassadors and more than a few doctors—would have done it for free. They knew me, you see.

So, thanks to everyone. Do the same for you sometime. It's kind of a nice feeling, knowing you've got friends around the world.

That doesn't mean I'll tell where we went or where we are now. For certain I won't reveal what I happen to look like this time around. Couldn't do that.

I will say: My new face could be described as rough. The doctors did their best under difficult circumstances, but none possessed Vincent Parry's special touch. Scar tissue is present here and there but the marks have faded with time. Mary says my face has the "lived-in look" of a longshoreman, or perhaps a retired, slightly corrupt union official. I find little to complain about in these characterizations. Of the three faces of me, this current one is my favorite.

Mary and I have traveled quite a bit in the past dozen or so years since my second mysterious disappearance from the silver screen. We like to arrive in a country, be it Laos or Togo, with only *The Lonely Planet Guide,* and take it from there: just two spry, American retiree-adventurers among the pert college students.

One thing I've noticed: Taylor Powell pictures have gotten more popular recently. You could call it a minirevival. I'm bigger than ever on the subcontinent, my half smile and wryly raised eyebrow causing a half billion Hindu ladies to rub their legs together under their saris. The U.S. market is also huge; they've got late-night Taylor Powell festivals on cable.

As for Collier Stone, he's a trivia question, nothing more. Talk about your one-shot wonders. *Hand on the Tiller* remains a prime industry mystery. No picture ever opened as big, held as steady, and then dropped so completely out of sight.

It makes sense. Beauty, even the randy shit Taylor Powell sold, is a constant-demand sort of thing. As for salvation, which is what Collier Stone offered, it's more of a one-shot deal, the conditions have to be right.

But that's cool.

Back in the jungle Vincent Parry said the face "is the front side of the mind." Fingering the now familiar contours of my thrice-born mug, I tell myself that's all it is: the front side. Here today, gone tomorrow, like a book and its cover. Mary and I, we take things as they come. Basically, what we need is each other, so we're happy.

We had a wonderful time last week. Dyson came down to our house on the island with his family. After a hitch as a merchant marine, he's opened his own carpentry business, doing well at it, too. I'm pretty proud of him.

I must confess to much spoiling of Dyson's kids, who are triplets. When they were born, I felt tense, remembering how the unfortunate persistence of my own genes had caused us so much distress. But Dyson's wife, Sherry, a luscious French Canadian, has some rather tenacious DNA of her own. The three kids, two girls and a boy, look almost exactly like her, except for those signature lips, which will be much fun for some lucky suckers to kiss about fifteen years up the road.

So that seems to be that. Life is going on. In celebration of Dyson's visit, Mary dragged out her old Casio. Together, we raised our voices in song: "There'll be peace in the valley, for me, someday . . . The host from the wild will be led by a child / And I'll be changed, changed from this creature that I am."

Acknowledgments

The author acknowledges the anthropology of Michael Taussig, for certain jungle concepts. Also: Mikey D, and The Sloan in the Kitchen team, friends in need, and deed, in a bumpy year: Hank, who came through, Will/Roy, who said to make it bigger, and Baum, for about everything.